# DRAWING RED

Adara Spence

Spence-Johnson Publishing

**Drawing Red**

*To Mr Spence, my family,*
*and anyone who looks for magic in the mundane.*
*You will find it.*

# CONTENTS

# CHAPTER ONE

# IN GOOD COMPANY

H er mobile buzzed in her pocket, guitars blaring. They always contacted unsuccessful applicants later in the day, as she'd learned from many near escapes. But now came the hard part: hiding her relief from her parents. Show time.

Dropping her pen on the pad, she put on her best hopeful expression and swiped up. "Hello?"

...

"Ah."

...

"No, it's OK. I understand."

...

"You too. Bye."

She sat her phone on her sketchpad then made a beeline for the kettle, praying her audience wouldn't see through the charade.

"Well?" her mother asked.

Lucy dropped a tea bag into a cup. She needed chamomile for this one.

"The manager said someone else was a better fit for the role," she said, fumbling as she put the box up on the rack.

"Again?"

1

Steadying herself, the teen turned to her mother, who stood in the doorway with her arms folded—the same pose she'd seen her give her failing university students.

With a rustle, her father folded the *Lombar Voice* and added it to his growing pile on the other side of the table. "Did you...freeze?" he asked, adding his own gaze, making her shift from foot to foot.

Freezing was Lucy's inbuilt self-defence mechanism. It stopped her before she said anything stupid—just shut off the sound of her voice mid-conversation. She hated it in the moment, but looking back afterwards, it'd always stopped her from putting her foot in things.

Her silence said it all. The kettle beeped on the bench, a chirp of moral support as it reached boiling point. Good old dependable Cross-Key & Co., just like their slogan said: Always in Good Company.

"You have above average grades and a perfect attendance record. These shops should be biting their hands off for you. Unless you don't want a job?"

And there it was. The accusation. The truth, of a sort. Lucy scrambled to cover. "It's not that I don't want a job! It's just..."

"Just?" her mother prompted, eyebrow raised.

She was cornered. After mentally racing through variables, she realised the truth was her only option and blurted, "I've been working on something else. It took six months, but I've finally collected all of my art into an online store. I can sell prints and take commissions, and I'll give you my profits."

A weight lifted from her shoulders but dropped like an anvil again when her mother's eyes narrowed.

"Just because your dad isn't working right now, you think we need you to provide an income?"

Lucy blinked. Wasn't this about money?

2

"You'd never earn enough for a flat," she continued, waving a hand dismissively. "Ben's almost nine months old. He can't stay in a cot in our room forever and this is only a two-bedroom house."

Lucy's mind raced. This wasn't happening. It wasn't. It was not happening.

Her father sighed. "You can't expect to earn enough to live off those cards and portraits. You need a proper job. Without a degree, the best you can do is to get your foot in the door somewhere and work your way up."

The gears in her brain sputtered. "What about the house move? I thought the plan was to move to somewhere bigger after Ben was born."

Two blank faces stared at her.

"A house move? Whenever did we say that?" her mother asked.

An image of their living room floor laden with gifts popped into her head. Christmas when she was five years old. At dinner her father announced, "Lucy, you're going to have a little brother or sister, then we'll move to a new house and you can both have your own rooms."

Lucy waited for her promised gifts for thirteen years. At long last, the first gift arrived nine months ago, and she'd been waiting for the second for months now.

"It won't be long before you get another job, though. You'll beat me to it," she said, deciding to ignore the fact that no publication would dare hire the disgraced senior editor of a failed newspaper. Even after the lawsuit against *Talking Point* had been dropped, the national witch hunt hadn't. Cancel culture at its finest.

"This is not up for debate." Her mother's words were dagger sharp. "How would we afford this magical house move? IVF is expensive, let alone six rounds. No one would dare give us a mortgage in this state. One working parent with two unemployed adults and a baby to support."

Tears prickled at the corner of Lucy's eyes, but she bit her tongue. Silence was golden. It always had been.

"You know," her father said, "It's getting harder to convince the neighbours you're on a gap year. The rest of your age group is employed or away at university."

Another stab to the gut. Her parents would have only been happy with acceptance to a top university, and never for 'soft subject' like art. She'd spared them all the embarrassment of rejection.

"Well..." he continued, shifting in his seat. "I was holding out to see how this interview went first, but I've got a friend looking for a spare pair of hands on his salmon trawler. They'd give you a lift over the Channel in exchange for some work, and we could set you up with £300 to get you started. You could earn your way as you go," her father commented.

Lucy goggled at him.

"Think about it. They leave in three days. I can drive you to the docks."

"Very generous considering his childcare duties and job-hunting, don't you think?" It was a statement, not a question.

She mentally counted to ten. They wanted to ship off a girl, who spent most of her life in her bedroom, across the globe on her own? She'd never even left the country! She knew people on travel vlogs who did that, but that wasn't her. What would happen if she froze? How long would it take her to get back?

Then realisation hit, sweeping in like a tidal wave. That was the point, wasn't it? To get rid of her. Never mind if they pushed her in at the deep end to drown. They could lie and brag about her success if she wasn't there, and still had child number two to show off. Meanwhile, she'd be lucky to find her next paycheck.

No. She clenched her fists.

She needed to stay. To be the doting big sister, with all the tabloids having her on speed dial for sketches of major courtroom cases. To see Ben's first steps, hear his first words.

"I'll launch my store tonight and keep looking," she said, voice low. "If I don't find anything, then..." She couldn't finish the sentence. Her dinner felt like it was creeping its way up and she bolted.

Lucy spent the bulk of the next two days scrolling through job adverts at her bedroom desk, checking every three minutes for orders. On the second night she'd dreamt her fish and chip supper had put her on trial in a courtroom. She'd woken up in a cold sweat.

The day stretched into the afternoon, and she craned her neck to the ceiling and sighed. Her dream of a big house on the outskirts of Garrowhead City was swimming off into the distance. It would have been a simple life, filled with Cross-Key tech. Top of the line TVs that autotuned to whatever station they wanted at the push of a button. No guessing milk or water temperatures for Ben...

She remembered her fascination with her mother's belly the first time it had grown round, followed by the crushing disappointment when her father said, "There's been a change of plan. The baby had to leave." Then a year later, it happened again. The swollen belly and the disappearance. And again.

Electric guitar and flashing lights exploded from her desk, her phone buzzing. She didn't recognise the number, but the area code looked familiar, so she answered.

A young male voice asked, "Hello. Is Miss Lucy Blakely available, please?"

"I'm Lucy."

"Fantastic! My name is Dave Crossley. I work for Cross-Key & Co. I saw your website and have a job for you."

She lost her grip on her phone, but grasped it tightly before slipping completely out of her hand. Cross-Key. *The* Cross-Key & Co.?

A small spark lit deep in her chest.

*Breathe,* she reminded herself. Oxygen was important. "Is this a one-time commission or a larger project?" She tried to speak like the people in those business pitching shows her dad liked, happy she didn't splutter.

"That would depend on you. We're in a unique situation with a role that's cropped up that we need filled as soon as possible. Could you come to our headquarters in Garrowhead at two o'clock tomorrow for a speed-sketching test?"

She sat up straighter. Speed sketching was her specialty. This could be her chance!

Lucy nodded before remembering she had to use her voice and forced out, "Of course," while her cheeks heated.

"Wonderful! Report to the main reception when you arrive. Bring any other work you think displays your skills, and photo ID."

"OK. I'll be there tomorrow."

"We look forwards to seeing you. Good day, Miss Blakely."

"Thanks. Bye."

*Click!*

She felt lighter than she had for days. Her website had worked, and she'd had a portfolio prepared since she couldn't remember when. But she'd need a lift. Surely her father wouldn't mind if it was for an interview—especially for an award-winning household name.

When she woke up the next day, seeds of doubt had crept in.

The large, muscular frame of Sgt. Sir! grinned down at her from his poster on her bedroom wall. He was the main character of her favourite childhood cartoon: *Sgt. Sir!* where actions spoke louder than words. But while the sergeant's story could be rewritten again and again, she had only one shot to make things work. She couldn't look at him, instead concentrating on changing into her own personal war colours of tan and cream.

The harsh January chill made her shiver as she climbed into the back seat. As they pulled away, butterflies burst into life in her stomach.

She puffed out her cheeks and lips and applied her mum's coconut balm, blowing kisses and funny faces at her miracle of a brother. Ben giggled in his car seat.

Out of the corner of her eye, Lucy saw her dad look, watching the pair through the mirror.

"Radio?" she suggested.

Her father flicked the dashboard.

*"...for the fifth week. Now something for the stargazers out there. This month's full moon is a Wolf Moon."*

"Another popular fad," he grumbled at the wheel.

"Next!" she called, and the radio flipped stations.

*"...and the dish ran away with the spoon!"*

Neither had the heart or gall to take *Tiny Tykes Radio* away from a key listener, who wriggled his approval.

The radio was a mystery of the universe. No matter how picky the person, or what mood they were in, it always found a station to suit the individual or group listening. Like all Cross-Key products, it was pricey but indisputably the best. No one disliked Cross-Key & Co., not even critics who made their living picking brands apart. They were untouchable, which made their pulling up to the security booth at the Cross-Key Industrial Park's entrance all the stranger.

Lucy licked her lips, resisting the urge to apply more balm.

Behind the black wrought-iron gate sprawled factories, office buildings, and warehouses. A guard pointed them towards a five-storey red brick office block near the entrance, screaming big business. Above a rotating glass door, a sign in large silver letters read *Headquarters Main Entrance*.

She stepped out of the car clutching her portfolio.

"I'm heading into town," her dad said, expression like his tone: unreadable. "Call me when you need me to pick you up. Put your best foot forward."

"Thanks," she said, equally blank, wishing she could read minds as he drove off.

She squared herself, turned, then walked through the revolving doors.

Behind a large slate reception desk stood a young woman with dyed caramel hair, not quite covering her dark roots. She had hazel eyes, a smooth complexion, and floral henna wove around her hands and wrists.

Lucy's heart danced the salsa against her ribcage. Why? Why her?!

"Hi!" she said cheerily, looking up. "I'm so glad you turned up. It's been forever, hasn't it? How have you been? Oh, just one sec. I'll let Dave know you've arrived."

Surprised by the enthusiastic greeting, Lucy took refuge by the water cooler as the teen rang through to a back room; the receptionist beaming all the while.

No. The cheer couldn't just be for her. It was her job as a receptionist to be nice to everyone. Not after the incident. But a flash filled her mind of two five-year-old girls leading an imaginary unicorn around in the playground.

The dreaded reality was confirmed when the receptionist turned around, her ID flashing in the light on her chest: Hina Usmani. Her former childhood best friend.

"Dave's on his way down," Hina said, putting down the receiver. "You're five minutes early. Prompt is good."

Condescension or genuine excitement? Lucy couldn't tell, but it felt like the interview had already started.

"You do remember me, right? From sch—" Thankfully, the phone rang, distracting the cheery teen, and Lucy quietly thanked whoever had interrupted them.

Then a man wearing a long white lab coat came out, clipboard in hand and pen poking out from behind his ear under a mop of blond.

"Miss Blakely?"

She nodded, recognising Dave's voice from his call.

"We're glad you could make it on such short notice. Please follow me."

As the pair walked—or ducked in Lucy's case—past reception, she glimpsed the word *interpreter* on the top page of the clipboard. Her skin prickled in horror. What on Earth did that have to do with drawing?

Two hours later, Lucy walked back out with an aching arm. After three rounds of speed sketching and the strangest inkblot interpretation exercises she'd ever seen, the job was hers. A literal artistic interpreter. Who in the world communicated only through drawings?

At least it wasn't speaking vocally. That was a small mercy! And who would live on-site who would need her 24/7?

Oh well. Best not look a gift horse in the mouth. She had a job, plus a roof over her head...for a week at least.

Two days later, Lucy walked into the common area of the Cross-Key & Co. staff's residential building, and wow.

A hot, sweaty auburn-haired teen lay on an exercise mat at the foot of the sofa. His grey tracksuit rippled across his torso as he reached up and brushed his fringe out of sky-blue eyes. He flashed her a bright mid-workout grin. "Hi. I'm Will. You're Lucy, right?"

Muscle function returning, she smiled back and nodded.

He gave a thumbs up. "Cool," he said, and her cheeks warmed. "I started just after New Year, so it's been almost two weeks for me." His eyes followed the workers carrying boxes across the common room to her suite and whistled. "That's a lot of stuff. I hope you unpack OK. I spend most of my free time here, so give me a shout if you ever want company."

"Thanks," she said, preparing to avoid him at all costs. A workman handed her a key for her suite, and she made her not-so-metaphorical run for escape.

The room carried on the same neutral Cross-Key colour palette. Standing in front of a generous double bed, she glimpsed herself in the wall-length mirror. At least her clothes would blend in there. Neutral, non-threatening, and part of the background. Exactly as she wanted.

Although her home away from home shouted modest, it was kitted out with luxurious Cross-Key tech. The white light turned on as she walked in, not too bright or dim. The water from the tap in her en suite was just right, too. It was all very welcoming and how she preferred. But it wasn't...home.

After an hour of unpacking her stomach growled. There could be ingredients in the kitchen, but they weren't hers. Perched on her bed, she connected her phone to the building's wi-fi and searched for nearby takeaways.

She wondered if she should order something for Will, too, as a goodwill gesture. Actions spoke louder than words. But she didn't know if he had allergies or what he liked. Plus, that would invite extra conversation. Words were a messy business. Resolving to offer in future when there were less risky variables, she placed her own order. She liked Will too much to chance sticking her foot in things so early.

Day 0 complete. She could survive a seven-day trial, couldn't she? She counted her lucky stars she'd be living on-site. Otherwise...well, that ship had literally sailed.

One pizza later, she'd set her alarm ready for day 1 and climbed into bed, wondering who'd made tea, and what time Ben had gone to sleep.

# Chapter Two

# A Trial of Ink and Blood

T he journey from the residential building to Cross-Key & Co.'s headquarters seemed to be in high definition. Damp tarmac clicked beneath her feet, and the wet grass lining the estate paths stung her nose.

It was Monday, day 1, and she had no idea what she was walking into. Who was the client she'd be interpreting for? Old? A genius? An investor? The job was a mystery, but the room it came with was too good to ignore.

Hina was already at reception when she arrived at 8:25 a.m. A wide smile juxtaposed bags not quite hidden beneath her eyeliner—hallmarks of a long weekend. "Hi, Newbie. Congrats on the new job. You were always good at drawing."

Lucy tried to smile, restraining the urge to tap her foot by vice-gripping her satchel. They paused for an awkward beat. Hina, thankfully, picked up her phone to call Dave, who arrived in a flourish with a white lab coat billowing out behind him and a clipboard clutched to his chest. "Lucy, glad to have you on board."

Lucy stuck out her hand and gave him a firm handshake.

"First, we'll get you your identification and access sorted, then I'll introduce you to your charge."

Lucy nodded and followed. Three flights of stairs later, they stopped at a thick metal door covered in all manner of security gadgets: a keypad combination lock, two keyholes, and if all else failed, Lucy observed, a chain. Security Department was embossed in silver along the adjacent wall, and beneath, a thumb scanner and card reader.

Dave didn't even finish raising an arm when the door swung open.

Inside, a wall of monitors stretched from floor to ceiling. Scenes of the estate played in real time of roads, warehouses, laboratories, and meeting rooms. Spotting the top of her head on one monitor, she looked up, following the perspective to the square ceiling panels. Nothing.

"Doesn't miss a trick this one, does she?" came a gruff, low voice behind Dave's shoulder. He was large, with the monitor light illuminating cool sepia skin. He wore a crisp black suit with matching sunglasses even though they were indoors, and his grey hair was slicked back to a bald patch. She remembered him standing in the schoolyard waiting for Hina at 3:30 p.m. Hina's father. She suppressed a shudder.

"Kamal Usmani, night security manager. I asked to work overtime so I could meet you. Fancy seeing you working here alongside my Hina. Thought you'd end up in academia like your mother." The comment hit harshly.

She stayed silent.

The manager looked stern, but at least it wasn't an outright scowl. If he held anything against her, he didn't show it. After all, Hina's and her friendship had stopped under strained circumstances.

"Enhanced starter package, please," Dave requested.

"Section?"

"Research and Development. Full. Twenty-four-hour access."

Kamal whistled. "Thrown in at the deep end." He moved behind a monitor.

Lucy heard keys tapping, followed by strings of beeps, clunks and...a laser?

Then he picked something up, blew on it, and handed her a metal badge displaying the Cross-Key & Co. logo. It read: *Lucy Blakely, Head Illustrator, Artistic Interpretation Division.*

She was a department head at Cross-Key. What did it matter if she was the only one in it? Resisting the urge to photograph it (she'd send it to her parents later) she pinned it to her blouse.

"That's a tracker device and your employee ID. We'll use it to log your hours and location."

The badge looked plain, and she couldn't spot anything that looked like a tracker. Then again, she thought, they had pretty much invisible CCTV.

Next, he handed her a lanyard with a plastic card attached. Her own face stared back up at her, literally up from when she'd searched for the hidden camera earlier; her button nose scrunched and mousy hair falling into her eyes. Bitterness it was then.

"This is your access ID," said Kamal sternly. "It will open every door in this headquarters other than on the managers' floor and the Security Department. It'll let you in the other office buildings around the site and into the Research and Development zone, both levels. Only a select few have access to the lower levels, and most employees don't know they exist."

What was she getting herself into?

"Lend no one your ID cards, especially the door access; and if you lose it, inform us immediately. We have a perfect record, and you don't want to be the person to blemish it, do you?"

"Yes," Dave said, waving a hand. "It's a wonderful record. Can I have the paperwork, please?"

Lucy let out a controlled breath as they left, then crossed half the estate back towards the residential building. They stopped at a large red brick factory. Engraved in the bricks above the door read: *Research and Development.*

Security guards waved to Dave as they walked into a gigantic hall. Doors lined the sides of the walls along with large windows showing smaller testing labs, and running down the hall's centre was a row of computers and whiteboards. Scientists bustled about all over the place, with the odd plain-clothed employee here or there.

Lucy watched in fascination at the trials being carried out, though she couldn't imagine what they were working on. Parents holding babies queued outside one room, and beyond the glass she saw adults trying to coax their babies to swallow spoonfuls of mush. She'd done plenty of that with Ben.

Dave spotted her glance. "We're attempting to create our own brand of baby food. We've got high hopes for another best-seller."

Lucy believed it. Maybe working here, she'd learn their secret to success. To perfection.

They stopped at the last doorway on the left, which opened onto a hallway. Halfway down, Dave raised his ID to open a door, and Lucy was yanked into a cupboard barely large enough for the two of them. She gasped and inhaled thick, dusty air—a stark contrast to the clean, pristine estate outside. A naked dim yellow light sprang to life as the door closed behind them, just enough to make out old Cross-Key & Co. products.

"Sorry, but pay attention," he said, and twisted a multipack of Cross-Key cat food. Then he gave the shelf a shove, and the stack swung open.

Light bounced around the underground dome, illuminating as well as any natural window or skylight.

"This is your office, so to speak," Dave said, pulling out a seat. Lucy followed his lead. "It's one of several vault rooms, and where you'll communicate with your charge."

He slid open a panel on the tabletop and pulled out a large oak-coloured softback notebook with a grey spine. After closing the compartment, he set the book down between them, flipping it open to a double spread of blank off-white pages. Then he placed a box on the table and opened it, revealing a vast assortment of pens, from cheap markers to high-end fountain pens.

"Please draw yourself standing with a hand against a tree trunk."

Lucy bit back her questions, and wanting to look decisive, reached for a black fine liner and began.

Her black-and-white image-self stood sideways, right palm outstretched, touching the bark of an enormous tree trunk.

Moving to turn it around, Dave cut her off, hand raised. "Watch and wait," he said, eyes fixed on the drawing.

For what? Right when she'd concluded Dave was crazy, the image faded into the paper, leaving the page blank again. She gaped.

"Amazing, isn't it? We've printed entire pages into the book and they all disappear without a trace. Wonderful picture. I liked it while it lasted," he said regretfully. "But at least we'll get to see plenty more, eh?"

Without waiting for a response, he produced a small plastic tube and removed the lid. "This device is used to test blood sugar levels. When you press the button, it gives your finger a small prick and a drop of blood will appear. We require a quick blood test before we can continue."

Was a medical test necessary for an artist? Dubious. Unwilling to risk rocking the boat, she nodded cautiously. He lifted a medical kit onto the table before wiping the tip of the pen with a sterilising wipe and handed it to her.

She placed it to her fingertip, braced, and pushed. Not bad.

Dave held out a test strip, which Lucy placed against the bleeding tip, covering it. Then she took an offered ball of cotton wool, pressing it against the wound to stem the flow.

"Alright, now you can meet your charge," Dave said, and wiped the strip with her blood onto the page. The blood faded as the ink had, and Lucy's eyes widened.

At the top of the page, a dot appeared. It expanded into a circle and kept growing outwards until the edges smudged. A blood red sun shone up at her. No. It wasn't blood red. It *was* blood.

Tingles trickled from her head down to her toes, as if someone had cracked an egg on it, then warmth suddenly enveloped her like a big hug. It was nice, comforting actually, and to her dismay, faded ten seconds later with the image.

"That's how Oda says hello," Dave explained cheerily.

*Oda?*

"How did...?" she trailed off.

Dave reached out and stroked down the book's inside cover. "When a Cross-Key employee discovered this notebook, he immediately brought it to our Research and Development department. They tasked me to head a confidential investigation. International relations are in my remit."

Noticing her slack jaw, Lucy hastily closed it and gripped her trouser legs beneath the table.

"We believe this book is inhabited by a tree spirit. While Western cultures usually imagine tree spirits as female fairies, dryads, and forest nymphs, we think this is closer to the Eastern version called a kodama. We call it Oda for short."

Lucy's mind reeled. Spirits and ghosts were nonsense. But then how else could she explain the disappearing and reappearing ink? A sick practical joke? Though she couldn't deny the warmth she'd felt was real. A tree spirit, though?

Dave continued, his pace quickening with enthusiasm. "There's intelligent life here. Oda responds well to pictures of trees, as well as the sun and rain, though our attempts to teach it the alphabet and words failed because it can't hear. With your drawing abilities and the blood bond you just made, we hope we'll be able to find out a lot more about Oda and their kind."

Lucy nodded while desperately hoping Dave would say something that made sense.

"Legends say a kodama sticks with the same tree until the end of the tree's life. We think when the tree was felled to create this notebook, the spirit inhabiting it stayed with it into death. We don't know why, but it's something we want to find out."

The door to the dome banged open.

Kamal strode down the staircase and crossed the room. He removed his sunglasses and his dark brown eyes fixed Lucy with a piercing gaze. Her face prickled as blood drained from it.

Dave, however, acknowledged him with a grin, pulling out the papers from earlier. "I was just getting around to it," Dave said.

"Not quick enough," quipped the security guard. "I was watching. Those should have been signed before your little demonstration."

This confirmed Lucy's suspicions. Others knew, and they'd been watching her. But who?

Dave handed Lucy a clipboard. "To continue your trial, you're required to sign this non-disclosure agreement. You may not say who you are interpreting for, and you will not talk about Oda to anyone who does not talk about it to you first."

"Of course," Kamal drawled, "even if you tell anyone about it, you'd be called crazy, and the weight of our global reputation would back that up."

Lucy gulped, holding back a sting of tears, but she bent forwards and signed her name. Dave took it with a smile. "Most kind. I'll drop this in to Human Resources."

Kamal huffed. "It's the end of my overtime."

"Vigilant as always. Thank you for your service," Dave replied before turning to Lucy. "As eager as I am to continue, I recommend you take the rest of the day off. It's likely a bit of a shock. Go and let things sink in, and keep an eye out for a delivery this afternoon. I'll send over a company pocket communicator. From midnight, we expect you to be on call."

All the way back to her apartment, Lucy replayed her morning. Then, as promised later that afternoon, a communicator the size of a black tablet arrived.

It beeped when she turned it on, and a small green envelope appeared in the centre. She tapped it.

Miss Lucy Blakely,

Welcome to your trial period at Cross-Key & Co. Please use this device for internal communications. Due to the on-call nature of your role, we request you keep this device charged and with you at all times.

See attached your proposed employment contract. Should both you and Cross-Key & Co. sign the document within the next six days, your position will be secure.

Until then, we request you report for enhanced security checks every day at Security Department (Headquarters).

Human Resources

❦❦❦❦❦ ❦❦❦❦❦

Tuesday broke to the bombastic brass opening theme of *Sgt. Sir!* the first series, something Lucy only deployed on occasions where she, too, felt like she was going to battle.

After completing her morning routine, she put her ear to the bedroom door and waited. Silence. One hastily tiptoed journey to the kitchen later, she retreated to her room.

Ducking past Hina at reception, she made her way to Security HQ, shoulders tensing as she approached. The door opened and—

A young man in a black suit sat hunched in front of the row of screens, curly blond hair hanging as limp as his frame. Although his eyes were hidden behind trademark security sunglasses, tiredness radiated off the slumped figure in waves.

"You the interpreter?" he asked.

Lucy nodded.

He scratched the back of a shoulder, sighed, then stood up and held out a hand.

"Alex Matisse. Day security manager. Sorry you had to put up with Mr Usmani yesterday. He's a bit uptight."

True, she thought, as images of the straight-backed, stern-faced night manager came to mind. But this man was so laid-back he may as well be lying down.

He reached into a drawer and pulled out a machine similar to a bar code scanner, ran it over the badge on her chest, and it beeped.

"All done, Ms Interpreter. Dave will tell us when you're finished work. Have a good day." Without waiting for a reply, he trailed off down the row of screens, stopped in front of a desk drawer, reached in, and pulled out a bag of fruit chews.

Lucy took her leave. Retracing her steps, she scanned herself into the Research and Development building and found her way to the cupboard and tins of cat food. With a twist and a shove, the hidden shelves swung open. Bottling her breaths to contain her excitement, she went through the doorway and down the stairs in the dome.

Dave was already there, typing rapidly at a computer display by one wall.

"She's your charge. Why don't you get her out?"

She? Did spirits have genders? She mentally resolved to stick with 'they' until she could ask Oda one day, then eagerly reached for the hidden panel on the work surface. With a gentle push, the hidden mechanism opened, and Lucy gently pulled out the notebook, smiling at the coarse surface beneath her fingertips.

"I'm glad we didn't scare you off," Dave chuckled. He wheeled a large projector and light over to the table so it looked down onto the centre.

"Put Oda in position. That's it. Nice and centre. So, our current theory is she's trying to communicate by mentally projecting her emotions. Did you feel her enthusiastic greeting?"

Lucy remembered the warm, invisible hug. Did this mean the tree spirit was psychic? Some sort of reverse empath? She nodded.

"Bearing that in mind, we'll need you to say what you feel when Oda returns an image. That will help us work out what she's trying to say."

"Sure," she agreed. Yesterday's butterflies had taken over her heart's quick step.

"Picking up from yesterday, she can't hear or feel. We've tried both and no response. Liquids, on the other hand, she'll happily absorb. Must be a tree thing. We drew a wiggly line in ink and she drew it back to us perfectly upside down."

Lucy nodded, trying to keep up with the torrent of words, most passing her by. What she did understand was Oda was unlike anything she'd ever seen. A brilliant, naive, innocent child. Like Ben. The world, and people, were harsh. Manipulative. Oda needed shielding, guiding, a friend. She could do that. Beneath the table, she clenched her fist. If she could last the week, her brain reminded her.

"Today's task is to find out how much she understands about time, so I thought we could start with ageing using trees and humans."

For the next three hours, Lucy sketched a series of images. On one hand: saplings, fully grown trees, and dead stumps. On the other: babies, children, teenagers, adults, the elderly, and a skeleton.

She left lunch early to practice speed-sketching the images. If she hesitated drawing them, Oda would think she'd finished and absorb it early, making every picture a race.

At 2:30 p.m. she drew her introductory image of herself pressing a hand against the bark. The image returned shrunk, with a small sun glowing above. This time the heat pounced, wrapping itself around her in a tight embrace.

"Oda recognised me," she said in awe. Then began the tightrope walk of drawing the images as quickly and precisely as she could.

After three false starts, arms zinging with adrenalin, the complete message was finally drawn, and Lucy watched it sink into the page in satisfaction.

The return came slowly. An elderly woman standing under a tree. That image faded, replaced with a seed cracking open and a baby next to it—both underground.

Lucy couldn't stop her giggle, and Dave didn't even try. He clutched his sides, gasping as he tried to speak. "Decomposing...when they die...enriches soil...but tomorrow...we need to explain...babies don't grow underground!"

Beeping cut through the laughter, and Dave looked at his wristwatch. "Sorry to cut this short, but I've got a meeting in ten minutes. Same time tomorrow."

Lucy stood, stretching her right hand. Laughter was excellent medicine, but now she'd calmed down, she couldn't ignore her throbbing cramp in her palm. She resolved not to draw that night and let it recover for day 3.

By Thursday, Lucy had formed a routine. She spent her mornings planning with Dave, after lunch practised drawing the planned images at speed, then mid-to-late afternoon she'd introduce herself to Oda with her customary image. That part could never come quick enough, and on the fourth day Oda welcomed Lucy by wrapping her in the equivalent of a thick duvet toastie.

Having explained babies didn't grow underground on Wednesday, she'd moved on to explaining humans got their nutrients from food instead of soil. She sketched a child putting an apple into their mouth, followed by a teenager who did the same, and lastly, an adult.

It was a gamble. Would Oda see the images as someone stealing from the tree's branches?

When the image returned, she sank back into her chair's metal frame.

"Oda's drawn a sun, which we know means well wishes, and is showing a child being showered with apples, like rain." Her words came out clunky as she tried to piece together her answer.

"That makes sense," Dave said. "The reason trees make fruit is for animals to eat. It helps the seeds to travel away from under the canopy of the parent so they're deposited in the sun when the animal...how should I say this? Defecates. A mutual working relationship between animals and trees. This is gold dust for my report." He picked up a clipboard and pulled out a pen from behind his ear.

"We're coming on in leaps and bounds. I think tomorrow we'll move on to birds. Thanks for your hard work today. I'll see you tomorrow, up with the larks," he ended with a chuckle.

Lucy put on a fake smile as she packed up her things. She knew nothing about birds. She didn't even risk drawing robins on Christmas cards. Waving goodbye, she walked away and tried to ignore the sickening pit of despair opening in her stomach.

Walking back to the residential building, she stretched her stiff hand. Ideally she needed to practise, but if she did so while in pain she wouldn't last the week in her job. It was a no-win situation.

She flopped on the bed and covered her head with her aching hand, wincing as a sudden jolt shot across her wrist. Definitely no practice. But she had to do something if she wanted a place to live at the end of the week.

Friday started like all the others—with a brass blast of *Sgt. Sir!* commanding Lucy back from the Land of Nod. She'd fallen asleep slumped over her tablet with tab after tab open on bird anatomy.

Day 5, and as far as she knew, she hadn't done or said anything too stupid or insulting. Just one working day left, then her future was secure. Right?

Violent buzzing tore through the air on her morning walk across the estate. A man in a harness up a tree tucked between two warehouses held a chainsaw up to a tree branch. The machine jarred as it hacked its way through the limb before an entire branch fell to the ground with a sickening thud.

Lucy tore her eyes away, clutched her satchel to her side, and tried not to break out into a jog. That was the sort of thing a government would do to force out tree spirits if they knew about their existence. She thanked her lucky stars that Cross-Key & Co. were the ones who had found the poor creature.

Her night-time study had paid off. After sketching out a few birds perched on branches, she drew a nest filled with eggs and a brooding blackbird—then promptly panicked, and prayed she hadn't just announced to Oda that she was pregnant.

"Something wrong? Do you need a break?" Dave asked, concerned.

Lucy's face turned cold, and she stopped like a deer in headlights. Dave kept looking, so she shook her head again, and mumbled, "I'm fine," then refused to look anywhere else other than down at the page.

With the confirmation of recognition that Oda understood birds could fly—and not just disappear and reappear on different branches, as the pictures suggested—Dave called an end to a long day's work.

# CHAPTER THREE

# SCRATCH THAT

There was no avoiding it. Wait any longer and she'd become a nuisance they'd have to chase up. Call too soon, and they'd assume she wasn't coping. The pressure to phone home had reached boiling point.

After heading into town to eat and avoid awkward common room encounters, she made her choice and headed back to the staff residential building.

Once safe in the confines of her room, she sat cross-legged on the fluffy duvet and dialled her house phone number for the first time. Although she'd had it drilled into her from a young age, there had never been an emergency for her to use it. It gave her a feeling of being on the outside—of being *other*.

Lucy's hands trembled when the dial tone ended, replaced by a breath and a male clipped, "Hello?"

She let out a breath, forcing herself to relax. "Hi Dad, it's me."

"Lucy." It was a statement rather than a question. "I saw you got head of your department in your photos. About time you got yourself a decent position, eh?"

Lucy paused mid-nod, closed her eyes at her own stupidity, and forced out a verbal reply. Next time she'd make sure to video call. "Yes," she agreed, fingering her head of department badge, and scrambled for something to say. Too much awkward silence and he'd suspect something was wrong. "Hina Usmani from primary school is here, working at the reception desk, and her dad works in security."

"Really? That's interesting," he said, but he didn't expand on how. Metal clanged in the background and she longed to ask what was going on. Not having automatic access to those details made the thirty-minute drive away feel like a different continent.

"How are you all getting on?" Her fingers ached from gripping the phone so tightly. She wasn't sure if she wanted an answer. If they were doing well, it meant they were better off without her. If they were struggling, maybe she shouldn't have left after all. She held her breath.

"Well, I've had several companies contact me, but they weren't what I was looking for."

Lucy read between the lines. No one was willing to give a managerial position to someone whose company went under during their leadership.

"Your mum's working all the hours under the sun as usual. She's a force of nature." Lucy could hear the accented tones of pride mixed with the disgruntled complaint. "Ben's just about ready to move into his new room. You caught me with a paintbrush in hand. It's a dark forest green, and we've got new furniture for it arriving at the weekend."

Her mouth felt dry, and she raised her left hand to her throat. The freeze was coming but was saved by a loud wail in the background. Ben had come to her rescue.

Her father huffed. "Duty calls again. Bye, Luce." *Click.* Silence.

A salty tang startled her, tears contacting her tongue.

They were moving on without her. Already. Her trial hadn't even finished, but they'd already painted her room and bought new furniture. Lucy learned from a young age that actions spoke louder than words, and this message was loud and clear. She wasn't welcome back. So she was on her own—sink or swim. Whether she drowned was up to her.

What did she have? An income and a roof over her head, at least until the end of the week, if she screwed nothing up. A position at a world-renowned company, if she kept her head down. Oda, a secret newly discovered being who was genuinely happy to see her, and a job that appreciated her drawing talents—if she could push past the cramps in her hand and arm.

Oda relied on that talent, on her, like Ben had been to survive, protected from a harsh, unknown world. They were innocent, vulnerable, and filled with curiosity to explore. They were the same. The newfound tree spirit and the miracle baby.

A jigsaw piece of resolve slotted into place. Her mission was clear. She'd be the best interpreter she could be, keep her job, and be so successful her parents would brag about her so the spotlight would never have to be shone on Ben in the first place. He'd get the freedom and leniency to grow and be what he wanted to be—something she'd always craved. She'd make them smile, so he didn't have to.

Her determination transformed into a rod of steel that ran down the length of her arm, stripping away the ache of the day's drawing. She picked up her communicator device, opened the contract she'd received on her first day, scrolled to the bottom, and signed her name.

❦❦❦❦❦ ❦❦❦❦❦

Lucy walked to work on Friday with her jacket slung over her satchel. It was unusually warm, and although it was a one-off, she longed for spring so the trees would come to life with buds and blossoms.

A rustling noise stopped her in her tracks. She felt the eyes before she could see them. She turned and looked over her shoulder, but saw no one other than the warehouse workers milling around on the other side of the street. Clutching her satchel tighter to her side, heart thumping, she took another couple of steps.

*Rustle.*

She glanced back again, and a short-haired black cat crawled out from a bush onto the path, staring at her with wide eyes. It froze, one white paw in front of the other, mid-step.

Lucy smiled and bent down, clicking her tongue, and held out her hand. Feeling her grip on her satchel slip, she took it off and shifted into a squat, clicking again, hand outstretched.

The fur ball edged closer, stopping and starting, until it stopped a whisker away from the tips of her fingers.

She didn't move. Its tail twitched, the only warning before it launched forward and slashed, and darted back into the bush.

Blood oozed from the three stripes of ripped skin; the sting was sharp. Cold tingles began at the tips of her fingers as the warmth seeped away. Why? Why did she risk it, even if the fur with eyes was cute?

She fumbled to open her satchel one-handed—trying to not get blood over her clothes or bag. The pavement didn't escape, spotted red. Grabbing a bottle of water, she poured it over her arm, then dabbed away the excess with emergency tissues, pressing against the wound.

Bundling her bag and coat under her good arm, she jogged the rest of the way to Headquarters. Silently chanting for Hina not to spot her, she ducked through reception to the adjoining public toilets.

At least it wasn't her right hand; then she really would have been out of commission. She peeled the tissue away, then held the arm under the cold water tap. After patting it dry, she fashioned a makeshift bandage, finishing it with tape from her arts supplies.

It wasn't worth risking her job over cat scratch fever, so she dug out her phone. 8:24 a.m. She knew she was too early for the surgery to be open, but she had to get to work. After leaving a message on their answer machine, she looked in the mirror.

It was just a scratch. She could get an emergency dinnertime appointment and take a long lunch.

Pulling on her jacket to cover the wound, she headed out to the main reception.

Hina stood behind the desk and waved enthusiastically when she saw her. "Day 5 already, new girl? Keep up the good work. Stay there. Dave told me to stop you on your way in," she said, then flashed her a thumbs up and picked up the receiver.

Lucy decided it would be a good time to examine a modern art piece next to the toilet entrance to avoid being drawn in to awkward conversation. She still hadn't worked out what to say to the girl, and she wasn't looking forward to it.

Dave entered with a spring in his step, his grin so wide it looked like it would split his face in two.

"We're thrilled you signed your contract early. This makes things so much easier. Our Chief Executive Officer wants to see you. I meet with her every day, and I've been telling her how Project Oda has been coming along—in leaps and bounds—all with your help. It's wonderful news. Come on. We'll take the lift. Top floor." Lucy could barely keep up with him; both words and strides as they entered a lift at the back of the building.

They stepped out into a short corridor with one ornate solid wood door at the end. The silver Cross-Key & Co. logo was attached in metal on the front and beneath that, written in gold ornate letters: *Margaret Crossley, Chief Executive Officer.*

Dave knocked, and a receptionist invited them into a small waiting room.

Five minutes later, the receptionist announced, "Mrs Crossley will see you now," and Lucy followed Dave into a small office where an older, rounder female stood, hand outstretched. Dave greeted her. Lucy shook it.

"It's nice to meet you, Miss Blakely. Please take a seat and we can start."

Mrs Crossley took the black executive office chair on the other side of an enormous desk and Lucy took the seat Dave indicated on his right. She sank into the black foam, one of the few focal points of the room that oozed luxury. The desk filled the room with a fresh pine smell and the award-lined walls were exposed brick. A gold-flecked Roman shade covered a ceiling-to-floor window, and the room was lit dimly by a papier mâché lamp that looked like a full moon. It was a terrible clash of time periods and Cross-Key perfection.

A slim figure stood in the left corner—a lady with blonde hair neatly tied back, wearing the same thick sunglasses as the security managers. A guard? Compared to the curvaceous Mrs Crossley, this lady had a lithe, svelte figure. Her pale skin bordered on sickly, but the rippling six pack beneath her violet pantsuit said otherwise. She couldn't place the material. Nylon perhaps? The short woman stood poker straight, arms crossed. The CEO's personal bodyguard?

Dave inclined his head to the woman, and she tilted her head in return. Not knowing if she should introduce herself or not, she placed her hands on her lap and smiled out into the room expectantly.

Mrs Crossley came to the rescue. "I was delighted to hear how well you've settled in. Dave's reports about you have been glowing. I'm over the moon that you decided to join us before the trial concluded."

Lucy's cheeks grew warm.

"Before we go any further, I have a brief formality to attend to." The CEO held out her ring-covered fingers and Dave handed her a collection of papers from his lab-coat pocket. Lucy glimpsed a familiar signature on the bottom of the cover sheet and her breath hitched.

"On the recommendation of Dave Crossley and having looked at your references and the results of your trial so far, Cross-Key & Co. would like to offer you an official position on Project Oda."

Lucy's heart hammered in her chest, beating a drum of victory as Mrs Crossley picked up a pen and signed her name with a practised flourish beneath Lucy's signature. Dave picked them up and said, "I'll hand this in to Human Resources on my way out. Lucy, I'll also arrange the payment for purchasing your business to be sent to your new payroll account."

Lucy nodded and choked out, "Thank you," which sounded like a squeak.

Mrs Crossley continued, "We're very pleased that Oda appears to have made a bond with you. We're keen to deepen the friendship between our two species. The Cross-Key motto is 'In Good Company,' even across species. How do you suppose our toasters work?"

Lucy blinked at the sudden change of topic, thinking back to the red toaster in her family's kitchen. Not wanting to admit she didn't know, she pivoted. "It always makes the perfect toast."

"Indeed," Mrs Crossley said, smiling. "The secret behind that perfection is a technology that no other company on Earth knows exists. We at Cross-Key research and innovate using technologies from other species."

Lucy's brain ground to a halt and her polite smile almost cracked. Was that a joke?

"They are the partners of our company—our '& Co.' I believe I can hand things over now to my guest for the next part of this explanation." She raised an arm and motioned to the pale woman who stepped to stand at her side.

"It's nice to meet you, Miss Lucy Blakely. I am Cecelia and I am here as an ambassador for my people." Her voice was high-pitched but as smooth as pearls. It sounded young, but her tone was all business. "It's my job to help maintain peace between our races, and to foster a productive working relationship of trade and research. I am a vampire."

*What?*

Lucy's mind ground to a halt, attempting and failing to process the statement in several ways.

It would explain the ultra-athletic physique—or perhaps not. Maybe there were overweight vampires, for all she knew? It was daytime, but the blinds were closed. Hiding away from the sun? A lamp was on, but Cecelia wore black sunglasses shielding her eyes—perhaps the lights were too bright for her? That didn't mean she was a vampire, though. Were fangs a prerequisite for being a vampire? She couldn't see any at this distance.

The only thing she knew about vampires was that they drank blood, and in all the films, they could smell it like sharks. She had to know if this was real.

As casually as she could, Lucy moved her arms behind her back, camouflaging her movement with a smile and tilt of the head. Using her right hand, she pushed up her jacket sleeve and pulled the makeshift bandage loose.

"That's not very smart, Miss," Cecelia warned, her voice deadpan.

Lucy froze.

"Margaret, your new employee is injured. She ought to take more care if she's going to act as interpreter for your people."

Mrs Crossley raised an eyebrow and stared at Lucy in a silent command that said, "Show me."

Cecelia knew. A fact that Mrs Crossley had accepted and not questioned. Trying to hide a slight quake in her left arm, she took off her jacket and showed the arm with the bandage to the room. She battled the lump of shame growing in her throat, coughed dryly, and uttered, "A cat caught me on the way in today."

"She speaks," Cecelia remarked, voice laced with exaggerated shock. "As quiet as a church mouse, this one."

Lucy froze, cheeks heating.

The CEO turned to the vampire. "Indeed. Please take her down to the medical supplies bay after our discussion. We can't have our interpreter without the use of her arms or hands."

"Of course," Cecelia replied curtly.

"Do you think you can wait a little longer?" the CEO asked.

Not trusting her voice, Lucy nodded.

"I appreciate this will come as a shock, so here's a bit of history to help clear things up. Cross-Key & Co. was founded by my ancestors. The phrase 'in good company' was coined in the early medieval period, as a sign of peaceful trading between humans and vampires, and later, werewolves. My family have safeguarded the existence of these groups ever since."

Lucy's eyebrows shot up. Werewolves, too?

"Little Miss," Cecelia chimed in. "Why do you think vampires and werewolves are merely things of legend? Tell me," Cecelia ordered in her high-pitched lilt. The voice danced in her head as she stiffened at the unexpected question. How was she meant to know? Then quickly berated herself for panicking.

Falling back on her anti-freeze training, she concentrated on releasing the tension built up in her shoulders, allowing her to think clearly. She dug deep into her past for a memory, where she sat on a carpet in a classroom, their teacher talking about stories. "Myths are just stories, but legends are meant to have a grain of truth," she recalled.

"Exactly. We do exist; we just don't live here anymore. In the early 1300s vampires and werewolves came under increasing persecution as the Church increased its hold across the world. Vampires do not sleep, so we dedicated ourselves day and night to finding a way out. While mankind was stunted in a theology cycle, we advanced. Harnessing our own energy systems, we cracked open the field of blood alchemy, which paved the way to new technologies. My kind have issues with sunlight, and werewolves like to be closer to moonlight, so just before the turn of the century we slid off into space in our first ever space vessel." Cecelia sounded bored, as if she'd just delivered a droll history lesson.

Lucy's mind cobbled together what she'd been told. Vampires and werewolves. In space. Vampires and werewolves in space.

"Of course, not everyone working here knows about this," Dave added, and Lucy jumped, forgetting he was there. Everyone kindly ignored it, and Dave continued. "Only Crossley family members know about this—and now you. No one in our immediate or extended family had the artistic skill set required to handle communicating well enough with our new tree spirit friend."

Her scalp prickled as the praise and responsibility hit her. She was honoured, but the familiar weight of burden closed in, moulding her wonder into frightened awe.

Mrs Crossley nodded, smiling encouragingly. "The next stage of the project," she said, "will be introducing Oda officially to the vampire and werewolf races. As was written into the Charter of Exploration and Secrecy

36

by my family so long ago, the first race to make contact with another intelligent species must do the formal introductions to the others."

Pain shot up Lucy's arm and she winced. Glancing down, she saw her knuckles had gone white; she'd been gripping her thighs so tightly. Loosening them, she tuned back in to the older woman.

"The meeting will take place at the Fleet. The Fleet is a group of twenty-two vessels, currently spread over three locations in space, which house the entire vampire and werewolf populations. We will be going to a particular vessel called The Bureau. They handle issues regarding species relations, law enforcement, defence, secrecy behind technology patents, and interspecies trade deals."

Lucy clung to the serious edge in the older woman's voice like a lifeline securing her to the ground, struggling to stop her mind floating away to images of faceless green aliens entering church buildings—rockets counting down to launch behind the steeple.

*Knock. Knock. Knock.*

Lucy jumped again. The door cracked open. At first all she saw was empty air, then a pleasant male voice said, "Biscuits anyone?" She lowered her gaze to find the voice and saw a familiar mop of brown-red hair.

"Will," Mrs Crossley greeted. "Do come in. We're almost finished."

A low rumbling sound brought the teen into view, propelling himself into the room in a wheelchair, a plate of assorted biscuits on his lap.

Lucy's breath caught, like someone had punched her in the gut.

"Fantastic. I'd love a biscuit," said Dave cheerily. "Would you like one, Lucy?" He took one, then passed the plate to Lucy, who took one without a word.

She shoved it into her mouth absent-mindedly and the biscuit stuck to the roof of her mouth it was so dry. Why was her mouth so dry? Oh yes, it was a sign of shock, wasn't it? Funny that. Why would she be in shock?

Dave chuckled, seeming to understand her predicament. "Water?" he asked.

Lucy nodded.

He stood up and walked around the desk to the customary water cooler that seemed to be in every room in the building. She took the offered cup and resisted the urge to drink it all down in one gulp, instead opting for small and frequent sips while her mind ran away in circles of impossibilities.

"As I was saying," Mrs Crossley continued, "The meeting to present Oda will take place next week. As interpreter, you'll be required to convey messages to and from the tree spirit. Cecelia will be working with you and Dave to help you prepare."

Lucy nodded, raising her glass to her lips for another drink. It was empty. When had that happened?

"Excellent. Our meeting is at an end. I have a stock check meeting with Will and Dave now, so would you please take care of our newest recruit?"

Cecelia curtsied at the request.

"Lucy, I know this is a lot for you to take in. You can always talk to Cecelia, Dave, and Will about this. I believe you also know Miss Hina Usmani on reception. You may also speak to her about this. She's a family member."

Lucy's legs felt like spaghetti when she stood up, but she still managed to stick out her hand. The CEO grasped it in a soft shake.

Cecelia glided towards the door with a swanlike grace. Lucy followed, wondering how Will was so calm about everything?!

# Chapter Four

# Moonlight and Beyond

B y the third dome Lucy was lost. Instead of heading outside to the Research and Development building, Cecelia had brought her through a network of underground corridors and chambers. Eventually, the pair climbed a staircase and exited into what looked like an empty hospital bay. Low humming reverberated around the room, but Lucy couldn't find the source. A large window and door led into a staff room where scientists bustled, cups in one hand and clipboards in the other, oblivious to the background noises.

"Have a seat. I'll get the supplies we need," Cecelia instructed, and Lucy perched on the corner of the bed nearest to the door.

The words rang in her head, *the supplies we'll need*. The vampire meant to do the healing herself, not some official human medical staff? The thought of a bloodsucking vampire going anywhere near her wound made her shiver.

When the lady returned, she didn't carry new bandages or cleaning materials, but a hand-size chrome box. The lid clacked open, and she pulled out a plastic strip of pills.

"Take one of these and you'll be..." she paused momentarily, "right as rain. That's it."

Lucy glanced around the room, searching for the water cooler.

"Simply chew and swallow like you would any other food," Cecelia explained, and Lucy questioned whether the vampire could read minds or if her face was just easy to read. "It's designed to taste like your favourite sweet—whatever that may be. It'll quicken the healing process and help your body wipe out any harmful bacteria or infections at the site."

Lucy popped the innocent white capsule into her mouth and her taste buds exploded, as if she'd eaten three of her favourite chews at once. If these ever made it into shops, they'd risk people eating them like sweets.

"It's good, eh?" Cecelia encouraged in a more conversational tone now she was satisfied that Lucy wasn't going to run away. "It's made from vampire technology—far superior to human tech by about a millennium, give or take a century, or at least that's what we predict."

Lucy reluctantly held out the strip of remaining pills, and Cecelia put it back into its box.

"Now we wait for five minutes, then check your arm."

A slight tingle began in her shoulder, then danced down to the fingertips. It felt like pins and needles, but it wasn't uncomfortable.

After a few minutes of awkward silence, Lucy trying hard not to openly stare at the vampire, Cecelia broke the tension, asking softly, "How is it now?"

Lucy pushed the sleeve of her jacket up her arm and took off the bandage, revealing smooth unblemished skin. Her eyes grew wide, and she held out her arm, flexing her hand. No pain.

Cecelia took a hold of the makeshift cover and took that into the staff room, too. When she returned Lucy had her first glimpse that she was definitely not human. The woman bent down to her level, lifted her arm, and sniffed it.

Freezing fingertips touched her wrist. She flinched, heart pounding in her ears. Would a vampire be able to hear her tachycardia? If she did, she had enough tact not to let on.

"You're in the clear. I can't smell any bacteria or infection." Cecelia retracted her icy appendages and Lucy dropped her arm. "You know, you can continue to use your family doctor if you're particularly attached to them, but otherwise we can handle all of your ailments right here. Cross-Key supplies extra medications for the Fleet, which is hundreds of years more advanced than what's in Earth's market."

A reminder rang in the back of Lucy's brain. She'd need to cancel her doctor's appointment. Clearing her throat to force out her voice, she said, "I have to make a phone call. I've got an appointment that needs cancelling."

The blonde smiled genuinely at that. "Of course. Remember, you're in good company here. The best of company, actually."

Lucy paused before reaching for her phone, speaking before her confidence failed. "Do you have any medications for pain?" She didn't want to explain about her arm cramps in case they thought she was too weak for the job.

Cecelia headed back into the storage room and returned, handing her a small box, no questions asked. "No more than once a week. It acts as a preventative, so make sure you take it like clockwork or else the symptoms will manifest."

*If I start tomorrow, every Saturday morning could work,* Lucy thought, standing up to leave. "Thank you, Miss Cecelia," she said, not knowing the lady's last name. Did vampires even have last names?

Cecelia shrugged. "This is a lot to take in, so I doubt you'll be at your best to start working right now. Have the day off to let things sink in."

Lucy nodded, but a pang of guilt ran through her. She'd taken a lot of half days already, even if they weren't her idea. The thought of more time off concerned her. She sucked in a breath, steeled her back, and said, "I'll come in tomorrow and Sunday."

"Then I'll see you in the morning. Bright and early." The vampire filled her last phrase with venom before bowing her head, and Lucy had to stop herself from running out the door.

Outside, the sunlight dazed her and made it hard to see her phone screen as she dialled the doctor's number. She scrolled past her home phone number, and imagined everything she wanted to but couldn't say to her parents.

Her job was drawing into a book to communicate with the tree spirit inside, at a company that uses vampire and werewolf technology, and she has to go and meet them in space next Friday.

She'd always wanted to do something extraordinary that would make them proud, but now she was she'd couldn't tell them—an extra layer of chains added to her already struggling voice.

When Saturday rolled around, Lucy could tell it wasn't the typical working weekday. A large convoy of vans and trucks were leaving the estate, one by one, out onto the main road; the large Cross-Key & Co. logo stamped on their sides.

She marvelled at the fact that the products built from vampire and werewolf tech were heading into peoples' homes, and they were none the wiser. What would her dad say if he knew his toaster created a vampiric link to work out his personal preferences? The secret wanted out—tearing at her insides, begging her to tell someone. She ran.

Her trial over, she headed straight for Research and Development. Holding her pass up to the security, she was cut off by a shout.

"Lucy!" Hina, dressed down in blue jeans and grey T-shirt featuring a pink heart motif, jogged towards her with a cheery smile.

Lucy simultaneously froze in panic and admired the girl's ability to run in heels.

"Hey." The energetic teen flashed a smile. "Congrats on being made permanent. Dad told me when he got back from his shift."

Stretching a polite smile, Lucy dropped her arm, badge in hand. How should she react? Hina was a 'safe' person to talk to, but... If only it wasn't her.

"Do you want to celebrate in town over a coffee?" A pitch of cheery hopefulness gave Lucy the impression that maybe bridges weren't as badly burnt as she'd thought, but she flashed back to the warning tones Hina's father had used and she wasn't too sure. She couldn't risk her position by messing it up and saying something stupid.

Fist clenched, she tried to summon her response. "I'm working today with Cecelia. Sorry. I hope you enjoy your day off, though."

Hina looked crestfallen, and Lucy's gut wrenched. The dejected teen forced a smile.

"OK. Maybe another time, then? Don't work too hard. Good luck and have fun." She gave an exaggerated conspiratorial wink before turning and heading towards the estate's main gate.

When the girl was far enough away Lucy let out a sigh, then scanned herself into the building.

Her satchel took up its usual place on the table, next to a mix of Lucy's own pens and Cross-Key supplies.

Not long after, Dave entered the dome with a goofy smile on his face and a stern-looking Cecelia in tow. Lucy straightened up as they walked in, forcing herself to look relaxed by giving a small wave. The wait, although short, had been agonising.

"Lucy, would you please bring out our guest of honour?"

Her chair squeaked as she jumped up at the invite, circling to the other side of the desk to the secret compartment. A chill ran down her spine as she gripped her quarry, reverently lifting the notebook out onto the table.

"Now that we're officially colleagues on this project, you have permission to interact with Oda whenever you like. Note that security managers will be monitoring everything closely."

An invisible weight lifted from Lucy as the news of twenty-four-hour access sank in, then promptly crashed again with the increasing gravity of responsibility. Sure, having full access was an honour, but if anything happened to Oda, it would come back on her.

She nodded her understanding, then opened the notebook and sketched her image of introduction. The resulting warmth enveloped her like an enormous reassuring hug. It was good to be back.

What with the madness of vampires and werewolves in space, somehow the tree spirit always kept Lucy grounded. Oda had no expectations of her at all, and to Lucy, that was a breath of fresh air in a world polluted with stifling demands.

"From what I have heard so far about the kodama," Cecelia chimed from a computer chair at the far side of the dome, "they're quite naive. I imagine it would be very easy to mislead them. That could be dangerous for the meeting."

Lucy tilted her head in question. The vampire lady continued, "Although I have not been introduced to Oda personally—that is, I have not touched the book—I have read Dave's reports for the CEO. We may have a bit of a handful with a few of the Council members at the Bureau."

Dave sighed. "I feared that might be the case." Running a hand through his hair, he turned to Lucy. "The Bureau was set up with one goal in mind: protect the existence of the Fleet. They don't take kindly to anything that may hint at the possibility of other intelligent species. They fear the questions won't stop with the new, and that the past would inevitably be looked at again. Oda could give the game away."

Frowning, Lucy considered the scientist's worries. Oda was naive and eager to talk to anyone, regardless of who. The kodama didn't seem to have any sort of filter, and they weren't sure if Oda understood the concept of secrecy. If Oda fell into the wrong hands, that could be a major security risk for the other species.

"Loose lips sink ships," Lucy responded.

"Indeed." A thin smile graced Cecelia's lips. "I haven't heard that expression in a while," she mused, then held up a finger. "But I'm afraid that the Bureau may take your words quite literally. Our Fleet is made up of crafts that could be referred to as ships. If the Bureau suspects there's any chance the kodama could give away our existence to the humans, as it already has itself, they may try to dispose of it." Cecelia said all of this in the same matter-of-fact tone she'd used to tell Lucy vampires existed, one that left no room for doubt.

She turned the finger around to examine her claw like nail. "We only put the possibility of humans making first contact into the Charter for equality among species, but no one ever actually believed humans would go and do it. We thought the Fleet would find extraterrestrials. Some will want to eliminate this uncalculated risk as soon as possible and by any means necessary. For example, trying to trick Oda into saying something wrong, using deceptions, double meanings, and wordplay. It's dirty and underhanded, but that's their job."

Lucy stared unbelieving at the woman who didn't seem bothered by this at all.

"That's where we come in," said Dave, waving his hand between himself and Lucy. "We need to help present Oda in the best way possible. Our job between now and Friday will be to help Oda navigate any potential traps or multiple meanings. Between the three of us, I'm sure she'll pick it up in no time at all."

"She?" asked Cecelia pointedly.

"Of course. Oda." Dave responded.

"How do you know Oda is a female? Or that kodama have genders at all?" Lucy gave a silent whoop as the vampire woman called Dave out on the same point she'd raised.

"Well, you know..." Dave gave a twist of the hand as if trying to catch an explanation out of thin air. "Dryads are normally depicted as female, and then you've got Mother Earth..." he trailed off, scratching the back of his neck.

"I will refer to this spirit by their name alone until my species has formally established a link between our races. I would advise you do the same," Cecelia intoned.

"Well, yes, but we haven't specifically drawn attention to the concept of gender yet with Oda. They're understanding. I'm sure Oda won't take too much offence by it. She seems happy to just have communication in the first place."

Cecelia said nothing, and Dave coughed. "Fine. Moving on, let's get to work seeing if this spirit has any concept of truth and lies."

As Oda's translator, it was her job to make sure no double meanings filtered through. She could and would do it.

She spoke. "How about a street swindler?"

After lunch the "swindler" evolved into a "con artist," and Lucy sketched out a comic strip of a rigged game of find the apple using three boxes and a table.

Lucy frowned as she struggled to draw out the sequence quick enough so that Oda wouldn't absorb it before she was finished.

It was her hardest task yet, and her hand flew across the practice paper. After three premature absorptions, Oda finally got the whole story on the fourth and Lucy collapsed back in her chair, stretching her hand. She smiled as the image (a con artist holding an apple behind his back while a lady pointed to one of the empty boxes) disappeared.

In response, Oda presented them with a picture where all three boxes had an apple beneath them.

She grinned. It was utterly adorable. Unfortunately, it still didn't show whether Oda understand the meaning of deception.

"Not to worry. I'm sure we're close to a breakthrough," Dave said with a chuckle. "Let's call it a day."

Lucy gripped her hand into a fist and made a snap decision. "I'll be here tomorrow."

"Oo, eager to get to work? Excellent. I'll be working tomorrow, too, so I can base myself down here for the day," Dave said, typing furiously.

Cecelia nodded, her expression blank and eyes still hidden behind her sunglasses. "Miss Blakely, a word, please?"

# Chapter Five

# Red Riding Hood

The office workers in the building were heading out for the day as Lucy trailed Cecelia for their private chat. Like yesterday's meeting in the medical bay, lead-weight butterflies took off in her stomach as she followed the summons of the vampire.

Lucy wasn't sure what she'd expected but being dragged into the ladies' toilets was not it. Cecelia stopped them in the doorway, smiling at people who gave her funny looks for wearing sunglasses indoors. At last, when everyone had left, she led Lucy in front of the stalls to the wall of mirrors above a row of cherry blossom ceramic sinks.

"What is this?" the lady asked, then ploughed on without a response. "This is a mirror. To you, it shows you a reflection."

Lucy nodded, taking in the pale pink doors of the toilet stall behind her right shoulder that she shouldn't be able to see because Cecelia was standing in front of it.

"To me it is not. For vampires, this is a door. A gateway, if you will. I can bend the metal's inherent light structures to create a portal to somewhere else. The simplest way I can put this is to call it one end of a wormhole."

An image of Cecelia climbing up on the vanity, feet balancing to avoid the sinks and taps, then sticking one foot into a mirror ran through her head. But that was absurd. Her brain substituted it with the vampire stepping into a floor-length mirror, like in *Alice Through the Looking Glass*. Spirits, paranormal creatures, and now mirror portals. How much had been hidden from her until now?

A shiver ran the length of her spine as the vampire tapped a finger impatiently on her wrist.

"The ability to use mirrors this way belongs solely to vampires. However, after years of experimenting with our abilities and by fusing it with our blood alchemy technologies, we created portals large enough to transport ships and other beings across space. We can program them to open and close at will. Cross-Key & Co. is home to the only portal in operation that has been extended to use by humankind, and that is overseen by the Bureau at the Fleet."

Lucy nodded, feeling more like Alice herself every second; a rabbit hole of memories she didn't want to follow. She had a sneaking suspicion about where this conversation was going.

"Humans send large polluting rockets blasting up into space. Such brute force and harmful waste. We elegantly slide to our destination. In order to get to the meeting on Friday, you're going to have to go through a mirror also—or, as I call it, a door. I believe Cross-Key refers to our ingenious magnificently complex key to the stars by some ridiculous human code name." At this, the posh lady actually rolled her eyes to the ceiling.

"Anyway, this is the primary method of communication between our two races. A few others exist on Earth in case anything happens to this one, but they're in different states of disrepair. You should know that for all intents and purposes, your only way of getting home from the Bureau is through one particular portal and it's heavily guarded so no one unauthorised can enter or leave the Fleet."

The lights in the room seemed to have become brighter, and her head spun. At least she could put images of large rockets blasting off to bed.

She'd never admit having looked up videos of space launches, but the notion had scared her almost to tears.

Voices of two women laughing became louder as they approached the stalls. Cecelia acted quickly and took Lucy's hand, wrapping her freezing fingertips around her wrist, and dragged her back out of the toilets just in time as two women gave Cecelia funny looks before entering themselves.

"See you tomorrow," she chimed, and strode away with all the intent and aura of the world's most obvious secret agent.

Lucy flashed them an innocent smile as she watched the retreating woman's back, then headed back into the stalls to sit and let the new revelation sink in.

The grey sanitary bin in the cubicle jumped out at her, and her breath hitched.

*How did you manage that time of the month in space? Would Cecelia know if she...?*

Once again, she forced herself to exhale and tried to rationalise. Surely they'd tell her everything important beforehand. What use was she to anyone locked away in a toilet stall?

With the promise of a cup of chamomile waiting, she counted to three and unlocked the door.

❧❧❧❧❧❧ ❧❧❧❧❧❧

By the time Lucy reached the staff residential building, her panic had lessened. The sights and sounds of the sky, cars, and people leaving the industrial park to go home brought her back to Earth. Although the fear had dulled, concern for Oda swam around her head like shark silhouettes.

She ascended the stairs on autopilot and opened the door to the common room without her customary ear-to-the-door check.

"Hey, Lucy," Will greeted her, raising an arm from his seat on the sofa. His feet were propped up on a velvet leg rest and the TV was on in the background.

Lucy froze, pulled out of her thoughts, and shakily raised a hand with a smile in his direction. The memory of seeing him in a wheelchair for the first time was still fresh, and she wasn't sure how to approach him. Instead, she pivoted to the kitchenette and her original goal—a refreshing cup of chamomile.

She couldn't just ignore him. But she didn't want to say the wrong thing, either.

As nonchalantly as she could, she brewed herself a cup and waited for it to steep.

Silence was golden. Perhaps she didn't have to say anything. She could sit down and draw something in one of the chairs. Then she'd get to watch him, too. As nonchalantly as she could, she ducked her head as if inspecting the progress of her tea, disguising her warming cheeks.

Lifting the cup, she took an experimental sip. Perfect as always. No need to wait long with Cross-Key products. Carrying it over to a cream high-back chair, she slipped off her shoes and pulled her feet up, settling in to revive an old project.

She pulled a drawing tablet out of her satchel and opened a sketch she was midway through, and began to shade, thankful again for Cecelia's wondrous painkillers.

The pair sat in a companionable silence before Will asked, "Are you drawing?"

There can't be much problem answering that, can there?

"Colouring. A scene for my little brother."

"Oh. Anything interesting?"

So, this was turning into a conversation. The stylus paused above a vivid block of poppy red. "I'm drawing a version of *Little Red Riding Hood*."

An unexpected grin spread over his face, and she tilted her head.

"You and your brother have great taste. So, you've got a thing for wolves, then?"

She almost spurted out a sip of tea but managed to stop it before it splattered across her tablet, forcing herself to gulp it down. "What?"

"You know, the fetching wolf who kills the axe murderer, saves the damsel, and gets treated to a gourmet dinner as thanks. The wolf."

What version of *Little Red Riding Hood* had he read?

"That's not the story I know," she confessed.

"Sure you do. It's a classic."

Acutely aware of them being alone on their shared floor, and of the potential hints being dropped, she asked, "Will, are you a...you know?"

She picked up her cup and gripped it with both hands.

Will muted the television, then carded a hand through his fringe. It was a sign of uncertainty that Lucy had never seen before on the boy whose happiness always rivalled that of Dave. "I've never had to say this to anyone before." Before Lucy's mind could run the one thousand possibilities of where that sentence could lead, Will blurted out, "I'm a werewolf."

Her flatmate was a werewolf. After vampires, tree spirits, and an upcoming trip into space, why not complete the set?

Like she had with Cecelia, she let her gaze run over Will fully for the first time, looking for any tell-tale signs. What would they be, though? Ears and a tail? A love of sausages? She saw an incredibly handsome teen with hair designed to run hands through and eyes that...

"I'm at Cross-Key doing three years of work experience," he said, emboldened by Lucy's lack of rebuttal, and she tuned herself back in to the conversation. "You know Cecelia? Well, I'm like her. I mean, not exactly—but the whole ambassador thing to represent my race."

The nervous, butchered sentences were cute, and she smiled in encouragement.

"My job isn't as glamorous as hers. She's a portal engineer and I check incoming stock to warehouses with Dave. Chasing up missing stock, writing emails, that sort of thing." Although he said it wasn't as important as Cecelia's, it sparked an earnest fire in his eyes.

Although she wasn't sure if he knew about Oda or not, maybe he could help her prepare? On second thought, it was better not to bring it up.

"So, you lived in space until now?"

"Sure did. You know about the Fleet, yes?"

Lucy nodded.

"Well, the stock I deal with here goes there. The Fleet gets a lot of fresh stock and specimens from Cross-Key. It's like a resources lifeline for us. It's an honour to be working here." His voice was climbing in pitch with the excitement, and Lucy was surprised he wasn't waving his arms around. Maybe there was a reason for it?

"Can you use wheelchairs in space?"

Will let out a barking laugh and Lucy saw him doubled over, blue eyes twinkling with mirth and wiping away a tear.

That must have sounded so stupid. Was it too personal? She was an idiot!

"I don't need to use that when I'm on-board Fleet vessels," he said, gesturing to a small folded chair tucked away neatly in a corner. "I know it sounds bizarre, but I only need to use it when I'm on Earth. My body's not used to the gravity here, so I get exhausted easily. It's called orthostatic intolerance. My body struggles to pump blood up to my head against gravity, so my heart rate quickens to compensate. Add dizziness standing up and fainting if I'm upright for too long. Your Earth astronauts feel the same thing when they get back from the International Space Station."

The tightness in her chest returned. Would that happen to her when she got back? She was too scared to ask. Once again she paused mid-panic. If it was going to be a problem, they would have told her already. Nothing to worry about.

Sensing the change in mood, Will quickly added, "I'm always super impressed by Dave, his mum, and the other humans who come to the Fleet every now and again. They go back through the portal and they can walk around in all this gravity like it's nothing." He even waved a hand through the empty air in front of him before letting it drop.

What a relief! She smiled gratefully, and he scratched the back of his neck with a sheepish grin.

Will continued, "I'll get my time when I can cope with gravity, though. The next full moon isn't too far away."

Lucy gripped her now stone-cold cup for comfort, poring over the latest revelation. So, werewolves do respond to the full moon. She locked the information away, then honed in on another nugget of information that didn't seem to fit.

"Dave's mum?"

"Mrs Margaret Crossley—the CEO of Cross-Key & Co.," he explained.

The short-haired older female Dave. Of course, it was a family company!

Silence once again helped to keep her runaway stupidity under wraps. This conversation had gone much better than she'd thought so far, but she didn't want to chance her luck for much longer.

Will, on the other hand, was keen to gossip.

"The CEO hasn't announced her successor yet, but I think it'll be Dave. I want it to be, anyway. He's a great guy, and I know he's working hard to prove himself fit for the post. I'm sure the CEO's been priming him for it, too, with key roles like portal management and Project Oda."

He knew about Oda. Safe!

Hina's face flashed across her mind, along with Mrs Crossley's words. Hina was safe to talk to. She's also a family member. So, what was she to the CEO to be in the know if Dave knew—Dave, the potential next in line?

She was snapped out of her musings by the sight of Will reaching up his arms into a stretch. His shirt lifted a fraction around his middle and her thoughts ground to a halt.

The pressure to not stick her foot in things snapped, and she leapt to her feet, putting down her cup of chamomile on the coffee table in front of her.

"Lucy?" he asked, and she paused mid-crouch picking up her satchel. Her ears burned.

"It's my birthday on Tuesday the 30th. I'll be having a party here in the common room to celebrate. I'd be happy if you came along. It'll be us and a few other work mates, as well."

Fireworks and alarms exploded in her brain. A social gathering. The thing she'd dreaded more than anything about joining the workplace.

She mumbled, "I'll have to see what I'm doing," then quickly retreated to her room door. "Thanks for the chat. Have a good evening."

He waved a hand, and she escaped behind the door, dropping her satchel to the floor, then sat on the corner of the bed as tight as a coiled spring. The butterflies in her stomach had taken up hang-gliding as Will spoke and were refusing to land.

Brass shattered the Sunday morning peace. The blaring *Sgt. Sir!* opening theme worked, waking Lucy up with a call to action. The effects hadn't worn off yet. Perfect. Rubbing her bleary eyes, she reached out and turned off the alarm, but squinted as a light continued to pulse on her phone's screen.

A message? They'd waited this long, surely they could wait a little longer? Then she carried out her morning routine: clothes on, make-up done, then squirreled breakfast back to her room to eat in private.

She sat cross-legged on her bed, cereal bowl in lap, and groaned at the blinking light and lifted it to her ear. Her father's stressed-out tones made her shoulders hunch.

"Lucy, your mum has asked me to let you know that she'll be presenting some of her latest research at a conference this Wednesday. It's at the Step-Ahead Hotel in Garrowhead East. It'll be an all-day thing from 9:00 a.m.–5:00 p.m. She wants you there." A loud wail broke through the silence, followed by a low groan. "Get the time off if you can." *Click.*

She couldn't just take time off a week before going into space. But not turning up would really upset her mother. If she did go, then something went wrong at the Bureau because they weren't prepared enough...

Close to seeing her half-eaten cereal covering her bed sheets, she shoved her breakfast away along with her dilemma for now. Work started in twenty minutes.

Oda. Yes. Oda needed to know the difference between truth and lies. The tree spirit's life was at stake. Mentally shutting out her parents' demands for now, she concentrated on the day ahead.

Maybe they needed to show Oda the story first with someone playing the game truthfully, and they could swap them out for the con artist?

The door swung closed behind her as she stepped out into the estate and set off on her seventh daily commute.

# Chapter Six

# Spirited Away

Lucy returned to her flat that night feeling triumphant after the day's possible breakthrough.

The common room was empty, and she wondered if Will had also had a weekend shift. Taking the opportunity of alone time, she pulled her feet up onto the sofa and pulled up *Little Red Riding Hood* on her tablet.

Her next scene was taking place; a dark forest trail with a cottage peeking out just beyond a bend in the distance. It was the sort of place she'd imagined going on a camping holiday with Ben and her family growing up. Looking at the image now, she could imagine the crunch of a wheelchair at her side, gallantly escorting her down the track.

But how could she continue writing this version knowing Will? She sighed and closed the drawing, resigned to never finish the story. A rumble in her stomach brought her attention back to her surroundings. It was dark outside, and there was still no sign of Will. Not that she'd know what to say to him if he were here but...

*...and gets treated to a gourmet dinner as thanks. The wolf.*

Looking up at the kitchen, she grinned in a light bulb moment. A quick stock check showed much more food than one person would need. The ingredients would need to be replaced, but she could do that, she thought, pulling up her bank details on her phone.

She blinked, then swiped the page to refresh it. The balance had four digits. Cross-Key's payment for her company had gone through.

Mind set, Lucy began pulling out pots and pans. The feeling was calming and familiar. The number of times she'd been left to cook for her busy parents...she'd turned it from a chore to time she could spend in her own thoughts. The kitchen grew hot under the heady smell of chicken, carrots, onions, and potatoes.

After a brief search, she successfully secured corn flour and added it to the mixture, thickening it into a soup. Bringing it down from the boil, she spooned an experimental bit onto her tongue.

Good, but the chicken needed shredding and it could do with some seasoning. She made the changes, and the second taste test brought tears to her eyes. That was it. Home.

Then realisation clicked. She'd been invited to Will's home, so it was only right she give him a flavour of hers. Reaching into the cupboards, she dug out some containers to portion it off.

Maybe she could box some up for her dad. Who knew what they were eating without her?

Unfortunately, her hunt yielded only cardboard, which would turn to mush on contact. Probably for the better, she mused. She didn't have the time to visit, let alone getting time off to go to the conference.

Ladling a portion into a bowl, she put the lid back on the pan. Moving to her satchel, she pulled out one of her sketchpads and tore out a page and pen.

Hi Will,
I made chicken soup using ingredients from the kitchen. Hope you don't mind. I'll put the money back for the ingredients. There's plenty, so help yourself! Reheat it on medium for ten minutes stirring occasionally and you're ready to go.
Happy feasting!
Lucy

Later, she lay in bed, staring at her phone. A few taps later, she'd sent a portion of her earnings to her parents' accounts. If she couldn't be there to physically support Ben, she could at least help out with costs for now. A cash injection that size would impress them, surely?

Putting the phone to one side, she covered her eyes, and finally admitted she was homesick. Couldn't her family have built an extension or found a cheaper house big enough for her, too?

Will flashed across her mind again. What right did she have to complain when he was so far away from home? He was incredible. She couldn't do that.

She remembered how naive and innocent Oda was, though, and now also felt the urge to protect the tree spirit just as strongly. She could earn money by drawing, and she was about to go on an adventure into space to speak to different races, whether she wanted to or not.

She fell asleep with 'what-ifs' and 'if onlys' playing through her head on repeat.

The whining tones of electric guitars dragged Lucy out of her groggy stupor. Blue flashes of light pulsed, intermixed with vibrations on the wooden table beside her pillow, threatening to topple over the edge with each buzz.

Grabbing it, she checked the caller ID and sat bolt upright.

"Hello?" she answered.

"Lucy," Dave said breathlessly, "Have you been communicating with Oda since we finished our session earlier today?"

Had she...what?

"No," she answered honestly.

"Have you been back to see Oda since we finished our session?"

"No," she replied again.

There was a pause while a few voices spoke down the line. Her mouth turned dry and she swallowed.

"We need you at the Security Department as soon as possible. Sorry to have to wake you up, but this is a potential crisis situation." Dave's voice wobbled as he said his last line. That was bad. Terrible. Nothing upset always cheerful Dave.

Potential crisis? What could she possibly do in a crisis?

"I'll be right there," Lucy said firmly, all traces of sleep gone. "I just need five minutes."

"Thank you. It's too dangerous to be out at this time of night on your own, so a car will be waiting outside for you."

*Click.*

Throwing on the same clothes she'd worn that day, she grabbed her satchel and tiptoed out of her room so she didn't wake up Will.

As promised, a white Cross-Key minivan was waiting for her—a member of the Security Department decked out in black sat in the driving seat.

The drive through the premises was quick. The paths and factories lit up in white patches from the estate's blue floodlights; her pounding heart was the only accompaniment.

Arriving at Headquarters, she showed her ID to another night security guard who radioed the security headquarters before admitting her.

After jogging up three flights, she knocked on the device-clad door. Entering, Kamal Usmani, Dave, and Margaret Crossley were all there, stern looks on their faces, with Dave fighting back tears.

Mrs Crossley looked up with a frown. "Miss Blakely. There has been a break-in. I'm sorry to say that our tree spirit has vanished."

❧❧❧❧❧ ❦❦❦❦❦

The screens in the Security Department displayed the interior of Oda's dome from seven different angles. Nothing moved. If Lucy hadn't seen the night manager pressing fast-forward, she would have assumed they were on pause.

Dave wiped away a sheen of sweat from his brow, even though the January air was bitter that night. "You and I appear to be the last ones who were in the dome; the footage verifies that. However, between now and then, Kamal went to do his rounds personally, checked in on Oda, and the desk was empty."

Lucy clenched her fists and stared at Kamal, who continued to forward through each video in turn. Dave continued, "I'll be happy to state here and now that I do not believe you had anything to do with this. You're not in any sort of trouble," he reassured her.

"Yet," added Kamal, still not looking away from the monitors.

Lucy wanted to sink into the floor and disappear. Did the man hold a grudge against her after what happened between her and Hina? Was he

61

looking for an excuse to get her fired? They could see on the CCTV she was innocent.

A light flashed above the Security Department's door and the CEO pressed a button next to it, then Cecelia stood in the doorway. "I've got the coordinates, Mrs Crossley," the vampire said, her lips pulled into a thin line. "I'm ready when you are."

The CEO didn't skip a beat. "Good. Dave, you are in charge until I get back. I want a full investigation launched. Leave no stone unturned. Good luck."

And just like that, the two women left, leaving Lucy with Dave, Kamal, and a few other guards, staring at monitors of their own.

Lucy didn't know how much the other guards knew, so she practised what she'd been taught: don't speak about it unless they spoke first.

Kamal turned to Lucy. "Locater badge? I need to verify your location since you left Dave's company earlier."

*You're not going to find anything there no matter how badly you want to,* Lucy mentally jabbed, unpinning the ID and handing it over without a word. Dave nodded approvingly, and it was slotted into a device attached to a computer.

A few tense moments passed then log lines appeared on the device's small monitor.

"The little miss went back to her apartment after her shift. As she wasn't on duty she wouldn't have been wearing her tracker, so her whereabouts until you called her are a mystery," Kamal said accusingly.

"Kamal," Dave said in a harsh tone, arms folded. "This is serious. You know you can cross-reference the CCTV footage across the industrial park with the time logged on her ID of her entering the staff residential building. Go on. Satisfy yourself so we can get to the real culprit. Time is of the essence."

Lucy's eyes widened at the man's demeanour. Maybe he had the makings of a strong leader like Will had said?

Shoulders hunched, Kamal moved his fingers over the keyboard with reluctance. Seconds later her own image flashed up on a few of the wall monitors, and she watched herself enter her apartment building. Her front, sides, and back all showed, then... That was outside her bedroom window! Her jaw dropped.

Kamal forwarded the footage at x64 speed. Will entered the building sometime later. Then there was a sizeable gap before the security car showed up and Lucy climbed in.

"The timestamp corresponds with the log and we never saw her leave the building after she got back from work. She didn't even climb out any of the windows. So?"

Kamal dropped his folded arms, then clicked the screens back over to Oda's dome once more. "No movement, Sir. She's clear," Kamal admitted dejectedly.

Although Lucy knew she was innocent, hearing the words made her heart flutter all the same after all the scrutiny.

The security manager cleared his throat, gathering himself after the defeat, then barked to the room, "Search down! Look for anyone suspicious. Research and Development building. Report back in one hour. I want you all to start your searches five minutes apart. Go!"

Every guard stood up and walked out of the room. Lucy couldn't tell by the name badges if there were any Crossley family members among the group but suspected there were. A chill of unease ran through her as it reminded her she knew more than family members themselves about what they were searching for.

"Right, now we can speak freely," Kamal said, perching on an office chair. "To be honest, we don't have a clue what has happened. I had thought Miss Blakely could have cast some light on the situation, but I'll admit it was a dim hope at best."

Dave raised a hand to his chin. "The HAT machine logs?" he questioned.

Lucy resisted the urge to raise an eyebrow at the term. HAT? Kamal, clearly expecting it however, handed him a printout.

"It's as I told Mrs Crossley, sir. The HAT machine has been inactive this evening from between you and Miss Blakely leaving the tree spirit until five minutes ago when Cecelia fired it up."

Lucy tried to follow as best she could. HAT machine...did they mean the portal? Cecelia's voice piped up in the back of her head. *A ridiculous code name.*

Dave, as per his unusual talent at accurately guessing what Lucy was thinking without her saying anything, confirmed and completed her suspicions. "Mrs Crossley and our vampire ambassador have gone to report the missing tree spirit to the Bureau. Cecelia said she'd already informed you about the machine?"

"Yes, but she didn't tell me what it was called," Lucy replied, tactfully leaving out the part about the vampire's disdain.

"Indeed. The marvellous HAT machine." Dave forced a smile. "It's short for Here And There machine. Before the industrial revolution when we were off through the portal, we'd say we were visiting the HAT maker. Fascinating history, no?"

Kamal and Lucy made no response and Dave coughed, his cheeks reddening.

"Lucy," he continued, smile drooping again, "you'll be placed on holiday leave until Oda is found. Until then Project Oda will be going on hiatus."

Her heart skipped. If they found Oda, she thought glumly. A little voice in the back of her head whispered it had all been too good to be true. She should have known better.

"We're truly sorry for the inconvenience," Dave said apologetically. "You should head back to your apartment now and try to get some sleep. I'll call the car again. We'll tell you as soon as we get any more information."

❦❦❦❦❦ ❦❦❦❦❦

The oppressive emptiness of Headquarters in the dead of night was deafening. Suffocating. Lucy's shoes clacked on the tiles that gave way from the carpet of the security headquarters—something she hadn't noticed until the regular hustle and bustle of the corridors had vanished in the dead of night—and a sound she may never hear again.

It was over. Oda was missing. What use was an interpreter without a charge to interpret for?

The door clacked shut behind her and she daren't glance back without tears spilling. She walked, shoulders hunched, barely looking at the route ahead. Not that anyone would be there for her to walk into. Not that she would see any of them again.

Without any leads, it was certain. She'd lost it all. Her job. Her income. Her apartment. Oda. Will.

She felt as low as the Sgt. in episode six when he realised he'd left two trainee soldiers behind at sea, pulled out in their life boats by the currents, never to be seen again. The *Sgt. Sir!* theme tune began playing on repeat in her head—a threat of a broken promise and of a future she'd fought against, instead of the usual morning rally call.

Raising her jacket sleeve, she wiped away the growing wetness on her sleeve, and bit her quivering bottom lip. It was just the cold. That's all.

Lifting her head, she noticed her feet had brought her to the central stairwell leading down to reception.

A night security officer sat behind the desk in place of the daytime receptionists and, glancing up from a magazine, he nodded to her in acknowledgment as she reached the bottom step. Giving him a silent wave she passed through the atrium to the front door, where an icy breeze stung her cheeks at the door.

The car hadn't arrived yet, so she paced, bouncing on the balls of her feet for warmth. She could imagine herself being watched by Hina's father, watching her walk out of the girl's life. Again.

Then there was Oda, who she'd promised to protect—and Ben, who had no idea he was growing up in a world of paranormal creatures.

A small black security van arrived, and the driver rolled down the front window. "Miss Blakely?" he asked.

Lucy stepped forward, hand outstretched, then paused.

No. She couldn't let it end. She hadn't left yet. Oda and Ben were both precious. Both innocent and completely dependent on others. Even if she was stepping into a world she knew nothing about, she wasn't so helpless and wouldn't trust so blindly. For them, she had to try.

Lowering her hand, she shook her head. "I'm sorry. I won't be needing a ride after all. I have more to do tonight."

The driver sighed, head tilted. "If you're sure."

With a quick glance directly into the CCTV above the doorway, she strode back into Headquarters.

# CHAPTER SEVEN

# IN THE FRAME

B y the time Lucy returned to Security Dave had left, leaving herself and Kamal Usmani alone.

The manager sat poker-straight in front of a large screen, playing the footage over on fast-forward from multiple angles. He didn't turn away, simply continued his search.

"I want to help," Lucy said bluntly to the back of the man's head.

"How? What special skills can you offer in this investigation?" he asked sarcastically, as if she'd said the sky was green and ocean violet.

After a brief pause from the sting, she replied, "Can I watch the CCTV footage with you? Another pair of eyes."

Another beat of silence, then the aged man turned and held out a remote. "Take that one. The footage covering the time period is loaded," he said, pointing to a small computer on a side wall.

Lucy nodded and took the control. It looked like they needed all the hands and eyes they could get considering she hadn't been thrown out. Sitting in a computer chair, she scrutinised the square monitor in front of her.

If it weren't for the timestamp in the bottom corner, she'd think she was staring at a still image.

Her eyes stung from lack of sleep, and she glanced at the clock on the wall. It had passed into Monday while she'd been looking. Twenty-five minutes.

Now and then, Kamal would grunt in frustration, only moving to rewind one of the ten screens he was watching.

She rubbed her eyes, then stared back at the screen. The sky-blue door to Oda's dome flickered for an instance. She screwed her eyes shut, shook her head to combat the fatigue, then rewound the footage and leaned closer. Pressing play, she stared at the door. It flickered again for a split second, and her heart leapt. A jump in the footage?

Clearing her throat to break the silence, chest tightening, she asked, "Can I have some headphones, please?" She hated how uncertain she sounded and tried not to shrink under the gaze he levelled at her.

He reached into a drawer and pulled out a pair of headphones that she took silently and then plugged them in and rewound the image five minutes. A few doors slammed in the distance, then at the moment of the flicker, *clunk*.

She rewound and repeated. Flicker and *clunk*. Pressing the remote, she slowed the footage down to half speed. The flicker became a brief shadow crossing half the screen. She bit her bottom lip as she slowed it down as far as she could.

The story played out across three frames.

Frame one: a humanoid figure entered through the now-open door.

Frame two: the shadow hunched over Oda's table.

Frame three: the shadow was by the door, object in hand, reaching for the door again.

Lucy raised her hand, voice shaking. "I've got something."

Kamal was up and over like a shot. She handed him the headphones, rewound the footage, and pointed to the flicker before showing the play-by-play.

He took off his glasses, revealing wide, tired hazel eyes, and picked up the remote, thumbing back and forth between the frames. "Dave Crossley, report to the Security Department immediately. I repeat. Dave Crossley report to the Security Department." Lowering the radio, he rubbed his sweat-covered forehead, and turned his full attention on Lucy for the first time since her return.

"This is all about to get a lot more complicated if what I think is happening is true. We're going to need Will here for this."

What was happening? And what did Will have to do with it?

Lucy sat up straighter as the man pulled out his mobile phone, not taking his eyes away from the screen. Three attempted calls later, Will appeared to pick up.

"Will, get to Security immediately. A van will pick you up in five minutes. We have a lead from this evening and need your opinion." Without waiting for Will's response, he shoved the phone back in his pocket and replaced it with a radio again. "Car Delta Papa Six. Report to the Avenue East Road residential building. Pick up Will Harven immediately. One wheelchair space. Destination Security Department."

"Roger that," came a short, sharp response, and Lucy wondered if it was the poor driver she'd turned away earlier.

Will arrived first, wheeled in by a guard, slumped in his chair, shirt dishevelled as if thrown on at late notice. He thanked his escort and dismissed him before propelling himself closer. "What can I do for you, Mr Usmani?" Spotting Lucy he sat up straighter, more alert. "Thanks for the soup. A real feast."

Lucy nodded in acknowledgement, glad he couldn't see her cheeks heating under the white-blue glare of the monitors.

"Will," said the manager. "Dave told me he filled you in earlier, so I'll get straight to the point. Watch this screen and tell me what you see."

Lucy backtracked the footage and played it at normal speed.

"Trick question?" asked Will, scratching the back of his head.

"Try again," Kamal said, giving Lucy a nod. She slowed the footage down, frame by frame.

Will leaned forward in his chair, eyes shooting open.

"Thoughts?" Kamal prompted.

Will gaped, his mouth hanging open before replying, "The only thing I know that moves that quick is a vampire. But how could they...?"

"You just confirmed my suspicions," Kamal said, "and I don't know, but it's my job to find out."

Will and Lucy gaped, then the door swung open again and Dave swept into the room. "What is it?" he asked, with all the sharpness of a CEO who'd been told his company was on the line.

"We, that is, Miss Blakely here"—Kamal brandished a hand in her direction and Lucy shifted in her seat—"decided that she would rather stay with me investigating than go to bed. She found this in the CCTV."

Kamal took the control and played the frames to Dave. "With Cecelia gone with Margaret, I can't guarantee it, but Will and I think we have a vampire on our hands."

The scientist furrowed his eyebrows, leaning closer to the screen. "I think you're right. No other being could move that fast. It sounds like a stroke of luck that Miss Blakely caught it."

Lucy cleared her throat and said, "The colour of the door flickered for a split second."

"Thank you for staying, and for your diligence, Lucy," Dave said, running a hand through his hair.

With Dave's agreement, Will seemed to grow in confidence. His shocked face grew serious and stern. "On behalf of the werewolves, in my official capacity as ambassador of my race on Earth, I have to officially advise you to report this to the Bureau as an interspecies incident." The words sounded like they were foreign to him. It was a level of formality Lucy hadn't heard from him, but it didn't not fit. In a strange way, it suited him. "Because of the magnitude of the issue, this should be reported in person," he continued. "As the one in charge when the revelation came to light, Dave needs to do it."

The man agreed. "I had a feeling something like this could occur. Call it a hunch, but I extended the HAT machine activation logs for the past twenty-four hours. The only activation was for Cecelia and Margaret, who went to report Oda missing. From that we can conclude that our vampire sneaked through on a different day, and that they're still on Earth."

A chill shot down Lucy's spine and she shuddered. A vampire was on the loose? Her eyes widened as her brain conjured images of back lanes filled with drained, blood-splattered corpses—a large man bending over the pile, sharp fangs glinting as he bore down on another victim in his arms.

She grimaced, thankful her family were safe in their own home. The old adage was that vampires couldn't cross a threshold unless invited, right? For the sake of fighting off rising panic she decided to believe it was true.

Dave broke through her reverie. "My mu-the CEO and Cecelia have already left to alert the Bureau of Oda's disappearance. It's very late and we all need our rest. The vampire will be weak from having crossed over into our world and will likely need time to get their bearings. Earth has changed a lot since they were last here after all. I think we should all get some rest, then assemble at 8:30 a.m., then head to the Bureau to make our report."

"Mr Crossley," the night manager said, gripping his radio in front of his chest. "Given the nature of the incident, can I tell the family members in my unit what they're searching for? They can keep a closer eye on things alongside the regular guards; with your permission, of course, since the CEO isn't here."

Dave brought a hand up to his chin.

"Although I'd rather wait to get clearance from the CEO, I admit it would be better to get as many eyes out for our thief as possible. You have my permission to spread the word through the usual family channels; restricted to the security team."

Kamal bowed to Dave, then reached for a communicator tablet similar to Lucy's and began tapping.

Lucy's breath caught when Dave turned to address her directly. "This will be a criminal investigation. As the person who discovered the footage, who knows Oda well, and as one of the last people to see the tree spirit, you'll be called in for questioning. Given all that, it would be worth you coming along for tomorrow's proceedings."

Lucy's mind raced. Saying what Oda said was one thing, but this was undoubtedly her speaking her own opinions. What if she messed it up? Said something stupid? Insulted someone?

At least she had a voice, her brain reminded her. The thought was grounding—a weight settling on her shoulders, running the length of her spine and down into the floor. "I'll go. To help save Oda."

Dave beamed at her. "Excellent. Then let's meet here at 8:30 a.m. sharp."

Lucy nodded, and Will punched the air.

Kamal had once again replaced his sunglasses, hiding his expression. Turning to Lucy and Will, he said, "I'll get the van to drive you two back to the staff residential building. Although the vampire is long gone from here by now, it's too late for you to be out on your own, and you'll need as much rest as you can get for tomorrow."

*That must be him in father mode,* Lucy mused as she watched him pull out a radio to order the car.

To Lucy's surprise and delight, Will transferred out of his wheelchair into the seat next to her in the back of the small Cross-Key passenger transport van.

The gravity of the night weighed on them both, and they kept a companionable silence during their short ride. When they arrived, the driver carried Will's chair to his door, and he hefted himself into the seat, panting from the exertion.

She knew his condition was tiring so what must he be feeling in the middle of the night?

"I could take you upstairs if you'd like?" she asked quietly, floating the suggestion to the teen.

He looked up at her, a smile returning to his face. "Thanks. I could use the help."

She nodded. "I never got my driver's license, so you'll have to forgive me if you accidentally end up in the rubbish shoot or with bruised toes."

His laughter chimed like bells. "If you do, you owe me another bowl of chicken soup. And breakfast."

She smiled back. "Deal," she said, then gripped the handles and pushed him through the building's automatic doors to the lift.

As they neared the top floor, the mop of hair in front of her said, "It takes a lot of courage to walk into another world, especially one with different species. But I know you'll be fine. You're a good person."

Lucy wanted to ask what evidence he had for that belief but offered a small thank you instead, and concentrated on navigating the narrow exit out of the lift into their corridor.

Will pushed the door to their common room open with one hand, and together they successfully manoeuvred him through the door to the sofa in the middle.

"Thanks, I'll take it from here. See you in the morn—no, see you later, yeah?" Will asked, acknowledging the ungodly hour.

Lucy smiled and nodded, swaying as the adrenalin from the night left her system and fatigue washed in.

***

Lucy lay in her bed, not sure what to do next. What did someone wear to go into space? Not a skirt, surely. What did you eat before going into space? How was she supposed to use the toilet in space?

Her initial tactic had been to drop her questions across the week she'd had left until the trip. That way it didn't sound like she'd been panicking. That plan now lay in pieces; she *was* panicking.

Assuming she'd moved on autopilot, she next found herself leaning on the kitchen counter with a bad case of jelly legs and plain slice of toast in hand. Wasn't that what they gave people with upset stomachs? Yes. Probably best to play it safe. Very safe. With everything.

She'd opted for flat shoes, a plain blouse, and black trousers, silently thanking her regular clothing style for being boring and practical. Safe. Safe is good.

Trundling and shuffling, Will entered the common room, pushing a lime green walker with a seat and handles. She could do with one of those right now, she thought, praying her knees wouldn't buckle.

Will beamed as he made his way over to the kitchen, looking like a puppy who'd been given a bone bigger than his head. "Morning," he greeted her, perching on the rollator in front of the counter. "That was one bump into the lift doors on exit, so where's my breakfast? Extra salt."

Lucy couldn't help but crack a smile. Even if she couldn't eat much right now, she'd hold up her end of the bargain.

"Salt?" she asked, silently trying to figure out why he looked so cheerful.

"Yeah. It's part of my on Earth diet. It's great for raising blood pressure, and that helps me stay upright."

Shrugging, she bent down and checked the fridge. "How about a ham and mushroom omelette with toast?"

The teen tapped his chin, pretending to think it over before giving a mock sigh. "I suppose that'll have to do. Thanks, chef."

Lucy's pulse raced in her ears for something other than nerves, and she set to work on her task, thankful for the temporary distraction.

After breakfast she slipped back into autopilot and in what seemed like the blink of an eye was walking into Headquarters reception.

Hina stood as soon as she cleared the revolving door, waving her over. "Lucy! Dave asked me to give him a call when you arrived so you could head up to Security together. It's a big day, eh?" she said, shooting her a conspiratorial wink.

Lucy tried to smile but couldn't manage and clutched her satchel tighter. The shakes had transferred from her legs to her arms at some point during her commute.

A blur of a shadow moved in the corner of her eye, then tight arms wrapped around her, squeezing. Daisy perfume wafted from the neck in front of her, mild and soothing. "Dad told me what happened. You'll do fine. I promise. Where you're going most people would give an arm and a leg." Lucy knew the logic of her old friend's words, and her tremors reduced to the odd small jerk.

"You know Will and Cecelia actually live in space, right?" Hina whispered in her ear. "If they can live there, you can manage a day trip."

Oh. She hadn't thought about it like that. Tension drained from her shoulders and she felt them lower, oblivious to their previous position up around her ears. Hina pulled away and Lucy give the girl an appreciative smile.

"That's my Lucy. Always defending the weak. Knowing you, you'll be all prepared," she said, then dashed back around the desk to answer a ringing phone. Lucy stared after the girl in wonder, marvelling at her unfounded belief.

# CHAPTER EIGHT

# THE HAT MACHINE

The grey jumpsuit zipped up to her neck—standard Fleet uniform according to Dave. It complemented her satchel well, which she slung over her shoulder. The bag contained her drawing tablet, with as many images as she could find from her work with Oda; evidence to help prove the spirit's innocent nature.

She'd presented it to Dave as soon as she'd arrived at Security. After a quick computer scan for viruses later, they cleared it for travel.

"Good thinking," Dave said. "I've also got the CCTV footage from Kamal," then handed her a metal suitcase. "Here. Put this on over your clothes."

She transferred her Cross-Key ID and locator badge from her blouse to the suit's chest, opposite an embroidered company logo. Her grip on the satchel made the dial inbuilt into the suit's fabric shine. Reaching out to touch it, she froze, uncertain. Knowing Cross-Key it couldn't simply be a timepiece.

Dave eyed Lucy with the cuff. "Are you sure you want to come with us? It would be great to have you, but we understand if you're not ready. Although I imagine the investigators would want to come and talk to you here instead if you didn't."

Images flashed through Lucy's mind: Oda, Ben, her parents being chased by a dark cloaked figure. *Will and Cecelia actually live in space,* Hina's voice reminded her. Then, she pictured herself floating in a grey jumpsuit, planting a flag on a white crater-covered surface. Silently, she thanked the other girl. "Yes," she answered as firmly as she could, which slid out as a squeak.

Will laughed from his wheelchair, tapping a foot up and down with the excitement of a trip back to his home. His suit sagged around his stomach and ankles, at least two sizes too large.

"Alright then, one last thing before we head out. That little dial on your suit cuff creates a personal gravitational field, a bubble around yourself. You can turn the gravity on or off, or anywhere between, depending on where you set the dial. On full it will simulate Earth's gravity so you won't feel the difference. The power button is on the side."

Lucy stared down at the little white circular dial, fascinated.

Alex, having taken over from the nighttime manager, looked exhausted as he led them out from Security. His back had taken on an extra degree of hunch, and Lucy thought if she took off his sunglasses, she'd see panda-worthy dark circles.

The group went down into the maze of underground tunnels, and from the time it was taking Lucy knew they couldn't still be under the Cross-Key estate anymore.

"Lights up," Dave called from the head of the group. The same white floodlights that lit the industrial land above illuminated a space the size of a shopping centre car park. Instead of vehicles it was lined with row after row of machines, all connected by a myriad of jumbled multicoloured cables.

Following Alex, they walked down a central path of machines out into a large open space, then Lucy spotted herself walking towards her. A floor-to-ceiling mirror took up an entire wall, bonded into the stone behind.

Wheels crackled over the concrete as Will pushed his way to a computer on an adjacent wall. He typed briefly, scanned his ID badge, and the computer's monitor sprang to life.

"We make most of our shipments to and from the Fleet from here," Dave said, flourishing towards a stacked pile of boxes, each displaying the Cross-Key & Co. logo.

"This HAT machine was the very first built. It's too small to actually launch a ship, but that's what our branch in Northern Europe is for. Less seismic activity there."

"But then we found a moon good enough to build a base," Will added happily as he continued typing. "Cross-Key sends us our parts through the portal, and we can construct them there. This is where I work most of the time." He grinned, as though Oda had not been stolen and there wasn't a vampire on the loose. Lucy simply stared.

"Aye," agreed Alex, bending his hunch into a curved recline as he stared up at the mirror. "It's good to know you're part of the family that helped to launch the original Fleet craft. I have an old diary that's been passed down through the family, and in it's a portrait of some of the original vampires who made the pact."

"You mean Jack John Crossley's?" Dave asked curiously. "Mum said that was lost decades ago."

"Nope," Alex said with a grin. "And what Aunt doesn't know won't kill her. Our night-walker friends took it back, then they passed it on to my dad during a visit. Cecelia doesn't look like she's aged a day. Don't tell her I said that, though," he added, putting his hands in his pockets.

Lucy remained frozen. She felt like she was intruding *in* a private family moment. Wait, so how old was Cecelia? The original launch was in the Middle Ages!

Oblivious to her shock, Will proudly kept typing what looked like long strings of code and flitting through settings, and she'd never felt more out of her depth.

The teen's voice echoed across the room, "We're going live in five." A large number filled every monitor in the room—all springing to life under his command. "Four, three, two, one!" A sound of a switch being flipped rang in the distance and a green light sprang on above Will's computer—the only signs that something had changed, until a coppery smell crept up Lucy's nostrils.

Alex strode over to stand behind Will and checked the screen. The guard gave him a thumbs up and Will wheeled back to Lucy and Dave.

"Coordinates are locked on to the Bureau. This feels odd, doing this without a vampire to oversee things," Alex commented as if he were pointing out an oddly shaped cloud. Nothing seemed to faze the man.

From her side Will coughed in irritation, a reminder that he was there, too, but it went ignored by the two men. Lucy locked eyes with sky blue. He flashed a grin at her, then huffed, sagging low in his chair with his arms crossed, and rolled his eyes at the ceiling. Her lips twitched at the antics.

"OK, team, the plan is to slide through the HAT machine into the welcome chamber on-board the Bureau. It's painless and safe and shouldn't take more than five minutes to get through. There's not a lot in there—just the endless black of warped space with some lights that we've erected so we can see where we're heading. We'll all go together."

Although Lucy nodded at Dave's plan she still didn't like the idea of walking through a solid mirror.

Alex held out a hand to Lucy. "I'll need the ID chip you have to give you clearance." Lucy raised her hands to take off the badge but was stopped. "Come here and I can scan it with this. You'll need to be wearing it for this to work, so keep it on you at all times." He raised what looked like a checkout scanner from a store, scanned her ID chip, and it beeped.

Will and Dave were next to get theirs scanned. Lucy looked at Alex to see if he was going to scan his own ID, but he didn't. At her glance Alex explained in a soft voice, "Oh no. I'm security. I'll keep guard here. That's my job."

Lucy felt stupid. No one had said he was coming, and of course they couldn't leave the portal—*HAT machine*, her brain reminded her—unguarded.

"Line up next to me," Dave ordered. Lucy positioned herself to his right, and Will flanked her other side in his chair. She stared forwards into the mirror and sucked in a breath. Her reflection was missing. It was just like Cecelia's in the bathroom mirror the other day. She clutched her satchel tighter to her side, a reassuring weight that told her she was still there even though her reflection had disappeared.

"You're taking your chair?" Alex asked.

"It's recommended," Will said, motioning to the mirror. "I won't transform until the other side, and the portal changes length depending on any large masses it needs to warp around when the coordinates are set. It's not worth being upright that long."

Lucy's mind reeled. A mix of vortexes, planets and black holes swam across her vision.

"Alright, let's walk. You won't feel a thing," Dave said with a grin too large to match their predicament, so Lucy knew it was for her benefit. Inhaling deeply, shoulders braced, she stepped forward.

First, Lucy noticed the lack of hair against her neck; the second thing was her satchel leaving a hole at her side as it floated away. Third, she reached to grab the deserting item and her stomach lurched. The ground disappeared, the momentum of the grab propelling her forwards into the beginnings of a somersault.

A steadying hand grabbed her flailing arms and tugged her back to the ground.

"I've got you. You're alright. Use the gravitational dial." Dave's steady tones washed over her panic, dampening it enough so she could bring the dial on her wrist cuff into focus. Punching the power button, the dial pulsed with warmth, and she rotated the dial to max.

Her satchel thumped back against her side, and her hair fell against her neck again. Breaking Dave's hold, she hugged the satchel to her side, then raised a hand to her hair and groaned inwardly. What a mess. Then she started combing her fingers through it in desperate hopes of flattening and detangling the newly knotted mass. She let her arms drop and smiled sheepishly at an amused-looking Dave.

To his credit, Dave said nothing, turning instead to her other side.

Lucy followed his gaze and froze. Her eyebrows shot to the ceiling. At her side stood a tall, muscular beast. His auburn hair swam around his head like a halo, uncovering mahogany fur-covered pointed ears that swivelled like radars. The fur extended down the backs of his fingers that sported pointed black claws.

"It's good to be back to perfection," he said in a gruff, contented tone, like someone returning home at the end of a long day. He flexed his neck from side to side, working out kinks with one hand, the other holding the back of a wheelchair, preventing it from floating away. His suit fit perfectly.

"Let me take that," Dave offered, nonchalantly walking over to take the chair.

"Thanks. Much appreciated," said Will with a wolfish grin.

Lemon yellow eyes sucked Lucy in, dancing with mirth. They were encircled by glittering sky-blue rims. He was striking, piercing, *other*. She shuddered from awe—or something she refused to name.

A loud crash made Lucy wince, breaking her eye contact. Dave was bent over the wheelchair that had returned to the ground, presumably as soon as he'd touched it, straightening it up and brushing it down. Then, like it was simply another day on planet Earth, he took up position behind it and wheeled it over to a screen embedded between metallic grey panels on the walls.

"Let's start the check-in process," he said, making the monitor light bright white by passing a hand in front of it, waking it up.

"Welcome. I am the customs program Be. How many wishing to board?" a high-pitched robotic voice rang around the room.

"Three," Dave replied.

"Can every member of your party swallow small solids?"

"Yes."

There was a loud clinking and clanging of gears, then one of the metal slats in the wall lowered like a drawbridge. Dave reached in and pulled out a black tray, then turned and offered Lucy and Will a cup of water and a pill each. "They're designed to disinfect foreign bacteria and infections visitors could carry on board. It's either this or spending two weeks in quarantine, and we simply don't have the time," he said, sounding regretful.

Lucy hesitated, watching Will and Dave take theirs first. Will licked his elongated jaw before popping the pill on his tongue. "Best part of inter-craft travel," he growled in satisfaction.

Dave also hummed in appreciation before taking a swig from his cup.

They weren't knocked out cold, weren't frothing at the mouth, and their pupils hadn't changed size, so Lucy concluded they couldn't be too bad. With a leap of faith, she popped hers into her mouth and an explosion of citrus burst across her tongue just like the anti-pain meds.

Perhaps the Fleet wouldn't be so bad after all. Even if Will was now a very tall half wolf man, his personality didn't seem to have changed. No. Not bad at all.

Dave returned their empty cups to the tray and closed the hatch back up. "WHAT IS THE PURPOSE OF YOUR VISIT?"

Another slat in the wall dropped next to the computer monitor, revealing a white panel with a rectangular screen above it.

"This machine measures a person's intent," Dave explained. "It uses the same vampiric technology we do in our products to measure a person's preferences. If it doesn't see you as a threat to the ship or detect any lies, it will clear you to pass."

"Shouldn't the reason we're here be..." Lucy lowered voice to a whisper, "private?"

The panel on the wall flashed red and Be's voice spoke crisply, "YOUR BUSINESS IS NONE OF MY BUSINESS, UNLESS IT IS MY BUSINESS, AND YOU'RE HERE TO UPGRADE, MAINTAIN OR FOR THE LOVE OF RUSTY PARTS IN A METEOR STORM, DECOMMISSION ME."

"When did Be get a sass upgrade?" asked Will.

Dave shrugged. "Don't worry. Privacy and confidentiality are coded into it. The vampires are a secretive bunch and wouldn't have agreed to this if it could pass on just data it finds."

It sounded incredibly political, but it settled Lucy somewhat. Having potentially insulted the machine, she fell back on her well-trained technique of shutting up.

"I've got this. One sec," Will said and approached the screen first. He hunched his bulky frame down to the mechanism. "Normally you'd need everyone in a party to declare their intentions, but as an ambassador I'm given certain privileges based on trust," he continued, then raised his hands in front of the panel, and gazed into the glass bar above. The smell of copper like the HAT machine seeped into the room and the machine whirred. About fifteen seconds passed before the white panel flashed green.

"APPROVED," chirped Be. "BE YOURSELF, BE TRUE TO YOUR NATURE, BUT ALSO BEHAVE WHILE YOU ARE HERE. IF YOU DO THESE THINGS, THEN YOU BELONG. PROCEED."

Clanking and grinding pulled Lucy out of her thoughts. On the far wall, a selection of metallic panels folded over one other, creating a man-size circular porthole that Dave herded them through. "Let's go. We don't want to block the portal for anyone else."

Instead of the hodgepodge of battered metal panels in the portal room, the reception was modern brushed chrome with sleek black and crisp white accents. It was the sort of place Lucy expected from the world's most luxurious hotels.

"Welcome to the Bureau. How can I help you today?" asked a gruff but feminine werewolf, launching into a rushed, rehearsed script. She had matching long black hair and fur that danced above her ebony skin as she moved. Her outfit was a grey one-piece suit with a cuff and dial on her wrist.

"Hello. Dave Crossley from Cross-Key & Co. Head of International Research and Development. This is my co-worker Miss Lucy Blakely, and you already know your own ambassador here." He motioned behind to Will, who was rubbing the back of his suit in a very inappropriate place.

A series of square lights sprang to life in the air, which Hina's werewolf counterpart tapped rapidly. "I don't have you down to arrive until Friday," she said, eyes narrowing.

"About that," Dave said and leaned over the white counter-top. "There's been an emergency. We have urgent information to add to the report about an interspecies criminal act."

The receptionist huffed then snapped, "Have you been summoned or invited directly to speak to someone on-board the Bureau?"

"No, but—"

"You are not the CEO of Cross-Key & Co. and therefore do not have the level of access required for admittance. If you wish to pass on information, please submit a formally written transcript via form 34CQ, then the investigations committee will contact you and assign a case number. Or you may return on Friday if you prefer."

The receptionist vanished the light screen with a swish of her hand.

"I may not be the CEO, but Will here," Dave wrapped an arm around said werewolf's middle, which Lucy was sure would have been shoulder height in human form, "is currently ambassador for the packs on Earth. Surely he has the right to come and go?" Dave pointed out.

"He is not—"

"Well, hello there." A devastatingly beautiful femme fatale sauntered down the corridor behind the kiosk. Her lips were thick and painted crimson, and her shoulder-length curls bounced round her cheeks with each step taken in shiny black heels and full gravity.

"Trisha?" the receptionist questioned, eyebrow raised.

Trisha's ice blue gaze locked on to Will's, and she smiled, approaching him with a swagger. "Hello, handsome," she said, before reaching up and kissing him on the cheek.

Will's eyes grew large, and his jaw dropped.

The copper-haired lady turned away, raised a hand, and silently beckoned the group to follow her back down the corridor.

"If that isn't an invitation, then I don't know what is," Dave said. "Look. She even stamped it," he said, tilting his head towards two glowing red arches on an increasingly rosy left cheek.

Lucy didn't know if she should laugh or cry and settled instead on admiring the woman's audacity as she retreated down the corridor. Actions spoke louder than words after all, and that woman was living, breathing proof of it.

"Well, we've got to be going. Don't want to leave her waiting. Bye!" Dave said, and Lucy followed his cue to dash past the now spluttering receptionist.

Lucy and Dave quickly caught up with Trisha, taking two steps for every one of Will's gravity-defying bounds. In other circumstances, walking as if she was on the moon might have been fun, but for now she had to look important enough to be heard, and using full gravity was apparently impressive to Will's people.

The group walked down a large grey metal corridor with up-lights in the floors lighting their way. It looked similar to the construction of the portal's chamber, but it was darker and thankfully clear of obstacles. Lucy made out apparent doors only from soft luminous signs lighting the walls at frequent intervals. Otherwise she couldn't distinguish wall from door panels.

They finally stopped at a door that read Grand Bureau Member. Trisha flashed an ID badge from her chest, similar to the type used at Cross-Key, and the group entered.

# CHAPTER NINE

# THE COUNCIL IS IN SESSION

A wave of heat washed over Lucy as they entered the office, away from the chill of the make-do metal-panelled corridor. She tugged at her sleeve, pulling it loose from where it stuck to her arm. As well as warmth, the office oozed luxury, albeit a mishmash of clashing pieces through the ages. It reminded her of Mrs Crossley's waiting room, bar two key differences.

Difference number one: *Trisha* was engraved in the Cross-Key silver font on the front of the receptionist's desk. The redhead, who couldn't have been much older than herself but oozing confidence, leaned casually on the front of the carved red wood masterpiece. She motioned them to sit, her movements much more animated and warm. Too lively for the undead.

Lucy's train of thought derailed when she spotted difference number two. A large rectangular window above the workstation showcased the inky black recesses of space, littered with small white stars like raindrops. She was in an office, on a vessel, *in space*. Of course, she'd known she'd be going to space, but now she *knew*, and the thought was sinking in while she sank into a foamy seat.

Lucy resisted the urge to take out her tablet and start photographing everything. This was what the inside of a spaceship looked like. They had put a lot more effort into the places where people would spend time—specific design choices she found utterly fascinating.

"Dave," Trisha grinned cheerily. "So lovely of you to come and visit. What a pleasure..." she trailed off, eyes lingering slightly too long on Will, who blushed again under the gaze.

"It's good to see you, too, Trish, although I wish it were under better circumstances," Dave answered, letting his I've-got-this persona crack, sighing and running a hand through his hair. "Thanks for the help. We're in a bit of a tight spot," he said, then turned to the two teenagers sitting opposite.

"Lucy, Will, this is Trisha. She's my cousin, and the current human ambassador stationed in the Fleet. She lives and works on board the Bureau. Her current role is secretary to the Grand Bureau Member. They're the person in charge of the Fleet's governing body called the Council. Imagine a prime minister or a president."

Lucy nodded, wondering how she'd gone from sketching in her bedroom to the office of the head of a colony of space-venturing paranormal beings.

Trisha typed something on a light keyboard like the receptionist had used, then vanished it over her desk and walked over to Will's wheelchair. "You want this secured?"

"Please," Dave said, happily relinquishing it to Trisha, who opened a cupboard door and buckled it inside. As soon as she let go it began to float but was tethered in place allowing her to close the door on it again. Then Lucy realised that everything in the room was fixed to the ground with small bolts she hadn't noticed. The sight of space was very distracting.

"How's work?" Dave asked, conversationally.

"The usual politics," Trisha said with a flick of the wrist. "The Grand Councillors are all out for Astra's position. A couple of the packs are trying to butter up the vampires for higher rank. Other than that, most of my time this month has been spent trying to track down missing stock arrivals and shortages on incoming supplies," she finished with steely tones, arms crossed and stared fixedly at Dave. "There's been a lot of pressure on me to sort out the discrepancies and a lot of comments made about my relationship with the Crossleys being a conflict of interest."

Dave winced. "Sorry, Cuz, but Will and I are working flat out to try to sort it out at our end. Will's your equivalent on Earth, and he's been learning all about the import process by shadowing me. You remember Duke, who held the position last year? Well, meet his brother."

Will nodded a bit too enthusiastically while Dave talked, and raised a clawed, paw-like hand in a wave at the end.

Trisha winked at him. Seated at Will's side, Lucy watched him freeze. Trying not to stare at the couple, she rearranged her hands in her lap instead.

Dave coughed, drawing attention back to himself. "To business, then. I am here today with Miss Lucy Blakely and Mr Will Harven to report an interspecies crime. It's in relation to the current report that Mrs Margaret Crossley, the CEO of Cross-Key & Co., and Cecelia, Vampire Ambassador, are here making. It's incredibly urgent."

Trisha took up position behind her desk, spread her hands apart in the air, and what looked like a ghostly computer monitor appeared in mid-air at her eye level. She swiped and tapped through several screens before making a pulling motion. Out of thin air popped a keyboard made of light, which glowed as her fingers flew across the keys.

"I've imported your Cross-Key & Co. employee files to the immigration system, and Be clearance should be enough to keep people off your backs for now. That, combined with character references from myself and Mrs Crossley, should do the trick." Trisha's all-business, no-nonsense attitude more than matched Dave's, and Lucy's awe of the young woman grew.

"Thanks, I owe you one," Dave said, breaking formality again with his trademark smile.

Placing her hand on the far wall, it beeped at her touch, and a once invisible door appeared on the surface. *Council Chamber* appeared engraved in swirling gold at the centre. Trisha pulled it open and disappeared without a word.

"I can't imagine they'll turn us away before hearing what we have to say," Dave said, sounding like he was trying to convince himself as well as the room. "A vampire breakout to Earth is a major incident. We'll be alright."

Not knowing how the Council worked, all Lucy could do was trust, but Dave's restless foot-tapping made her resolve to take his reassurances with a grain of salt.

"I've never been so close to the Council before," Will said, seemingly oblivious to the mounting tension. "We might actually get to meet Astra. She's the Grand Bureau Member. It's an honour," he said, rubbing his hands on his thighs, leaking barely contained enthusiasm. Lucy eyed his movements, wondering how his claws hadn't shredded the material yet. Excitement rolled off him in waves, and it was contagious.

Picking up on his positive vibes, Lucy tried to channel them. Will might be star-struck, but she had a job to do. She spent the next ten minutes planning how best to show off Oda's good nature.

The time passed with only small comments here and there before Trisha popped her head around the door again.

"They will hear Dave now. Will, you're officially shadowing, so you can come, too." The pair stood and headed to the door, Will punching the air as he went. Lucy smiled nervously.

"Lucy, you'll have to sit tight a bit longer. I'll get you when they're ready for you."

Lucy nodded at the lady and when the door thudded behind them launched to her feet. After an uncomfortable few minutes pacing alone with her thoughts, she wandered over to the window.

She couldn't see any constellations she'd been taught as a child. This was far, far from home. She was far, *far* from home. Her heart skipped at the thought, and she drove down a rising wave of panic.

Humming the *Sgt Sir!* theme, she imagined she'd been posted to a secret military base hidden on the far side of the moon. The next time she watched the *Sgt. Sir!* hour-long off-world special, she'd view it in a completely different light. Getting into character, she turned on the microgravity from her dial and bounded across the room, launching with focus and intent. She was on a mission. A rescue mission. Although she didn't have an anti-gravity super bazooka, her tablet was full of sketches.

Settled, face set, she returned the gravity dial back to Earth and dug her tablet out of her satchel. Booting it up, she looked through Oda's images and contemplated a game plan.

It wasn't long after when Trisha poked her head around the door again. "The Council will hear you now, Miss Blakely," she said formally.

Clearing her mind like she did before school assemblies and job interviews, she forced a breath out and her shoulders to relax.

"You'll be fine," Trisha reassured her. Lucy desperately wanted to believe those words were true and marched, back ramrod straight, into the unknown again.

The stuffiness of the room hit Lucy first, like a heavy blanket pressing in on her already sweaty fingers. The source of the heat: a sea of yellow and red eyes looking down at her from tiered semicircle stands.

At ground level, seated at a table with their backs to her, were Dave, Will, Cecelia, and the CEO, who also turned to look at her as she entered.

Trisha walked past her to a strikingly tall and muscular woman. Her frizzy black hair was as thick and wild as a wolf's winter coat, her skin ebony, showcasing glowing amber eyes.

"Grand Bureau Member Astra, Ministers and Councillors, this is Miss Lucy Blakely—employee of Cross-Key & Co.," Trisha declared.

Astra curled her lips upwards, flashing two canine fangs to Lucy. Amazingly, Trisha didn't even blink at the imposing woman standing head and shoulders above her. Lucy could feel the effects of Astra's intimidating aura halfway across the room.

"On what grounds is a non-Crossley human doing here?" the wolf asked, her voice low and gravelly.

"She was one of the last people to see the tree spirit before it went missing," Trisha explained. "Her background check has been patched through, including her contract, and she holds Be clearance."

"I see. Return to your duties," Astra dismissed, her voice deep and gravelly.

Trisha nodded, then walked back down to the entrance they had just used, giving Lucy the subtle Crossley wink as she passed.

Then she was alone in the crowd. What was she meant to do? Approach? Offer her hand? Astra was the leader, so surely she needed a bigger introduction than that?

Not trusting her voice or wanting to move anyway nearer to the woman uninvited, she bent herself forward into a bow. She'd seen Cecelia curtsy once but had never done it before, so avoiding it seemed like the safest bet. She couldn't imagine these enormous figures doing anything so dainty.

"Thank you," Astra replied, taking the action in stride. "Take a seat." The wolf clicked her fingers, and a chair rose out of a now flipped-open panel in the floor. It hovered for a moment before Astra touched it, then it crashed to the floor in her microgravity field. "Please," she snapped.

Lucy took the offered seat exactly where it dropped, then Astra began to circle her.

"We have heard," she proclaimed, "that a most unfortunate incident has happened at Cross-Key to a person you were employed to work with. This is of deep concern."

A low murmur of agreement spread around the benches.

"Tell us, what was the nature of the relationship you had with this person? It must be incredibly special for the Crossley family to break the Charter of Exploration and Secrecy." Her eyes narrowed, and a chill ran the length of Lucy's spine.

This was it. What she'd prepared for. Time for action.

Her lungs burned, constricting, as she bent over and plucked the tablet from her bag. Loading up her and Oda's introductory image, she offered it up, arms trembling.

"Explain," Astra said simply, while in the background, small strands of commentary trickled down to her every now and again.

Silence reigned as her throat closed, mouth running dry. She forced through the oncoming freeze.

"Cat got her tongue?"

"How primitive."

"What languages does she speak?"

Lucy counted backwards from five, ignoring the chatter from the audience as she pulled herself together. She wasn't speaking. She was interpreting. That was her job, and she was good at it.

Imagining the warmth of the room instead as Oda's welcoming mental hug, she zoned out everything around her so it was herself, Dave and Oda once again down in her research dome.

"This is the way I greet Oda—the kodama. I am employed as Oda's interpreter. I draw into the notebook Oda inhabits and Oda draws back to me."

Another round of excited murmurs and a few gasps broke out.

"Communication via pictures? How can a kodama draw and how do you interpret pictures?" Astra asked, glancing up from the image. Her tone and face had gone completely blank into the perfect poker face.

Lucy bristled. These questions were off the point. Cross-Key and Oda weren't on trial here. They had a vampire to track down.

Clenching her hands, she replied as calmly as she could manage. "Oda would absorb the ink into the book, then rearrange the ink into a picture and displayed it back to us on the page. I looked at the drawing and tried to decide the meaning of it."

The explanation was butchered, but she didn't trust these people enough to tell them about the blood bond. They didn't sound ready to help her, so why should she trust them?

Astra swiped through the images on the tablet. "These pictures are mainly puzzles. Would the kodama be able to answer direct questions?" she probed.

"That depends," Lucy said, thinking quickly. "If you set out a story or series of events to show the question, then Oda could tell you what they would like to happen and give you an ending."

Seeing confusion, Lucy continued, "For example, when we were trying to find out if they knew how to count, they rearranged the objects we wanted her to count into a circle instead."

A male voice in the back muttered, "Selfish."

"And do you think," Astra continued, "that if anyone other than you were to ask Oda a question they would always answer?"

The question confirmed everything Cecelia had thought about the Bureau. They wanted to know the likelihood of Oda being a threat to the discovery of their existence. Assuming her line of thinking was correct, she took a gamble. "I can't say for sure," Lucy answered, "but Oda only knows about humans. I don't think there's any risk of stories being told about you and your people. Perhaps we could teach Oda—"

"That's not the point." A short man with vivid red eyes—a vampire—stood up from one bench. "There's no way of telling purely through pictures if this creature is capable of deception. Not to mention the very existence of a self-drawing notebook. That's evidence enough of the paranormal."

A dam broke, and a wave of arguments and concern filled the room, rising gradually in volume until Astra raised an arm. *"Enough!"* Immediate silence fell. Her voice lowered again. Astra walked around Lucy's chair and looked her directly in the eye. "Do you have an answer to these claims?"

Her brain wanted to answer. It did. She'd prepared answers for this; she knew she had! But what were they? There was...technology...projections...and what else was there? This wasn't interpretation anymore. This was her *speaking*.

The world started to swim.

A screech came from Lucy's left, and she was thankful to see Dave up and on his feet. "My colleague is tired, and I believe this line of questioning has gone on long enough. There is still the matter of a vampire on Earth to be dealt with, and as part of the investigation we request aid to help apprehend the criminal."

Lucy's heart slowed and her vision focused again as she heard Dave's words. He'd done it. Made the request they'd come for.

Mrs Crossley stood up next to her son. "If you recapture the vampire, then you also recapture the kodama. Once it is back in our custody, all of your concerns can be laid to rest."

Astra cut off the tide of murmurs before they started with another raise of her arm.

"Thank you for your input. The Council members and myself will deliberate on what you have said. Please stay aboard the ship until we come to a decision. If we require any more information, we will call for you," Astra said, then handed the tablet back to Lucy.

"Thank you," she said. "Dave made copies of all of my sketches for you."

Dave grinned. "I did indeed. They're on this drive, along with a copy of our CCTV footage, for your vigilant perusal. We hope your deliberations go smoothly," he said, handing over a black plastic chip.

"Thank you. Why don't you go for an early lunch from the canteen while you wait? You did come all this way after all. We have to look after our guests."

It wasn't a suggestion, and they were promptly escorted out of the room by a group who Will whispered were the Guards.

On her way out, Lucy looked back at Astra and saw glimpses of her mother standing authoritatively. Both women were fierce, commanded respect, and took safety to a degree off the charts. Both women wanted the best for the people they were in charge of, and she couldn't help but smile at the thought.

Following her gaze, Will whistled. "Incredible, isn't she? She's only six-ty-four, you know."

Lucy almost walked into one of the very rare corners of the circular ship. Only? She didn't look a day over thirty! Her eyes grew wide as they walked back into Trisha's office. How long did wolves live for?

# Chapter Ten

# Pack Lunches

Barbecued meat filled Lucy's nostrils as the group entered the food court. Margaret and Cecelia had opted to go their own ways and eat in the privacy of the cabins they owned on-board, leaving the original trio of herself, Will, and Dave.

Long tables ran the length of the room, where groups of werewolves sat on matching benches. Vampires sat on their own, dotted around the canteen. Everyone wore a standard grey jumpsuit, but the sea of hair and shades was never-ending: browns, reds, blacks, greys, and even whites, swam in varying states of gravity. Judging from the amount standing on end, mild gravity looked like the preferred setting.

As they passed, Lucy saw werewolves with plates piled high with meat: chicken legs, pork ribs, and a lot of beef steaks. None of the food was flying across the room, so Lucy assumed the tables must have gravity set as a default. What she couldn't see was where the food was coming from. There weren't any servers or cooks.

Dave directed them to a table in the centre of the room, took a seat, then stroked the surface of the table in front of him. A hidden compartment flipped up, revealing a screen with a scrolling menu.

"This is how you order," he explained. "Tap the box next to the food you'd like. When you're done, you tap the top of the monitor." He ticked

99

a few boxes, then tapped the top of the monitor, which folded face down back into the surface as if it hadn't been there at all.

On the other side of the table, Will wrinkled his nose as he scanned the menu.

Lucy swallowed her embarrassment and stroked the table in front of her. To her delight, the screen popped up, showing a variety of foods and drinks available. The touch screen was intuitive, and she quickly scanned through starters, mains, and desserts. Opting for a lighter fare, she chose something familiar: chicken soup with crusty bread and water. Her stomach rumbled happily as her tap sent the order back into the table.

No wonder Will had eaten hers; he'd probably eaten it in space, too. Could you keep a farm on a spaceship, though? An image of a room filled with floating cows bouncing off walls made her giggle. The sound startled her and she caught herself, covering her mouth, eyes wide.

"Well, that was a pleasant sound," Dave said in a soft tone. It was the most relaxed she'd heard him since they stood in front of the Councillors. "You should do it more often. Laughter is good for the soul."

Lucy glanced at the table, her cheeks heating.

Taking pity on her, Dave changed topic. "It won't be long before we're served. It takes around the same time to get your food here as it does from point of order at an Earthen restaurant."

Lucy nodded, then let her eyes wander the room as nondescriptly as possible. Now and then groups of wolves broke out into loud, low laughter. They dwarfed the vampires who sat alone, their pallor pale and eyes glowing red. The smaller beings nursed—Lucy sucked in a breath—glasses of red.

She slammed the rising panic down. Cecelia had a glass of red at the dome, and that wasn't blood. It didn't have to be. And she tried her hardest to convince herself that was the case.

Straining to tune into the gravelly conversations around her, she jumped when a loud grinding whir came from the table. A hole appeared in front of Dave and a tray of food rose in front of him, like her chair in the Council's chamber. She was thankful they seemed to store most of their items away, otherwise she could have been attempting an obstacle course.

Dave happily dug in to a large portion of fish and chips, and not long after, Will licked his lips as a bright pink steak appeared. "Well done. Just how I like it," he said, causing Lucy to raise an eyebrow.

Dave turned to her between mouthfuls of crispy batter. "I should have said before. Don't get the steak. Here, well done means rare. Medium done means it's slightly been heated at room temperature. Rare is pretty much the next best thing to the living animal."

Seeing her blanch, he quickly added, "But don't worry. I'm sure the psychic fields would have picked up on that. And it's not like they're literally killing animals down in the kitchens. They grow vegetables and body parts of animals on one of the Fleet ships. Stem cell technology."

She vaguely remembered something in school about stem cells but not enough to understand what he was talking about. Thankfully, a well-timed bowl of creamy chicken soup appeared to distract her. As expected, it was perfection. The bread was perfect for dunking, with a tough, chewy crust for easy holding and soft mixed grain inside to cling on to as much soup as possible. One bite later, and she was transported to another world.

The glass of water was more than welcome after the heat and vocal workout in the chamber. As she ate, the food never grew cold. It put her own cooking to shame, and even more embarrassingly, she'd fed it to Will.

As expected, Dave finished his meal first, having been the first to arrive. He turned to her and spoke gently. "Lucy, I'd like to say something. You don't have to talk. Feel free to listen and finish your meal."

She nodded, trying to ignore the creeping dread by tearing another bread chunk.

"Just know that whatever today's outcome, I'm proud of you. You did your best, and you should be proud, too."

What if her best wasn't good enough, though? She dipped and reloaded her bread.

"As your mentor, I think you spoke incredibly well today, and you'd do well to speak out more. I know that when my family introduced me to the 'real' family business, I desperately needed someone to talk to. It will be a shock to your system. Please, use me and Hina. Will—well, his culture shock goes the other way. But I encourage Will to ask questions, and I want you to feel comfortable asking questions, too. I see them, bubbling beneath the surface. A creative like you couldn't not."

Lucy felt like they'd caught her with her hand in the cookie jar.

"In our line of work, there's no such thing as a stupid question. Acting out of ignorance, however, could get you killed. One's far more preferable than the other."

Lucy sat in silence, mulling over her employer's words as he vanished his tray with a stroke of the table.

It was all well and fine, people saying she had said the right things, but ultimately things always went better if she put up and shut up. She couldn't risk looking stupid, to say the wrong thing, to lose her job and reputation.

As for conversation, her parents weren't around, but she wasn't lonely, was she? She had Oda. No—had had Oda. She just needed to get Oda back. Resolved to ignore any other outcomes, she spooned up the last of her bowl.

Four werewolves shouted across the canteen, snapping her out of her reverie. "Hey, it's Will! Look, he really is here. How's it been?" Their silver

Guard badges glinted as one by one they bent to give Will high fives and hugs, then sat around him and began to chat.

When Will introduced her, she tried not to physically shrink from the attention. Three pairs of bright yellow eyes looked at her with curiosity, having never met an actual human before.

The fourth had amber eyes and made his way down towards them, hand outstretched.

"Dave, it's good to see you, but I take it you're here for the emergency meeting." Unlike the reunion of excited puppies, his tone was edged with concern.

Dave grabbed the offered hand and yanked, pulling the wolf into a hug. His fur had the same colouring as Will's, but he was taller and bulkier.

His impressive stature was ruined by the startled, wide eyes and a bristled mahogany tail, fanning out like a brush. Lucy choked back a laugh. So that was why Will was poking at his behind when they arrived.

"Duke, on the case as ever," Dave said, breaking their embrace to look him up and down. "That badge suits you," he said, poking at the Guards's symbol on his chest.

Duke took an offered seat next to Dave, and the pair caught up.

Not wanting to seem obvious, Lucy looked down at banishing her dishes while looking from the corner of her eye. So that was Will's brother, the previous wolf ambassador. He was impressive, but she preferred Will's more light-hearted nature.

She turned his way just as a loud cheer rang around him, with shouts of *Congratulations* and *Happy Soon Birthday*! The group clapped Will on the back and happily drank in the attention at the centre.

Eventually, the pair walked over to his brother, and the pack parted with one word from Duke.

Lucy watched, fascinated, as he sat next to his smaller brother; the mood of the group subdued until Duke nodded, granting permission for them to continue.

Will beamed at his brother, then started waving paws, introducing Dave to the group. He looked the picture of happiness, so Lucy made a snap decision. Pulling out her tablet and stylus, she sketched.

As time passed by, the Guards ate and went back to their work, only to be replaced by more who came to greet Will; word of his arrival had passed down the grapevine. Every now and again she overheard a comment like, "Wow—ancient tech," but thankfully none of them approached.

At what Lucy thought was the hour mark, Dave resumed his seat at her side, handing her a cup of water and staring down at the screen. "That's brilliant," he said. "Is it for..." he nodded over to Will, and she smiled silently back.

"He'll love it. Listen, I'm going to go check in with Cecelia and M—er, the CEO. I'll check if there's been any progress. Stay here with Will."

Lucy downed the glass of water, overly aware of her new position of only human in the room. Dave left, and with a mental shake, she returned to sketching.

The next twenty minutes dragged, and when Dave finally returned, the canteen was all but empty other than herself, two werewolves who sat with Will, and a vampire staring at a light screen by one wall.

"No decision yet, so they have advised us to leave. I expect we'll hear back tomorrow."

Lucy's heart panged. Indecision was not the answer she'd hope for.

Having overheard, Will bounced up, and the other wolves clapped him on the back.

"Good job," one said.

"Do us proud," said the other, then they left, leaving Lucy and Will to follow Dave out into the curved grey corridors of the ship.

They stopped in front of a door with *Earth Ambassador* engraved in bronze and knocked.

"Come in," said Mrs Crossley crisply.

Upon entry, Lucy recoiled from blinding white. Blinking her eyes back into focus, she focused in on a giant white-and-grey speckled semicircle filling an entire wall. Mesmerised, she walked over to it.

Will settled by her side and raised a hand reverently to the transparent wall. "My ancestors left planet Earth in search of a place where we could live in our perfect form all the time. The optimum blend of human and wolf, neither fully one nor the other. It's tidally locked. Half in perpetual darkness, half perpetual night."

Lucy let the words sink in as she stared at the half-moon.

The older woman warbled from her desk, "Beautiful, isn't it? They spoil me with this view. It's one of four the Fleet orbits. Four sectors of space."

"Werewolf's choice. It's like a religion," Cecelia chimed in.

Will dropped his hand and spoke softly, "There are fanatics who say the Gods made us as superior beings, the next evolution from humankind. I'm not sure, but it doesn't stop me being thankful for having lycanthropy, getting to live in this powerful body, seeing stars every day. I might not be so religious, but I still feel blessed, and I wish everyone could be so content."

"It would be nice if everyone was," Cecelia said dryly. Her mouth curled up at the corner. "Anyway. *Ship 1*, this sector's explorer vessel, is chartering its return from their latest recon mission, over a week late. The reports of their findings are trickling in as we speak, and there's a lot of buzz about it. That's what's holding up the Council's decision making."

"They're looking for traces of salt on the surface," Will supplemented and Lucy turned away from the window to look at him. "Or at least that's what the official mission was. Everyone knows they're really looking for a planet to settle down on." His expression darkened, eyes narrowed, and for a brief second Lucy thought she saw his eyes turn from lemon yellow to honey.

"It's very human to not be satisfied with the status quo," Dave commented. "It's a trait that binds us together, I think. But for now, let's make our way back to Earth. Cuz, could you fetch Will's wheelchair, please?"

Trisha gave him an overexaggerated salute, followed by a smile. "Meet you by the portal," she said.

A short walk later, Lucy's nostrils filled with copper again as they approached the receptionist's desk, and she realised that the copper had been throughout the entire ship but in varying degrees. It occurred to her as their IDs were scanned that the vampires must have incorporated their blood magic into the technology that made the ship. Pushing down a mental image of bleeding walls, she forced herself into a polite smile for the receptionist, who seemed a lot more eager to help with Mrs Crossley and Cecelia around.

As soon as they scanned her ID, her reflection in the wall-size mirror vanished and the desk behind her appeared in its place.

Mrs Crossley left first, walking through the metal as if it were a walk in the park. Will went next and Trisha swooped in, bounced up using lower gravity, and kissed him on the cheek. "Because I heard tomorrow's your birthday," she said. Will blushed, then quickly launched himself at the mirror, lifting his chair with one arm.

Lucy resisted the urge to squirm. Maybe nerves about the trip back through the portal had settled in?

"You next," Dave encouraged Lucy softly. "Just like before."

She clutched her satchel, squared her shoulders, and stepped into the mirror.

A small homely breeze brushed her cheeks from the not-underground-car park as Lucy stepped out of the HAT machine onto home ground once more, and was forgotten just as quick when she saw Will sprawled on the concrete down by his wheelchair.

Mrs Crossley was bent low over him. "Vasoconstrictors and salt. Quickly," she snapped, and Cecelia vanished.

"Lucy, water." Snapping her head up, Lucy frantically searched the cavern before zeroing in on a water cooler five pillars away and took off at a run. Filling two cups, she power-walked her way back as fast as she dared without spilling.

Kneeling by his side, she saw dazed blue eyes looking up to meet hers. "Hello, Red."

Lucy felt cold. She wasn't a redhead. Trisha on the other hand... He was clearly confused and not all there. She presented the drink out to Will's hand.

Mrs Crossley clutched Will's hand around it and coaxed, "There you go. Can you lift your head enough to sip? Just one. It'll help. That's it."

Will shuffled up, lifting a shaky hand for a sip before crumpling back onto his side. "The gravity won't let me."

From his seat where they left him, Alex explained, "Orthostatic intolerance. Illness of the astronauts, also known as postural orthostatic intolerance. POTS for short. The werewolf transformation itself is exhausting. Add a lack of blood supply to the head and let's just say I really wouldn't want to be him right now."

Lucy started as Cecelia popped back into existence at her side, holding a box of tablets and a pack of processed meats.

Will locked eyes on the vampire's hands like the goods were treasure and tried to prop himself up again, reaching for the medication.

"I brought beta blockers, too," Cecelia said, sounding bored. She and Alex could have been a double act. Lucy's eyes narrowed. Couldn't they see Will was suffering?

Pill in mouth, the teen reached out and Lucy steadied the cup and water into his hands again. He was cold. Too cold. He gulped down the cup, then reached for a second pill. Will exchanged the empty cup for another full one and swallowed, then lay back and grinned. "A much better sight than I'm used to. Ceilings start to get boring. The sky isn't bad. I like the sky."

Even if he was delusional, she felt a wave of contentment that he was happy while ghosting the edge of consciousness. Cecelia sliced open a pack of ham with a nail and Lucy stood up with the empty cups, searching for a bin.

Dave stepped out of the portal last, waving. He took one look at the sight and said, "You're a tough one, aren't you? Alex, third draw on the right."

The security guard pulled out a blood pressure monitor and Dave expertly hooked the werewolf up, as if it was an everyday occurrence. The arm cuff inflated with a hum and Lucy held her breath, waiting for the outcome but not knowing what she was waiting for.

"Low, but not too bad. We can give it some time before we head back up."

She exhaled in relief, then felt the weight of the past day and night crash into her, and she wished she could lie on the floor at Will's side.

The CEO nodded and strode over to the computer terminal. "Shut it down," she ordered, and Alex began pressing buttons. Heady earth slowly took over the distinctive copper in the air. Looking up, Lucy spotted her reflection in the mirror again.

"I think it's time to call an end to a very long day," the elderly woman declared. "Thank you all for your assistance. I'll relay the outcome to you tomorrow. We can do nothing until then. For now, get well-earned rest."

Rest. Rest sounded heavenly, and Lucy was certain that Mrs Crossley was a genius for thinking of it.

Cecelia placed a hand on Will's cheek as he polished off a third slice of ham. "Want some help to get to the surface?" she asked.

Will managed to focus on the blonde and nodded, his attention sharper as he was coming around.

"There's no rush. I'll call a car round when Will feels ready to sit up again," Dave said, throwing a walkie-talkie into the air and catching it midfall.

"Alright, you lot," Alex drawled from his terminal. "Strip. If I don't have those suits hung up and charged by 7:00 p.m., I'll get an earful from Kamal."

Twenty minutes later, Cecelia took up position at the wheelchair's handles, and with inhuman strength and ease, gracefully manoeuvred Will to the entrance. Lucy and the group followed, fighting for every step.

The brass refrain of *Sgt. Sir!* played on repeat as she trudged forward—a silent call of strength and a victory of surviving her foray into space.

Alex joined them in the security car, and Will nodded off during the short ride back to their apartment complex.

"I'll take care of this one," Alex said softly, lifting Will from his chair and spreading him out on the sofa. "Go get some rest."

With one last look at the sleeping angelic teen, she nodded and disappeared.

The sun as it sank beneath the horizon cast her room aglow in a warmth that the light of the moon at the Bureau lacked. How far away from that sun had she been today? She reached for the blinds and drew them closed.

She collapsed onto her bed, tired tears freely flowing in the privacy of her bedroom. Her bedroom. At one point, having a bedroom had never been in question. It was the place she'd planned on launching and managing her career. Ultimately, that dream had been crushed by an even bigger goal: keeping her parents happy. Her goal of being there to watch Ben grow up? It wasn't the same, but she could be there for him from a distance.

Her days of living obliviously were well and truly over. As Sgt. Sir! said in every tight spot: prioritise the essentials.

Time to prioritise. A roof over her head. So she'd need money to keep a roof over her head. For that, she had to find Oda.

Oda. The tree spirit inhabiting a notebook, and everything that came with it: vampires, werewolves, secrets, spaceships, and broken-out criminals.

It may not be the other side of space, but her old bedroom felt farther away; maybe because her situation was so far-fetched?

Since moving into her new accommodation, everything had changed. Or had anything changed at all, really? Was Cross-Key simply a dead-end dream about to be snuffed out, too?

She wanted to go home but didn't know where home was anymore. Images of her old house, kitchen, living room, and bedroom all swam in her vision. The latter no longer existed. A memory of Ben in his high chair. Oda presenting her a pile of apples. She sobbed again before taking in a heavy breath to calm herself. Alex was on the other side of her bedroom door in the common room, and she daren't risk being overheard. Closing her eyes, she curled up and sent a silent plea to the heavens.

*Please let us find Oda. Send help!*

# Chapter Eleven
# Queen of Paper Hearts

Good morning Lucy!
 There have been no further updates regarding extra support for Project Oda. We will notify you immediately if this changes.
 Dave

What did people say—that no news was good news?

The lights in Lucy's bedroom weren't as kind as the auto-dim feature on her work communicator, and an ache stabbed behind her eyes as she sat up. Where were a pair of Cecelia's sunglasses when she needed them?

Picking off yesterday's clothes, stuck moulded to her skin from the night before, she hobbled into the shower, changed, then entered an empty common room.

Pouring a bowl of cereal, she glanced at Will's closed bedroom door and mentally projected healing vibes.

Safe knowing he'd be crashed out most of the morning, Lucy planted herself on the sofa. Spoon in one hand and drawing tablet in the other, she flicked through the images she'd outlined on-board the Bureau.

She stopped on a picture of Will, his brother Duke, and three other wolves laughing in the canteen. Yes, that would do nicely.

Retreating to her room, she spent the morning firming up the outlines. A few hours later, she glowed with satisfaction at the five solid laughing figures.

Bringing up a fresh palette, she selected a range of greys, off whites, and blacks. Then, for the fur, she selected a range of wooden tones with pops of auburn.

Hovering over the eyes, she stopped, stumped. What colour were Will's eyes? As a human, they were sky-blue. But as a wolf she was certain they'd started out a bright lemon yellow, but when they stood looking out over the moon, she could have sworn they were a darker honey tone, closer to Duke's amber.

She didn't have time for this. Tuesday, and Will's birthday party had sneaked up on them all, so she only had hours left to finish. Trying not to imagine the evening's party, people, and subsequent conversations, she chose a shade between lemon and honey and set back to work.

An hour later, a rumble prompted Lucy to move to the on-site canteen, grabbed lunch, and headed down into what was once Oda's dome for printer access and privacy.

After scanning in, she opened the door to an eerie, empty silence. A sense of wrongness shrouded the room without Dave, Cecelia, and Oda to keep her company. Oda. Another thing she refused to think about until they'd received word. Instead, she took her usual seat at the desk and got to work on the drawing once more.

Hours passed until finally she hit print, then picked it up and examined it under the light. Not bad for a day's work. Pulling out a gold marker, she signed her name in the bottom corner, then left to face the music.

It was already dark outside when she left, so she jogged across the estate to beat any arriving guests, then shot straight into the safety of her room. Not twenty minutes later, the sound of laughter filtered through her door as people arrived. She didn't have to be there for the entire thing—just enough to show her face, hand over her gift, then escape before any awkward conversation attempts.

Lucy drowned them out by throwing on some headphones and settled in to watch the *Sgt. Sir!* moon special. The graphics on the special were ultra-realistic. The motion of the animated clothes in microgravity—

Cheesy pop music began thrumming over the top of the explosions and barked orders through her headphones. The whiff of pizza and chips with a barbecue tang slithered through the gaps in her doorframe and she knew she was done for. Once again, she'd forgotten to bring food back to her bedroom.

The final nail in the coffin of her isolation attempt came with a brisk knock on her door.

"Lucy? Come and join the party."

Hina.

If she stayed silent, maybe they'd think she wasn't there and give up? She'd left her light off to make her absence more convincing.

"I know you're there. Dad told me you were."

Lucy cursed the man's name under her breath. Well, she was hungry, and she wouldn't have to speak all that much. And she could count on freezing up before she said anything too stupid.

Groaning, she shut down her show and picked up her satchel. The door was barely open before she'd been grabbed into a crushing bear hug by two henna-covered arms, the scent of lilies wafting up her nostrils, making them itch. Giving in to the inevitable, she let Hina manhandle her into the common room, her door banging closed behind her.

Will looked up at the sound and grinned from the sofa, waving her over. Lucy's cheeks heated, but she let herself be pulled over to a chair opposite the teen.

The recovering teen had bags under his eyes but seemed to be in a good mood, with his feet propped up and a cup of something red and bubbly in his lap.

Lucy scanned the room. To Will's left sat Dave, who didn't show any signs of tiredness at all. In the kitchen area, a group of men who Lucy remembered passing at the warehouses stood surrounding a counter littered with takeaway boxes.

In a corner, as far away from the sound system as possible, stood Cecelia, glass of red in hand, her stony face keeping a few curious scientists from approaching. Oblivious to this, Alex stood at her side, one hand in a pocket and the other pointing to an enormous banner with *Happy Birthday* scrawled in green.

The wolf took a sip from his cup and smiled from ear to ear. "Thank you for coming."

Lucy gave Hina a look, and the fashion-conscious teen smiled innocently back.

Dave cleared his throat, breaking the tension.

"How could we not gather to celebrate the birth of our well-travelled Will? The boss, good old Mother Dear, said it would be a pleasant distraction while we wait for a response. What did she say? 'A morale boost for the workforce.' And don't we all need a morale boost?" He elbowed Will.

Hina giggled. "Yeah. Maybe Trisha will volunteer to come and tell us the outcome?" she teased.

Will spluttered and choked down a sip, wide-eyed and red-cheeked.

An ember sparked in the pit of Lucy's stomach, and she moved.

After a quick glance to make sure they were in the clear, she declared, "Happy Birthday," and held out her gift over the table.

He tilted his head like a dog, making the tips of Lucy's ears burn, before taking the sheet of paper. He unfolded it, and his eyes turned glassy. Dave leaned over to look, and Hina stood to stare, as well. She whistled then whispered, "Now that's what I call art. Is that...you know? From yesterday?"

"This is incredible. I saw you on your device yesterday. Did you do it then?" Will answered in question.

The tips of her ears burned. Not wanting to attract any more attention, she raised a hand level and wobbled it in a 'shaky but close enough' kind of gesture.

"Thanks. It means a lot to have a bit of home here," Will continued, staring slack-jawed at the portrait.

Lucy nodded and smiled but shifted her weight under the attention.

"You always were incredible at art," Hina commented, "but this is unreal; unreal because it looks so real. Didn't I tell you she'd be good?"

"You definitely found us a good one," Dave agreed, smiling at Hina, then Lucy. "Hina here recommended you for the job when we were desperately searching for our artist-interpreter hybrid."

Her heart skipped a beat. Hina had been her reference? But they'd stopped speaking when they were six.

"You said you wanted someone local," Hina explained, waving a hand dismissively. "Lucy always had a talent for drawing, and I knew she still lived in the area. I kept watching her produce these amazing portraits at community fairs. Whenever someone gets a quality hand-drawn card in Lombar, you know who it's from and it takes pride of place on the mantelpiece."

Lucy didn't know what to do with herself under the girl's gushing and wished she could turn invisible.

"When your shop popped up online I couldn't believe how much you'd grown. I had to point it out to Dave."

It almost sounded like Hina had been keeping tabs on her over the years, even though they weren't speaking. But...

A brief flutter of hope rose in her chest, and Lucy grabbed it with both hands, stamping down the doubt. Hina had watched. She'd cared. And now it turned out Lucy owed her once best friend a lot.

It was too much. Far too much.

Standing abruptly, Lucy rushed out, "I'm off to get pizza," then fled to the kitchen area and attempted to distract herself with pizza toppings.

A box slid along the bench under her nose. "You want this one," Hina said by her side, lifting the lid of a box. "You always liked ham, and you used to pick the peppers out of our school dinners."

The girl's observation skills were impeccable. No wonder her father was a security manager. Heartened, she reached for a slice, her eyes downcast. She didn't know what to do.

"You know, everything worked out for the best," Hina said solemnly, and Lucy's ears pricked up. Had the radio got louder?

"I know you wanted to help me, back then. It's not your fault your mum wanted you to be the Queen of Hearts."

Tears prickled the corner of her eyes as the memory sent her back in time.

Lucy's promised Christmas present never arrived. But it wasn't just her present, it was for her mum and dad, too.

After the baby went away, her mum cried, her dad shouted, and Lucy made it her goal to make them smile, no matter what.

During winter, she made them paper snowflakes. In spring she offered to help water the plants and drew pictures of daffodils that got stuck on the fridge.

Now, her class was about to find out what their end-of-year play would be.

"Everyone will get a piece of paper with the name of two characters I think you'd like to be. Put a tick in the box next to the one you want to play the most. I'll gather them back on Friday to help me choose who takes which part," Miss McGill explained, walking around with tiny slips of paper.

Next to her, Hina started crying and covered her face.

"What's wrong?" asked Lucy, putting a hand on one of Hina's sleeves.

"There'll be lots of people coming. What if I forget my lines? I can't do it!" Tears racked her slight frame as she choked back sobs.

Lucy put her hand up, and Miss McGill came over and crouched down next to her distraught best friend.

"Don't worry. I've got you two minor roles that don't have many lines, so you won't have to speak much. OK? It'll be lots of fun. I promise."

Lucy prodded the girl. "See? It'll be fun. Miss McGill promised."

Hina wiped a tear on her jumper as she moved to take the offered paper from the teacher.

"Lucy, Lucy…" Miss McGill leafed through the pile, then pulled out a slip with her name on top next to the title *Alice in Wonderland*.

That was her mum's favourite story! Surely that would make her smile.

Hina leaned across to look at her slip. "Who did you get? Can we stay together?"

Her eyes cast down the options:

*Hatter*

*Queen of Hearts*

She gulped. They were big roles, but she started bouncing when she saw Hina's.

"You got the Dormouse! I got the Hatter. They have a tea party together. We can be together!"

"Really?" the shy girl's voice wavered. "That's good. Please stay with me."

Lucy put a hand on the tear-soaked sleeve. "Sure, but I'll need to find a big hat to be the Hatter."

At the end of the day, Lucy ran to her mum, who stood next to Hina's.

"Look! We got this for our class play," she said, shoving the slip of paper into her mum's palm.

Beside her, Hina did the same.

The woman glanced at it, then pulled her daughter into the first hug she'd received since Christmas.

"Miss McGill has good taste," she said with a smile, and a burst of glee made Lucy bounce on her heels.

"Alice is one of my favourites. She has good taste in people, too. These are two big parts. Of course, you'll want to play the Queen of Hearts."

Lucy froze, just like Hina feared doing on stage.

Hina and her mother stared, the little girl waiting for the promised confirmation of Lucy's support.

Her chest tightened, and she struggled to breathe. Nothing she could say would please them both. Hina's wide brown eyes looked hopeful, but this was the first time her mum had hugged her in months.

And hadn't Miss McGill said the play would be fun? Adults didn't lie.

Unable to talk but still able to move, she nodded her head. Yes.

She couldn't look Hina in the eye as her mum took her hand and walked them back to the car.

Lucy received her chosen part, and for the next month, practised her lines over and over—and over.

"Off with their heads!"

Every time, her mum would stop what she was doing and break out into a grin or say, "My little queen. I'm so proud."

Lucy didn't—couldn't—speak to Hina at all. Every time she tried, her mind would go blank or suddenly she'd choke.

The night before the play, Lucy's mum cheerily tucked her into bed, reading her *Alice in Wonderland*.

"You'll do great," she said.

"You're coming?" Lucy asked for the third time.

"I wouldn't miss it for the world," she said, dropping a good-night kiss on her forehead.

Lucy rehearsed her lines for the entire day before the play began. They got changed, their class was called, and next thing she knew, Alice was standing up onstage.

Lucy scanned the audience. Hina's mum was there, waving at her as she spotted her, and Lucy gave a tentative wave back. But where was her mum? Maybe she was sitting in the back row.

Then, Hina the Dormouse walked onto the stage without Lucy and cowered, covering her face with her eyes. Miss McGill sat trying to mouth the lines encouragingly at the girl. It wasn't fun at all.

The Dormouse whimpered, and the teacher signalled Alice to continue the scene, skipping her lines entirely.

Lucy was close to tears. She'd wanted to be up there to comfort the girl, but The Queen of Hearts didn't appear until later.

At last, it was her turn, and The Queen of Hearts strode straight-backed across the stage.

The Hatter, March Hare, and the Dormouse—no—Hina, stood in front of her, acting scared. But Hina wasn't acting. The March Hare had dragged her to stand next to Alice.

Looking her friend in the eyes, Lucy spoke to the girl for the last time for twelve years.

*"Off with their heads!"*

Hina burst into tears, and Lucy turned away, looking again for her mum through the thundering applause. A void opened in her chest. Her mum wasn't there.

Lucy didn't manage her last line.

***

"I prefer *Through The Looking Glass* anyway." Hina's voice snapped Lucy back to the present.

"After that disaster, I was enrolled early into the family martial arts programme to help me build up my confidence. They also hired an acting tutor for me who worked with me one on one. Well, it clearly worked, what with me being a receptionist social butterfly and all."

Not knowing what to say, Lucy let the girl ramble. "So, in a roundabout way, it was thanks to you I could learn to speak in front of crowds. So thanks for that," she finished, pulling out a large slice of vegan cheese and tomato pizza.

The awkward silence stretched on, until Hina said, "I didn't learn about the miscarriages until I was older. I'm sorry for your losses."

Dropping the slice of pizza she'd been holding, Lucy reached out and pulled the girl into a long overdue hug. "We have Ben now," she choked out. "Less than a year old. He's got my room."

The pressure building for over a decade spilled, as Lucy confided once again in her childhood best friend.

"Thanks for getting me this job. I was facing time on a fishing trawler otherwise," she joked.

Hina untangled herself from Lucy's hold and took a large bite of pizza, looking her up and down appraisingly. "Sorry, Hun, but you don't have an ounce of physical strength in you. Even I could grapple you into submission, and that's saying something. I honestly couldn't say about sea legs, but yellow rubber overalls would clash horribly with your skin tone."

It was as if a small piece of jigsaw had slotted back into place, and Lucy grinned.

"So..." Hina trailed, then coughed into the crook of her arm. "Did you meet Duke while you were at the Bureau?"

Tilting her head at the sudden change in conversation, Hina continued, "He worked at Cross-Key before Will did. He's Will's brother."

She nodded her understanding. "I met him when he dropped by to speak to Will. I drew him in Will's birthday picture," she said.

"Really?" Hina asked, eyes bright and alert. "I saw his human form at work and he was hot. He didn't need a wheelchair like Will, but he had this really stylish black cane," she gushed.

A small spike of resentment stabbed in her brain. What did the girl mean, 'didn't need a wheelchair, like Will?'

"And?" she sniped, emotions boiling over. "Go on. What's wrong with needing a wheelchair?"

The teen spluttered. "Uh—there's nothing wrong with using a wheel-chair, of course. I bet we'll probably end up using one when we're older. What I meant..."

Lucy arched an eyebrow.

"Sorry. What I meant to say was I never saw Duke in his mid-trans-formed state, but I bet he's all muscle. I'll get Will to point him out to me later."

As time went on, it became clear Duke was one of Hina's favourite topics, and she didn't seem to be about to stop anytime soon. Resisting the urge to roll her eyes, it hit her that she'd verbally challenged the girl. She'd spoke out, and once again made Hina uncomfortable. Yet a small part of her was happy she'd done it, and she'd do it again. Her hands twitched and she reached for another slice to occupy them, but the smell made her nauseous. Pungent, like the power of her words, and oh, how easy they'd came to her. She looked down at the toppings, intent on losing herself in them.

"I met him during my work experience week when I was fifteen, and I think he put in a good word for me with Dave because I got offered an apprenticeship here when I was sixteen. Customer Services. He was so smart and—"

The back of Lucy's neck prickled with cold sweat. Small talk. She couldn't stand it. Or gossip. It never got you anywhere but trouble, in the end. Words making things awkward again.

The longer Hina went on, the harder it became for Lucy to swallow. A freeze was coming, pizza crust sticking to the roof of her mouth as it got drier.

"...of course, I work with him now," she continued, oblivious to Lucy having tuned out halfway through, or the tension growing behind her slowly furrowing eyebrows.

"I think he likes me. I was in my full-time role when he went back to the Fleet, but he changed jobs. He emails me now at work, sending me special instructions for deliveries. Although he hasn't said it outright, I think he got his current job just so he could stay in contact with me."

Lucy's thoughts began to cloud, and she struggled to catch her breath, drowning in a wave of voices.

"I'm sorry," Lucy cut in. "But I don't feel well. Headache. I'm going to go back to my room—to the quiet," she rushed to explain before her mouth completely disconnected from her thoughts.

It was blunt but effective, and she hoped the smile she gave would lessen the rudeness of the abrupt interruption.

Yes, she wanted a friendship with the girl, but it was too early to risk with accidental wrong words. Too much talking. Too many words.

"Oh, I'm sorry to hear that. Maybe some water would help? The pizza is quite salty. You could be dehydrated. But I suppose the music is rather loud. Do you need help back to your room? I can ask them to turn the music down if you'd like."

The flitting about of the girl warmed Lucy's heart, like when Oda projected their concern into her head.

Lucy shook her head then all but ran to the safety of her bedroom, slamming the door behind her. She collapsed onto her bed and took in a long, shuddering breath.

She'd told another lie. To Hina. What had she ever done to deserve a second chance from such a kind girl?

Electric guitar struck through her foggy brain, and she covered her ears and froze, letting her phone ring until, at last, the caller gave up. Then an explosion of fireworks broke the silence.

Mum flashed across the screen and Lucy dropped her head into her hands. Of all people, why her, and why now?

Heaving herself up, she plugged one ear and pressed play.

# CHAPTER TWELVE
# ONE STEP-AHEAD

"Hi, Lucy. I'm speaking at a conference tomorrow at the Step-Ahead Hotel. You know the one, at Garrowhead East. I've added your name to the list; don't thank me. It's from 8:30 a.m.–5:00 p.m. Make sure you get the time off. Your dad said you haven't been back to visit yet. Hard work is good, but he'll need your support with Ben while he's job hunting. See you at Step-Ahead."

Her mother's clipped tones cut off with an abrupt click.

With everything going on, the conference had been the last thing on Lucy's mind.

Flopping on her back, she sank into the duvet and covered her eyes with an arm.

Could she do anything that would make her parents happy? If she said yes to visiting home, they'd think she was homesick and slacking off from work. If she said no, well... Her mother was one to talk. She may as well live at the university. At one point the coping strategy may have worked, but when Ben arrived the woman was crawling up the walls, and cut her maternity leave short. Too many nights Lucy had stepped in to make dinner, with her mother coming home after 8:30 p.m.

With a groan she turned herself over, thoughts turning to the conference. Technically, she was lucky that she wasn't actually working, but the

125

thought of having to mingle with so many people made her heart attempt the foxtrot. Her mother would parade her around during the breaks, bragging that she worked for Cross-Key & Co.

At one point she would have leapt at the recognition, but if they didn't find Oda soon it wouldn't last for long; one more secret she couldn't share. One more potential slip-up with the wrong word.

She didn't need the added pressure of her father's job hunt while her own hung in the balance. Oh, she heard the unwritten code in the message. Come and babysit. She'd give anything to be there for Ben, but they were expecting news at any moment about Oda.

She couldn't afford to waste time helping her father chase a position that didn't exist. But she couldn't reject her parents entirely. Her priority hadn't changed. If she wanted to shield Ben from their expectations, she had to draw their attention and be exceptional.

Slowing her breathing, she calmed her panic with the *Sgt. Sir!* method. Reflecting on what she had to work with, she landed on time. The first half of her day she'd spend working on lesson plans for Oda. The second half, she'd face the conference.

Deliberating over every word, she composed a text.

> Hi Mum,
> All settled in. Very busy here. Only managed to get tomorrow afternoon off. See you then.
> Lucy X

Words meant lies. She hated it, but clicked send.

Wednesday began with a scrap of paper pushed under Lucy's bedroom door. Scrawled was:

> Lucy,
> Thanks again for the beautiful reminder of home.
> It can get lonely here sometimes.
> Don't be a stranger. I don't want you to be.
> Saved you some cake!
> Hope you feel better soon,
> Will
> P.S.: Alex reheated the last of your amazing chicken soup for me when we got back from the Fleet. What a feast!

Beaming, she propped the note up on her bedside table. Hina must have told him why she'd left, and he didn't sound too upset about her leaving before their raucous round of "Happy Birthday."

Looking back, last night was probably a piece of cake compared to today: a conference and potential Oda news. Thinking of cake, hunger panged.

With her mind set, she went out into the common room and hunted for the leftover treat. She was an adult, living independently, so why not? Having been pushed from her family home, she was allowed a little happiness, wasn't she?

After five minutes of rummaging in the kitchen area, she found a hunk of chocolate cake left in a tin. She scooped her sickly sweet prize with a fork straight out of the container.

*Yes,* she thought, eating Will's birthday cake. He didn't want her to be a stranger. Her parents would have to take a back seat this time.

After her choice breakfast, Lucy packed a bag with everything she'd need to create lesson plans for Oda's return. A beep made her freeze, one hand closing the satchel lid, and paused, then pulled out her communications device.

The message was brief:

```
Lucy,
A meeting has been called regarding updates
and will be held at 9:30 a.m. at the CEO's
office.
    Thanks,
    Dave
```

Her breath hitched. News?

She glanced at her watch: 8:42 a.m. Eagerly, she stuffed the tablet back in her bag and headed straight to Headquarters.

Entering the building, Hina raised a shaky hand in greeting. The girl wore thick eyeliner, attempting but failing to cover up the signs of a late night. Pulling a bobby pin from her lips, she attempted to soften the just-woke-up look by pulling her dark messy curls up into a bun. "Morn-nnnun," she said, stifling a yawn.

Happier than ever that she left the party when she did, Lucy smiled brightly back and gave a wave. After all, she'd need a clear head to deal with whatever the update meant.

Exiting the lift on the top floor, she was invited into the CEO's waiting room by her receptionist for the day. Will came rolling in fifteen minutes later, with Dave behind at the handles.

At 9:25 a.m. came the unusual sight of both security managers walking side by side—Kamal upright and stern-faced, Alex laid-back with his hands in his pockets. Mr Usmani didn't look as tired as his daughter following his night shift, but then again she supposed those black sunglasses could hide anything. They placed themselves next to both entrances to the room.

The receptionist opened the CEO's door five minutes later and let the group in.

Crossing the threshold, Lucy tensed, back straight. Last time she'd been in this room she'd been told vampires and werewolves existed, hiding in space. Would today reveal more life- altering information?

Cecelia stood unnaturally still in the same corner she had last time behind the CEO, who stood up and shook everyone's hands in greeting as they entered and took up the extra seats that had been brought into the room. The effect was cosy.

A quick war of words played out between the two guards before Alex all but shoved Kamal down into a seat, saying the man had technically finished his shift. The bald man sighed and acquiesced. Maybe he was more tired than he'd let on.

The door shut behind them and the temperature of the room spiked, so Lucy helped herself to a glass of water, happy to have something to do with her hands in case the news was bad, but it still didn't ease her growing queasiness.

"The Bureau has made their decision," Margaret intoned from her seat behind her desk. "Cross-Key & Co. has received a monetary fine for disallowing a meeting between another paranormal species and the Council to take place. They claim negligence on our part and have invoked a term from the Charter."

No one spoke or moved, their faces stern.

"In their opinion, they let us off lightly. That is something I vehemently disagree with, but we need to move on." Turning to Cecelia, the CEO continued, "I'll be arranging the transfer of monies when this meeting is complete."

The vampire inclined her head. "As ambassador of vampire-kind I hear your oath."

Margaret then turned to Will, who responded, "As ambassador of the packs I hear your oath." The formal tone sounded foreign, coming from the easy-going wolf. His voice wavered as he said his piece, but the old woman smiled understandingly at him, and he perked up, flashing her a winning smile in return.

Lucy was glad that she wasn't the only one who found speaking a source of discomfort, even though his only related to formal settings.

"As per our request of help in apprehending the thief, the Bureau has deemed it too much of a risk to send additional vampires and werewolves to Earth, for risk of exposure. We will have to use our own means to track down and apprehend the culprit, after which the Bureau have requested his immediate return to the Fleet to stand trial. If we fail, we'll face further sanctions."

Lucy's heart sank, and to her left, Will's jaw dropped.

Dave balled a hand into a fist and replied, "I didn't want to think that it would come to this, but I knew it."

Cecelia's singsong voice came from the back of the room. "I told you so," then began examining the nails on her left hand. "The Councillors only worry about their own seats in power. They'd never take the fall for something like this. It would harm their careers too much."

Kamal coughed, gaining the attention of the room. "For all intents and purposes, we are facing a kidnapping, so time is of the essence. Let's get to work immediately. Miss Cecelia, would you accompany myself and Alex up to Security and examine the CCTV footage?"

Cecelia looked up at the man. "Certainly," she said curtly. "To the Als it is."

"The Als?" Alex repeated, eyebrow arched.

"Why, of course," she replied. "You're Alex, Al for short. He's Kamal, Al for short. You both work in the same place..." she trailed off, her hand winding away the explanation.

Lucy couldn't wrap her mind around the woman. How could she be so calm? Or was humour just her way of coping? Then, with a glint in her eyes and the flash of a fang, Lucy knew the blonde was a predator ready for a hunt. "So, to the Als?" she repeated.

Margaret nodded her approval. "I want to be informed every step of the way. Go."

Cecelia and *the Als* left.

It was happening. They were moving. A tremor ran down Lucy's spine. She had to help get her friend back.

Resolved, she drained the last of her cup, took a deep breath, then said. "I would like to help." Margaret locked gazes with her, and she continued. "This job, my home, and Oda—I don't want to lose them. Please." Her cheeks grew warm under the stares of Dave and Will.

A single clap from Dave broke the tension. "Well said. I saw in the logs you've been clocking into work still. What have you been working on?"

Relieved that it wasn't an immediate dismissal, she answered honestly. "Lesson plans, for when Oda comes back."

Across the desk, Mrs Crossley nodded her approval.

"Other than those in this meeting and Hina at reception, you're the only other person at Cross-Key who knows about this. Anyone who can boost that count without divulging our secret partners is more than welcome to help."

The elderly woman placed her elbows onto the desk and laced her fingers together. "I'm officially changing the status of Project Oda from hiatus to a rescue and retrieval mission. I can't guarantee your safety, however Cross-Key will try to the best of our ability."

Lucy smiled and nodded.

Then it was Will's turn to receive the CEO's attention. "Tomorrow's the big night. How do you feel? I trust Dave has everything in order for you?"

The teen's eyes lit up. "I'm looking forward to it. Duke told me stories, about the wind at his back and the freedom to run. And I'm thankful that Dave's coming with me."

It took a moment for Lucy to realise that they were talking about Will's full moon transformation. She'd seen Will in his mid-transformed state on her trip to the Fleet—'perfect' they'd called it, but she wanted nothing more than to see him as a 'complete wolf.' Would he stand on two legs, like in horror films, or look like a typical wolf on all fours? Would he be bigger than normal? After all, he towered over her at the Bureau.

Dave reported as if it was any other typical workday. "I'll be using the same protocol I did with Duke. We'll fly up the coast to Cross-Key's private beach by helicopter. The area's been given advanced warning to evacuate, and we have plenty of food to keep him occupied and from straying."

The CEO smiled at them both. "Excellent. Now, until 'the Als'" she chuckled, "give us an update, I need you to continue tracking the missing stock. I appreciate it's a headache, but something has gone wrong and we need to pinpoint where."

"Yes, ma'am," Dave said, cheekily.

Refusing to rise to her son's bait, she continued to Will and Lucy, "And I'd like you two to head up to Security. They'll be heading the rescue operation."

⁂

"There you go," said Kamal, gesturing to Cecelia with a control in his right hand. "What do you make of him?"

The security managers and Cecelia huddled around a screen as Lucy and Will entered. The rest of the room was empty, as the Guards were probably out on patrol again.

Cecelia squinted. "It's very blurry and only in black and white. Is this the only footage you've got?"

Kamal huffed, but Alex stepped in. "Please forgive my colleague. I believe he thinks we're living in an age of detective noir stories. Just a sec." He moved off to a computer by the side of the screen and typed.

The screen image changed, sharpening as the seconds passed, like an image reloading repeatedly, with more pixels and added layers of colour each time.

"That's better," Cecelia said, while Kamal stared, open-mouthed.

"How did you do that?" he snapped.

Alex waved a finger back and forth like speaking to a child. "It's a little something Duke and I worked on before he left; a form of AI for the cameras. They've been learning over time about their immediate environment, and to recognise foreign objects. He said something about quantum mechanics and stem cells."

"That's my brother," Will commented flatly, and Lucy could almost see waves of jealousy rolling off him. "Computer science was always his strong

133

point. Then again, what wasn't? He could do anything. Won awards for his programming, though."

Cecelia whistled. "I'll have to ask him about it next time I visit the Bureau. Anyway," she paused, and the group looked at her expectantly. Clearly enjoying the fact that the group hung on her every word, she smiled, completely contrary to her next sentence. "Bad news." She motioned to the screen. "That's Fane. He's an ancient who lived for hundreds of years on Earth before going through the portal, so he'll know how to interact with humans and blend in. Although, he should be on *Ship 12*."

Will covered his mouth, and Kamal and Alex sucked in deep breaths. Lucy tilted her head in question.

"For the benefit of the non-family member here, *Ship 12* is the Fleet's prison ship," Cecelia explained. "Still got a century of his sentence left to serve."

Lucy's gaze darted to the screen.

The kidnapper wore a black version of the standard Fleet jumpsuit with a thick collar. Long chestnut hair fell unkempt around his ears, a lock falling between two glowing vermilion eyes, with contrasting pale pearl skin. His main identifying feature was an overgrown matted moustache that merged into what once may have been a goatee.

"We've got problems now," said Cecelia in a singsong voice. "That collar should have prevented his escape." The vampire took the control from Kamal and zoomed in to the top of the turtleneck.

"Aren't they meant to be trackers?" Will asked.

"The signal will be starting to fade, but it's worth a shot. The Council's bureaucracy had put us at a disadvantage time-wise," she commented.

Lucy mulled over that. Maybe they didn't want them to catch Fane? It certainly didn't seem too high on their list of priorities.

Seeming to disappear into thin air, Cecelia vanished. The only sign she'd gone somewhere was the open door. Three minutes later she reappeared at the door holding a device that looked like a complicated calculator with a large screen and two metal prongs at the tip.

She pressed a button and a map lit up on the display. Another press of the button made a small red dot appear, and it beeped intermittently. Spreading her hands in the air above the device, Cecelia zoomed into the map.

"He's just across the city. The sun must have been a shock to his system and slowed him down. The signal's weak. That's the diameter of the circle. The dark red indicates he's helped himself to a few meals while he's been here. Its brightness correlates to physical strength."

Lucy's brain conjured images of unsuspecting shoppers being grabbed into the shadows of back lanes. A shiver ran down the length of her spine.

"On the plus side, it doesn't look like he's moving. Probably trapped by the daylight," Kamal said.

"Yes, but I can't leave during the day, either. You won't be able to apprehend him without my help, so that means we'll have to wait until sunset," Cecelia pointed out.

Alex groaned and scratched the back of his neck. "And then he'll be able to move, too. At least we've got the address, so we can stake it out and hold him there until you arrive and physically bring him down."

Kamal puffed up his chest. "Now that's more like it. Let's do it. Where's the mark?"

"The Step-Ahead Hotel, other side of Lombar."

Through a mental fog, Lucy's thoughts began to move. They had an address and a plan. Brilliant. One more step towards Oda. Step. Step ahead. Step-Ahead...Hotel!

Lucy launched to her feet. "I have to go to that hotel."

The room looked towards her as one.

"My mum is holding a conference there this afternoon, and she put me on the guest list. I can get in."

Kamal scratched his chin. "You sure you know what you're getting into?" The concern in his voice made her think that perhaps he did care a little about her.

She nodded. It was a no-brainer. Her mother and Oda were there.

Cecelia whistled. "Then thankfully for you, little mouse, the signal isn't flashing. That means he's put himself into a resting stasis for now." Pocketing the device in her lab coat, the vampire pulled out an overly large pocket watch and screwdriver from another, then pried the back off the device. "I can send you in with a more accurate scanner. The closer you are, the more precisely we can monitor his state. Alert us immediately if anything changes, no matter how small."

Lucy nodded, balling now sweaty hands into fists around the strap of her satchel.

Pulling out a bag of purple fruit chews from a desk drawer, Alex offered one to Kamal, who refused, before unwrapping one for himself, as if he were watching a particularly interesting film. Still sucking on the chew, he commented, "He'll know his collar is a tracker, so perhaps the biggest question is why hasn't he removed it yet?"

The petite lady smirked, lips curling to reveal the tip of a fang. "See the tube into his neck? He's part of a circuit. If he attempts to break the circuit it detonates in a small controlled explosion, and bye-bye, vampire."

At Lucy's side, Will gulped.

A vampire was bad enough, but a vampire with a detonator?

She glanced at her watch. No time to lose. "The conference ends at 5:00 p.m., so after that I'll have to hide in the toilets or something."

"Actually, considering the stress of the situation, that's a long enough shift for one person," Kamal said, eyebrows furrowed.

His daytime counterpart chipped in, "We'll call in the extended family for this one. We've got generations ready to jump at a moment's notice if we ask them to. Unfortunately, the Fleet knows who they are, so Fane will, too, and if we send them in too early, the jig is up."

Cecelia, who had steadily been dismantling the device in her hands, looked up. "Miss Blakely—the secret weapon. Has a nice ring to it."

Lucy thanked and cursed the fact that she wasn't a Crossley family member. Although she was glad she could act, every Crossley member had self-defence training.

Lifting the screwdriver behind an ear, the vampire pulled out a small spanner. "No time like the present. Get ready to leave for your conference. I'll have this treasure ready to go in five. After that, I'm entering rest stasis 'till sunset."

Lucy nodded, and Kamal said, "Yes, Miss Cecelia," raising a hand into an actual salute.

Alex unwrapped another chew. "Will and I will update Dave and Mrs Crossley about the plan. Kamal, you alert the family," he said, handing over a mobile phone.

It was happening. This was it. She would—

Her stomach grumbled, ripping the wind from her sails. Why had she only eaten cake for breakfast?

"Can I take you back to your apartment for some lunch, first?" Alex suggested, much to her embarrassment.

"Ah, yes. I'd forgotten how often your kind liked to eat," Cecelia commented.

"Please, thank you," Lucy answered, her voice barely more than a whisper.

Will piped up next to her. "Oo, can I come?"

And so her last meal before going head-to-head with a vampire became, itself, a challenge of social horror.

# CHAPTER THIRTEEN

# FANE

The scanner in her pocket pressed against Lucy's leg through her beige linen trousers. Although silent, the thought of it suddenly vibrating made her palms sweat. Surely if it started vibrating, people would think it was someone's phone. Not entirely convinced, she turned her attention back to her mother.

Dr. Angela Blakely addressed the room of university researchers and rich archaeological enthusiasts. A throng of admiring students lined the back seats, and Lucy planted herself seamlessly between them. They were her age, and perhaps in a life without art, could have been her cohort.

Her mother flicked to the last slide. "So, our best chance of finding new life isn't to invest in the stars but instead explore our past."

The room burst into enthusiastic applause, and Lucy forced herself to join in, scared of accidentally pressing the scanner, as if it were a bomb. Nursing a cup of water, she watched and waited while her mother mingled with potential sponsors, completely oblivious to the danger they were in. It took the woman less than ten minutes to spot her and begin parading her in front of investors.

"Yes, my daughter."

"Don't you just value creativity? She's the head of an arts department."

"Yes, Cross-Key & Co. She's flown the nest."

Lucy knew the game well; one they'd played since she was little. Although her mother never congratulated her for anything to her face, she wouldn't pass up the opportunity to brag to others about her perfect family. Who wouldn't want to invest in a person who balanced work with a successful family?

She shook hands and nodded when required, but her movements were wooden and her smile strained. How could she relax, standing in the middle of a feast for a rogue vampire upstairs? Given the circumstances, she was amazed she could move at all.

Six introductions later, her mother pulled her by the arm behind the projector screen into a dark nook.

"Glad you could come. Now, your dad needs a babysitter for tomorrow. He's got a job interview and I'll be—"

*Sgt. Sir!*'s bombastic theme blasted from Lucy's chest pocket, making her jump. She froze.

"Well, answer that! It's impolite not to," her mother sniped, answering her question. Of course, they could never see the daughter of Dr. Angela Blakely being unprofessional, especially a working woman. Lucy resisted the urge to sigh. One week ago she'd been told that ignoring her mother would have been rude.

Dashing out of a side door, she swiped the screen. "Hello?"

Will answered, and he sounded stressed. "Lucy. Change of plan."

Lucy's breath caught.

"Dave's been arrested. Two vampires came and took him to the Bureau. Something about fraud and supply shortages."

In Lucy's chest, a butterfly took off, and she felt her pulse spike.

"The Council ordered all the Crossley family members back to Cross-Key to help with the fraud investigation. I'm sorry. Mrs Crossley's gone through the por—er, the HAT machine—to find out what's happening, and Cecelia can't leave before sunset. They've ordered me to stay put, too, in case I'm called for questioning."

Lucy saw red. They wouldn't send vampires to retrieve a vampire, but they'd send them to apprehend Dave. Then she paused, anger doused by a horrific realisation. The Crossleys weren't coming. She was alone. The butterflies in her chest attempted to jettison, and she covered her mouth to hold back vomit.

Will's voice trembled, soft and low. "You can always come back, too, if you want. We don't want you to be in danger. We'll come up with something else."

Closing her eyes, she took in a deep breath, and forced herself to calm down.

"Thanks," she answered, softly. "But I have to stay here. My mum's here, and Oda, and so many people who don't know, but I do. Fane doesn't know what I look like, so I won't be an immediate target. Just please, get Cecelia here as soon as you can."

"I like her," Cecelia's voice chimed in, and Lucy realised Will must have her on speakerphone. "Have I said that I like the little mouse?"

"You're brave, but I wouldn't expect anything less from you," Will said.

The impact of the praise was lost on Lucy, though, as a strong vibration buzzed against her thigh, followed by rhythmic pulsing.

Lucy's arms shook. "Um. How good are vampires at hearing things?" she asked, ripping the pocket of her seam in her attempt to wrench out the scanner.

"Great," said Will.

"Exceptional," replied Cecelia.

The round display showed the outline of the building, and where she stood, around the corner from the main entrance, was marked with a white cross.

A pulsing vermilion light beeped directly on top of the cross.

"He's awake," Lucy said, staring up at the window two floors above, open a crack, where a silhouette had appeared at the curtains.

"I think he heard us."

<hr/>

"Bang goes the element of surprise," Cecelia exclaimed. "Mouse, get everyone out of there. Now!" A wailing siren sounded down the phone.

"Hold on!" Will barked, and the phone went dead.

Lucy's mind raced. *Get everyone out. Leave. Fire!*

She sprinted through the lobby, praying that if a vampire's hearing really was as good as Cecelia claimed, then maybe her insane half-baked plan would work.

Sprinting through the main entrance, she left a sputtering receptionist and hurtled to the nearest flight of stairs. At the top of the stairwell before the first floor, she found it. Satisfied there wasn't any CCTV, she hefted the dense hand-size hammer out of its claw-like stand; she clenched her jaw and swung. The glass shattered, and she slammed her hand against the button. A loud bell rang through the building.

"Please evacuate the building. A fire has been detected. Please evacuate the building. A fire has been detected..."

From her vantage point, Lucy watched people snake out of the building's fire exits. A couple left their room, and Lucy hid behind the fire safe door by the staircase. When the grumbling couple had left at the opposite end of the hall, Lucy moved back to the window and scanned the crowd. A familiar brown bob led a group of university students across the road to safety. It wasn't an ideal parting by any means, and Lucy knew she'd have to make up for her abrupt departure later. Maybe say they had called her back into work? It wasn't entirely a lie.

Pulsing blue flashes brought her out of her thoughts. Two fire engines had arrived. She had to hurry, or else they'd turn off the siren!

Taking the stairs two at a time, she continued climbing. This was her chance. While he was down, she'd grab Oda and run! Setting her trembling hands to work, she gripped the bannisters tighter to propel herself forward.

The vermilion scanner pulsed, racing like her adrenalin-fuelled heart. Almost there—silence. The siren had stopped, leaving heavy, ringing silence.

*Scrape, clatter, bang!*

Lucy stilled, heart hammering and a hand over her mouth, hiding behind the corner at the top of the second-floor stairwell.

Silence.

Forcing her legs to move, she crept to the corner and peeked. Two figures stood in the corridor, one bent over the other. Scarlet eyes glanced up and bored into her. The escaped convict held a slumped, suited man by the waist.

A trickle of crimson leaked from two puncture wounds at the man's neck, and the vampire lapped at the trail, stopping it short before staining the white collar.

Oda was nowhere in sight. Her eyes darted down the row of doors. Which was his room? She needed to get past him. To stop him. She needed more noise.

Sucking in a deep breath, she readied a scream but choked, the muscles in her throat paralysed. She froze and raised a hand to her compromised vocal cords. Forcing a pushed scream produced only a puff of hot air.

The one time she didn't want to be mute!

Mentally cursing, icy dread sank into her chest, and she lost her words completely.

Images flashed. Her mother by the lake; watching her mother through a window; a window in a stairwell; a fire alarm attached to the wall.

With a stagger she backed up down the hall, not blinking as she stared the predator down.

Approaching the second-floor stairwell, she found her intact target and again shattered glass.

The lever came down, sirens blared, and a scream erupted from around the corner, followed by a thud.

Peeking her head around again, she saw him doubled over, hands over his ears, his victim unconscious at his feet. The vampire groaned, his eyes screwed shut in agony.

She tensed, sprang forward, then silence. Again. She screeched to a halt not a metre away.

Fane lowered his hands, shook his head, and opened his eyes. "Please don't do that," he said in a low, guttural voice. "It hurts. A lot."

Drawing himself up straight, he wiped a smudge of blood off his mouth onto his sleeve, narrowed his eyes as he looked at her, then crouched, arm pulled back, ready to rush her.

*Crash!* The window at the opposite end of the corridor smashed, and a figure covered head-to-toe in silver foil rolled across the ground, helmet and arms expertly tucked across her ribcage.

As graceful as a medalling gymnast, they arced into the air and landed steady, angled sideways and pointed what looked like a sort of gun. It whirred, then beeped.

"You're under arrest, Fane," came a familiar female voice, then what looked like blue lightning fired straight towards the convict. It hit, and Fane collapsed on top of the suited man.

Removing her helmet, Cecelia flashed Lucy a winning smile. "Sorry I'm late, or am I early?" she asked.

Lucy's jaw dropped, a hand still held tight against her throat and failing voice box.

The crowds dispersed within minutes of the police arriving and swiftly moving them on, cordoning off the hotel. The firefighters followed not long after, which Lucy put down to the Crossleys' powerful connections.

"We are still trying to determine the cause of the fire. A damaged window indicates an escape attempt." After that, all anyone would get out of the police was, "The investigations are still ongoing," so the media left.

Lucy sat in the back of the abandoned conference room under a silver shock blanket, staring around at the haphazardly strewn chairs and half-drunk hot beverages littering the tables. Not thirty minutes ago, the place had been full of potential victims.

Will and the Crossleys had descended en masse about ten minutes after Cecelia. Lucy watched him pick at the leftover finger sandwiches, before wheeling over to her side.

"Want some?" he offered, pointing down at a plate on his lap. Suddenly hot, Lucy shook off the silver blanket, and shook her head, turning away, as if examining the remains of the buffet.

From the corner of her eye, she saw him scratch the back of his neck. "I'm so sorry I lied to you. Dave wanted to lure him into a false sense of security. He planned it after you left, but then he really did get arrested. Fraud. That's the biggest pile of crap I've ever heard."

Lucy dropped the beef sandwich she'd picked up. So, they hadn't abandoned her after all? As she caught his gaze, he squirmed.

"We couldn't risk waiting until after sunset or Fane would have escaped. Luckily, Cross-Key's been working on a suit to protect vampires from the sun's rays for decades without the Fleet knowing. A present for the eight-hundred-fiftieth-year anniversary of the Charter's signing, Dave said. Anyway, we had to wait a bit for it to charge before Cecelia used the prototype."

His eyes clouded, watery, and Lucy's heart hammered against her ribcage.

"I was really worried about you. Even though we had a plan, I really wanted you to leave and be safe. Far away." His knuckles turned white from the force he gripped his paper plate. Lucy reached out, placing her hand on top of his, absorbing his repressed tremors.

"Thank you," she said earnestly, stroking the back of his hand, silently waiting with him for his trembling to stop.

The air grew thick. Will opened his mouth but closed it again, holding her gaze.

Snare drums and a bombastic trombone burst through the silence as a startlingly familiar tune broke the spell. Will plucked his phone out of his pocket, as well-ingrained lyrics rose to Lucy's lips. He answered, cutting off the original ending theme of *Sgt. Sir!*

Grinning like a loon, Lucy turned away; and that's how Hina found her when she walked in carrying two lidded paper cups.

The girl's eyebrows rose in silent question, glancing between Lucy's side-splitting grin and a stern-looking Will, none the wiser, in a call. "Want to chat? I got this for you," she whispered, holding out a cup in offering.

*After days filled with vampires, werewolves, space, and missing tree spirits, yes,* thought Lucy. Human company, her own age and female. That would do lovely.

Leaving a half-filled plate behind, she waved goodbye to the busily chatting Will, who turned and waved back, then followed Hina out a side entrance.

The pair crossed the main road in front of the hotel, and headed to the nearby Garrowhead Park, a spot famous for feeding ducks. Sitting on a bench at the lakeside, Lucy took the warm cup to help fight the winter chill.

"You seem perky," Hina commented. "Something *good* happen?"

Had something good happened? Yes. Fane was apprehended, and she'd made a very interesting discovery. Taking a sip of bitter latte—not Cross-Key perfection, Lucy noted—she nodded but said nothing.

"Are you going to tell me what?"

She thought about it, then shook her head. This discovery warranted extra investigation.

They sat in companionable silence, watching a police van drive away from the hotel, and her body grew weary as the remaining adrenalin left her system.

Loosening her scarf from her neck, Hina sipped her own hot beverage and cradled it to her chest. "I'm sorry I got you involved in this mess," she said into her cup. "If it weren't for my recommendation, you'd never have gotten involved with my crazy family. I lost you once, and..." the girl paused, before saying shakily, "I never want that to happen again. But it almost did."

Lucy heard the sincerity in the words but knew nothing she could say would put her friend at rest. Instead, she plucked the cup out of the troubled teen's hands and pulled her into a rough hug, answering with the strength of her grip.

"You know," spoke Lucy in a deadpan voice, "That's the first time I've pulled a fire alarm," and Hina leaned back and laughed.

"The Goody-Two-Shoes finally did something detention-worthy. Pretty sure you'd get out of it, though, the self-defence argument and all that," she said, putting the lid of her cup to the test as she waved it around.

Happy that her ice breaker had worked and her throat was playing ball, Lucy continued, "I'm glad you did suggest me for the job, so I can go visit Mum and Dad in person, as well as support them financially. And it'll be nice to see Ben."

"Support them?" Hina scoffed. "Like you haven't already tried making them happy for your entire life. You"—she poked Lucy in the chest—"need to live for yourself."

Her tone was fierce, defensive, and Lucy felt like the luckiest person in the world.

"Thank you." She took another swig of much-needed scorching caffeine. Her limbs were turning to lead in the winter chill as the adrenalin left her system.

Hina pulled out her communicator and Lucy glanced at it. "Any news?"

"Alex is in there at the moment with Cecelia," the teen said, stopping her scrolling and pointing back to the hotel. Police surrounded it, their vehicles spilling out into the side streets. "He says they haven't found Oda. Oh, they've put him in charge of Oda's rescue while my dad's been put in charge of investigating Dave. Did you know he's been arrested? What a load of rotten, backstabbing, two-faced tripe."

Lucy's eyes widened at the girl's righteous fury. She looked ready to take on the world. Her childhood friend wasn't a child anymore.

Hina launched to her feet, hand outstretched. "Come on, let's see what the kidnapper has to say for himself. We've got special clearance as Cross-Key staff. You up for that?"

A pearly white face and vermilion eyes swam across her vision and an echoing wave of residual terror washed over her. But no. She couldn't live in fear. Will and Cecelia thought she was brave, so she'd try not to let them down now. And Oda was still out there. They had Fane.

There was still a chance.

Clearing the dregs of her cup, she stood, and the pair walked back together to the hotel.

# Chapter Fourteen

# Eye for an Eye

They found Alex and Cecelia in the bedroom Fane had been hiding in. His victim had gone.

Hina explained, "He's alive. I spotted a few distant relatives taking him into the back of a truck. No body bag, so he must have been knocked unconscious. The Fleet will authorise a memory wipe, then he'll leave thinking he had the worst headache of his life."

The idea of a mind-wipe was one Lucy was sure would haunt her dreams for weeks. Would they mind-wipe her if they didn't recover Oda, and she was no longer needed? Hina's father had threatened no one would believe her, but if she was this far in, maybe there'd be no other option. She wasn't a Crossley after all.

No Fleet, no Oda, no job, no Hina, and no Will.

Cecelia held the taser she had used earlier on the vampire, who sat scuffed, tied up on the suite's floor.

"For the last time, where's Oda?" Alex demanded.

Fane shrugged. "Probably gone. I'm just a hired hand, see. In exchange for breaking me out and getting me to Earth, all I had to do was steal the book, and leave it at reception for the person to pick up. I don't know who they'd choose to pick it up, or where they'd be now."

Lucy's heart sank. Were they really back to square one? They'd been so close! She gave her best scowl at the man.

Alex went to the door of the room, cracked it open, and instructed the guard stationed there to retrieve a copy of the hotel's CCTV footage for the past week.

"Who was your accomplice?" Cecelia demanded, twisting a dial on her not-gun, making a light on the side flash green. "You'd better answer me. I'm in a foul mood already," the irate blonde snarled, baring her teeth, making a distinctly chipped fang flash in the dingy halogen light. "See this? When I get the medical bill for this, you'll be watching an enormous chunk of credits disappear from your tab."

The idea of a vampire visiting the dentist was absurd. If it weren't for the seriousness of the situation, Lucy was sure she would have liked to have used it as a punch line.

"I already said, I don't know who the person who bargained with me was, but they said they knew people higher up who could negotiate my freedom." Fane's voice turned harsh. "When I find them, though, I'm going to gut them. The deal was that I would go free and no one would follow me, not even Cross-Key. That oath-breaker will rue the day they tried to backstab me." The harshness of his tone made Lucy believe it.

"It sounds like your powerful friend underestimates their jurisdiction. The Bureau will always place the threat of our discovery above everything else, even *you*," Cecelia spat.

It was the first time Lucy had ever seen the woman so angry. She didn't just dislike this man. She loathed him.

Alex sighed and leaned against a wall beside the curtained window. "What do you know about the missing stock between Cross-Key and the Fleet?" he asked.

What? Wasn't that Mr Usmani's job to investigate? Or were the two cases related somehow?

Fane tilted his head. "Go on," he prompted.

"The Bureau has accused Cross-Key of short-changing them on their ordered stock, and supplies have been going missing before going through the HAT machine. What did you do?" he asked.

"Very interesting." The vampire flashed a menacing smile. "Very interesting indeed. Admittedly, I know nothing about that, but thanks for the gossip. It's good to know that my oath breaker, as high up as they are, must be having a nightmare of their own somewhere."

Alex scrunched up his face in disgust.

"That's about enough from you," Cecelia snapped. "Between you and me, there's only room for one vampire here, and that's me. Who'd ever want to make a deal with you? As if we'd believe such a blatant lie. You'll be coming back to Cross-Key, and you'll stay there until the Guards come and haul you back off to *Ship 12*."

"Isn't that a shame," Fane drawled. "But we have so much to catch up on, you and I. Interesting suit you've got there. Foil. Either you've developed a bizarre fashion sense, or that suit allows vampires out during the day. Which is it?"

Cecelia's face didn't crack, in fact Lucy didn't see it twitch, before she said, "It's sunset. Time to go," and pulled the trigger. A small zap of blue lightning landed where his feet would have been, but he'd jumped up just in time.

Alex signalled over his radio and guards (Crossleys, Lucy assumed) swarmed in and surrounded him. Under Cecelia's instruction, they herded him out of the room.

Turning to a wide-eyed Lucy and starry-eyed Hina, he explained. "We've got special holding cells in the domes back at the estate. He'll be holed up there until the Guards collect him."

"What is that suit?" Hina asked.

"It's called a cam-suit. It shields vampires from sunlight while giving them protection of camouflage," Alex answered. Then he put a hand in his trouser pocket, as if it was just another day at the office. "I have to get an official report from you," and pulled out a voice recorder, flicking it on. "Tell me everything you've done in the past twenty-four hours."

The girls groaned.

᷼᷼᷼᷼᷼᷼ ᷼᷼᷼᷼᷼᷼

After questioning, Lucy tried her hardest not to feel like a spare part. She headed back out into the cool cloudy air and to the lake she and Hina had sat at not too long ago, feet full of purpose and head full of fog. Every step was a fight against gravity, and once again she felt sorry for Will.

Party poppers and fireworks exploded from her pocket. Bringing out her phone, the screen flashed Mum.

Swiping, she opened the message.

```
Shame the fire alarm went off today. We'll
need you from 4:30 p.m. tomorrow.
  Mum X
```

That had all happened today. Another never-ending day. She'd circled the lake and took up her earlier bench position, phone gripped tight.

This was what she wanted, wasn't it? To stay with Ben. To be close enough to help when needed. But now she had Oda, who was missing and wasn't safe. Ben's immediate safety was assured.

A father and daughter walked by, the young girl clutching eagerly at a bag of birdseed and the father pointing to the ducks who had remained for the winter. No one came by to feed the Lombar ducks in winter, but Lucy saw how the ducks eagerly snapped to grab whatever the duo gave. She'd be there for Oda like the little girl to the ducks.

Letting herself sigh, she glanced down at her phone and swiped through to the image she'd drawn at the Fleet. Werewolves, vampires, tree spirits, spaceships... She'd accepted them all for the sake of her family. How much else would they take from her?

Something flitted across the corner of her eye, pulling her out of her thoughts. Hina puffed out a breath, visible with the onset of early evening air, as if neither of them had moved at all. She'd lost Hina once. Her parents would have to settle this time because she wouldn't lose her again.

Looking up to the tree canopy, Lucy ruminated, hoping for any signs of tree spirit to give her response.

"Do you want me to take you home?" Hina asked. Lucy smiled—the type that couldn't reach her eyes because of budding bags appearing under them.

Letting herself be led, Lucy found herself standing in front of a small daffodil-yellow car with bees painted cutely on each door. Raising an eyebrow in silent question, Hina flashed a grin and pulled out a set of keys. Thoroughly impressed with her friend's newfound skill, she climbed in the front passenger seat.

"Your kitchen looked stocked last night, but no cooking for you. I'll make us both something. I'm sure Alex will make sure Will's taken care of. And I'll ask Great Aunt Margaret if you can get a raise. I think today went a tad bit beyond the pay scale of a drawing interpreter," the girl commented as she drove them back to the Cross-Key estate.

"Thank you," she said. Today had been an eye opener, for the amount other people did for her, and where her loyalties ought to be.

Pulling out her phone, she typed:

```
Hi Mum,
Sorry, busy working tomorrow. I've trans-
ferred you enough to cover the cost of finding
a babysitter. Tell Dad I say good luck!
Lucy X
```

It's what any brag-worthy, successful businesswoman would do, right? It's what her own mother had done to her so many times.

She stuffed the phone back in her pocket just in time to climb out in front of the residential building.

"I think I'll check myself in here for the night," Hina commented, then whistled, swinging her keys in hand and opening the front door.

Lucy knew the girl was doing it was for her benefit, even if she didn't say it. With her feet curled up on the sofa, she watched Hina rifle through the cupboards.

"I've stayed here twice, when I had to meet Father at the end of his shifts," she said conversationally. She was no Oda with a psychic link, but the teen knew Lucy wasn't up to talking, and removed the pressure of chatting back by putting on the radio and dancing while she worked.

Earthy curry wafted through the flat, and Lucy was thankful that she'd gotten her friend back. Yes, even as Hina murdered the high note of a ballad.

⚜⚜⚜⚜⚜ ⚜⚜⚜⚜⚜

The next day brought the beginning of February, but instead of a fresh new start, Lucy trudged down to Oda's dome, clinging on to her work like the dregs of winter.

Did Oda understand the difference between trees and flowers? Petals and blossom? Lucy spent the morning crafting lessons for her missing charge about fauna until her communicator pinged shortly after lunch.

```
Hi Lucy,
There's been a development. Come up to
Security HQ asap.
Hope you've had a good morning,
Will
```

The pair hadn't spoken since Will's phone call the day before, and considering everything happening, Lucy wasn't certain how to broach a topic as major—minor—as their potential mutual love of retro family action TV.

The door opened as she approached, illuminating Will and Alex beneath the monitor glare. For once, the manager had his glasses off, and rubbed at heavy-lidded eyes, his cheek puffed with some sort of sweet. The poor man must have pulled an all-nighter, she mused.

"Thought you'd like an update in person," he said, pointing to a chair next to Will's. Lucy took it without a word. At her side Will beamed so surely it was good news?

"Dave returned half an hour ago. The Council kept him in overnight for *extensive* questioning. Aunt's given him the day off to recover." It wasn't like him to make a slip of the tongue, referring to the CEO so familiarly, even as laid-back as he was. Her heart went out for the man before something else he'd said struck her.

*Extensive. Recover.* What exactly did questioning at the Fleet entail?

"Good thing, too," Will said cheerfully. "He's meant to be coming with me tonight for the big one." His sky-blue eyes glittered animatedly in the computer light.

Big night... Wait—Will's first werewolf transformation!

Just then, a husky female voice rang from the other side of the room. "I had to pull in a number of favours that I'd been saving to get him out. He owes me big time." The red-haired femme fatale stepped out of the shadows, wearing tight black pants, matching kitten heels, and a loose cream blouse; the outfit screamed pirate glam.

"Surprise! How've you been holding up?" Trisha asked, holding a hand out to Lucy, who shook it, wide-eyed.

Forcing herself to clear her throat, she croaked, "Fine."

"Yes," Alex drawled, turning the attention back to himself. "Now that we're all gathered, let's get this party started," though his tone sounded like he'd rather crawl under a duvet. A button press later, and the regular CCTV of reception was replaced by Cecelia in an underground dome.

Pressing another button on the remote, he spoke. "We're all set. Take it away."

Cecelia, who could apparently hear what he said, gave the corner camera a thumbs up. "Trisha. As thanks for returning Dave, I thought you might like to bring in this. Call it an exchange of sorts."

Alex pushed a button and the camera panned, revealing a set of bars, and behind them sat Fane, legs crossed, on a bed.

Trisha's jaw dropped. "You did it? But—don't tell the Council I said this—I was certain they were setting you up to fail. What about Oda? Oh, I can't wait to see some of the higher-ups' faces when they find out," the woman gushed.

Alex filled her in. "He insists he doesn't know where Oda is, but we think that's a lie."

"We caught him at sunset, and vampires are too risky to move freely at night. Sorry, Cissy," Alex said.

"Cissy? *Cissy?*" screeched an irate Cecelia, and in the background Fane gave a low chuckle.

"So," Alex continued, "We waited until today to turn him in. Want the honour, Cuz?"

Trisha licked her bottom lip. "Well, isn't it unfortunate that he doesn't know where Oda is? I'm sure the Guards will get the information from him. Following protocol, I believe they'll use vampires for the interrogation, and I know a few who'd love to sink their teeth into you."

Lucy shuddered, but Fane just huffed and rolled over on his bed, ignoring them.

Then, all business, Trisha said, "As human ambassador to the Fleet, I'll return with the good news. Expect the Guards after sunset. Although you think it's dangerous for him to be moved at nightfall, the Guards will also be at their strongest then."

Alex clicked a button, and the screen switched back to the reception in real time.

"The collar still works, but he managed to drink fresh blood," Alex reported.

Trisha tapped the gravitational dial on her wrist, bringing out a flat screen of light and scrawled on the screen before banishing it with a flick of her wrist.

"Got it. Thanks for your work, and for the work." She pulled the frazzled man into a tight hug, then released him, popping a sweet into her mouth. "Careful, Matisse. You're slipping," she taunted with a smirk, and once again Lucy found herself intimidated by the Crossleys.

Replacing her expression to one of innocent sweetness, she bent down to Will. "Care to see me to the HAT machine?" she asked, winking at him.

It was too much, and Lucy absorbed herself into the grey office tiles.

Alex gave a strained laugh that came out like a wisp.

"I'm sure he'd be glad to. Won't you? When you're gone, I need to catch up with Lucy."

Lucy tilted her head in question, while Will gave a thumbs up and propelled himself over to the door. Pulling on a small rope tied to the handle, he yanked and the door opened. "After you," he said, motioning to the threshold.

When the sound of clacking heels grew distant, Alex moved to close the door, leaving the pair alone.

"That's not all that's been happening," he said, running a hand through his hair in a Dave-like fashion. "Fane's requested to speak to you, and only you. Do you know why that might be?"

Her chest tightened as she remembered vermilion eyes. Why her? A grudge, perhaps? Stumped, she said, "No. I've never spoken to him before."

Alex sighed and put his sunglasses back on.

"He's asked repeatedly for you all morning. We checked with the CEO, and she said yes, providing you consented and stayed out of reaching distance through the bars."

Lucy's mind raced. What could he possibly want with her? No. It didn't matter what he wanted from her. Could she get Oda from him?

"I'll do it," Lucy said, clutching her satchel to her side.

"He stipulated he'll give you alone information, but with no cameras, microphones or bugs. The CEO and I decided, given the nature of his request, to keep this on a need-to-know basis. Me, you, Aunt, and Cecelia who'll be backup outside the door. Which he's agreed to since it's vampire-proof against sound."

Lucy's head swam with the information.

"You're sure about this?" he asked, his lips thin. He looked like he'd aged a decade or two, and she desperately hoped Hina's dad turned in early for his shift to give the poor man a break.

Face set, she stood up. "I'll go."

# Chapter Fifteen
# Ready to Run

A thick steel door carved into granite completed the impression of a dungeon, but then opened into a smooth white dome. One section of wall had monitors from floor to ceiling, and beside that was a desk, chair, and kitchenette facility, where Cecelia stood nursing her red mystery drink.

Running down the centre were thick silver bars, and beyond them, sitting on a crisp white-sheeted mattress, was Fane. Beside him was a small toilet and sink.

Fane sat slumped on the bed's edge, head in hands, but glanced up when he saw them enter.

"Lucy," he intoned. "Lucy. Lucy Blakely," he said, sounding like he was saying it for the very first time. "The rest of you can go now. I want privacy. No privacy, no information. That's the deal."

Lucy raised an eyebrow. He was the prisoner. Who was he to make demands?

Cecelia knocked back the rest of the liquid and spat, "Why not say what you've got to say in front of us. Something to hide?"

Fane's expression didn't change. "The girl only. That's final," he said flatly.

With the courage of a hundred lions, Alex tugged the sleeve of Cecelia's coat and directed the fuming blonde to the exit.

"You've got ten minutes tops, then we're breaking the door down. Lucy, if you need us, hit the button at the top of your communicator. It's a panic button," he said, then heaved the solid steel door shut with a bang.

"Alone at last," he said, sighing in relief. "I can tell they're not snooping in on us; I have my ways." The vampire swooped his legs up beneath him on the mattress, never breaking eye contact with her.

Lucy gulped but said nothing.

"I've wanted to chat with you ever since the kodama told me about you. At least I think it's a kodama. It certainly has all the hallmarks of one," he said. "I travelled for a time in Japan, you know. I'd love to see it now," he said, much to Lucy's confusion, almost wistfully.

For being such a violent monster, the civil conversation was unexpected. It was like a calm had descended on the room. It was inviting. Settling. Like his voice wove a charm.

"Oda is my friend, and I'd like them back," she said, surprising herself with her ability to articulate. What was Fane doing? Was this another psychic vampire thing? Or was she no longer a selective mute?

"Oda? A fitting name," he replied, his voice lilted with honey. "Oda told me all about you, all good things, I can assure you," he said, raising a hand and smirking.

"You spoke to Oda? How?" she demanded. That had been *her* task with her drawings.

Another wave of calm washed over her, and her limbs went slack, the tension in her shoulders disappearing.

Why had she been angry again?

This was fascinating.

Another way to speak to Oda!

"One drop of blood was all it took to establish the link," he answered. "Telepathy is a trait shared by all vampires, fuelled by something in our blood, though we're still working on what that something is. Anyway, I misjudged the distance between two rooftops, dropped Oda in the fall, and got a particularly nasty scrape. When I picked up the book, the cover came into contact with my blood."

"You fell?" Lucy asked, incredulously.

"Earth's gravity is tough to get used to again," he snapped. Then his gaze grew distant, and he looked down at his palms. "What a curious creature," he commented to himself. The words were soft, curious, and it dawned on Lucy in that moment that Fane was as enraptured with the tree spirit as much as she was. Her gut stirred at the thought, and she snapped back to attention.

If he liked Oda, was that enough to keep them safe?

Lucy broke the silence, aware of time escaping. "What did you want to tell me?"

"Oda," he tried out the word, "spoke about you. About your loyalty, your warmth, acceptance, your teachings and patience. From the description I got, it sounded like rainbows would bloom wherever you stepped foot. In short, curiosity."

Warmth glowed in Lucy's chest at such high praise, and tears prickled at the corners of her eyes. "I want to see Oda again. What do you know?" she asked, and cringed as her voice warbled pathetically. Why couldn't she be stronger, like Alex or Cecelia?

"You're a good person. Kind and loyal."

Her betrayal of Hina came to mind, and she shook her head.

"Oda begs to differ, and I'm inclined to believe them. There aren't many people out there like you, so I'll tell you a secret," he said, then stood and approached the bars.

Lucy stepped back an equal amount.

"I lied. Oda wasn't taken by anyone. Instead, I buried the notebook beneath a tree. Hid it for insurance in case someone betrayed me, and I was right. Lucy Blakely, here's the rub. The Grand Bureau Member herself broke me out. The deal was the notebook for a life on Earth. She's your red-haired friend's boss. Trisha. Yes? Surely her own secretary knew."

She sucked in a deep breath. Astra! Could Trisha have known? As secretary, she'd be close, but she'd looked gleeful when she'd seen they had captured him. As if it was a big break for her. Her head spun, and she focussed on slowing her breathing as he continued.

"I planned to live on Earth in secrecy. I have killed no one since I've been here, and I don't plan to." He waved a hand. "That all changed as soon as the Bureau allowed Cross-Key & Co. to come after me. Trisha knows what's going on, but she's still calling the Guards to take me back. I can't have that."

Question after question ran through Lucy's brain until her unusual ability to speak blurted one out at random. "How did you get through the HAT machine? It's guarded, and turned off when not being used."

"HAT…" Fane trailed off, his brow furrowed for a beat before his eyes lit up and he barked out a laugh. "Is that what they're calling it down here? Astra would be thrilled. As for your question, it's also locked down and manned on every ship in the Fleet. Only someone with an insanely high clearance level could have authorised my cell door being opened. The person was hooded, but stank of nervous wolf." He wrinkled his nose, as if something foul had leaked through the bars.

When he spoke again, he locked gazes with her, and another wave of infuriating calm damped down her anxiety.

"You have no affiliation to Trisha or the Bureau, and you aren't a Crossley family member, not to mention you have Oda's trust. You're the only person I feel comfortable making a deal with."

Lucy straightened, lost in two pools of vermilion.

"You help me get out of here before the Guards turn up tonight, and I'll return Oda to you. Then, I'll be out of your life for good. You'll never hear from me again. Sound good?"

*Oda. Oda. Oda.* Her mind repeated the words as if in a chant. She could get Oda back. Keep her job. What did she owe the Fleet, anyway? They'd refused to help apprehend Fane.

Apprehend. On the run. Criminal.

Jamming her eyes closed, she broke eye contact. He was a criminal. His words were sweet but if it really was making her forcefully calm...

"Why should I trust you?" she asked, legs shaking as adrenalin returned and her brain woke up and took stock of the situation.

"Because Oda wants me to give you apples."

The simple sentence drove a knife into her chest, and she cupped her hands together, covering it. Daring to open her eyes, she looked at the vampire again. He looked earnest, almost pleading. And she believed him.

If she agreed, they got Oda. It was simple.

Lucy pulled out her employee ID access card, thankful her tracker was separate from her lapel's name badge.

She threw the card to his feet, and he dove to pick it up, shoving it up the tatty prison suit's sleeve.

"That will get you through the doors, but how you get out of this cell is up to you. Cecelia wore a prototype sun protector suit to catch you. They're somewhere in the domes beneath Research and Development, but I don't know where."

With a flourish, Fane bowed deeply, looking up at her. "Thank you kindly. Oda will be yours once again."

His words forced down a rising wave of her nausea, and her stomach moved from spin cycle back to cotton wash. She couldn't look at him, and headed for the reinforced steel door and knocked. Alex flung the door open, Cecelia popping up behind his shoulder.

"You alright? Did he try anything?" the security manager said, checking her over for wounds and scrapes.

"What did he want? He would never give information up for nothing," Cecelia said darkly, and Lucy was touched at the pair's concern.

Mind racing to find an answer, she picked up the lead Alex had dropped.

"He—" Her throat had gone dry, and she choked on her words. Back to awkward speaking again, then. Sputtering to clear her throat, she tried again. "He asked to drink my blood. I think he was messing with me. Revenge for pulling the fire alarm."

Lies. More lies. But she desperately hoped they believed her.

"The charges just keep piling up. Bartering with an innocent for blood," Cecelia said, her almost girlish voice at odds with the fist she punched into the granite wall, leaving a dent. Lucy flinched. They definitely believed her.

Alex placed a hand on her shoulder, and she jumped again, like a wound-up rabbit. "I'll take you back to your apartment, and Cecelia will stay with our deviant. Don't worry. He won't be going anywhere."

Lucy nodded, unable to look him in the eye, and followed him down the tunnel without looking back.

Wishing the day away, Lucy preoccupied herself by sketching, forcing her focus onto the cup in front of her; but her movements were mechanical, stiff, forced.

*Bang!*

Lucy jumped, eyes darting to her closed room door.

When she heard shuffling, she threw her tablet onto the duvet and tiptoed to the door, silently cracking it open to look.

Will stood stooped beside his wheelchair, one hand on his forehead, the other outstretched for balance.

Pain laced the pads of her fingernails as she gripped the doorframe, but released it when she saw him shuffle and collapse onto the sofa with a contented sigh.

He breathed hard, as if he'd run a marathon, then reached out to his wheelchair and heaved.

Yes. This was exactly the distraction she needed, and strode out towards the teen.

"Need a hand?" she asked, motioning to his chair.

He turned around and smiled. "If you don't mind, thanks. Didn't mean to bother you."

"Not at all," she reassured him, and pushed the handles of the wheelchair together, compacting it, and wrangled it to his side, her heart dancing the flamenco all the while.

Trying not to show her jitters, she took a deep breath and forced her voice to slow. "Do you want some tea? I was just going to make a cup," she offered, mentally calling herself a liar as she walked away from the abandoned mug in her bedroom to start anew.

"Thanks. I'll have what you're having," he said sheepishly, and Lucy busied herself making a second and third cup of chamomile tea in fifteen minutes. She held up the milk carton and sugar bowl in silent question.

"Milk and two sugars," he answered, the voice of innocence compared to her deceit. If he knew what she'd done, he wouldn't talk to her at all.

Taking the finished cup, he took a careful sip, then poked his tongue out. "You like it hot," he noted, and Lucy's mind ran rampant.

*It's only the tea,* she admonished mentally. *Calm down.*

"It's what happens when water gets to a certain temperature," she blurted, then cringed inwardly. That was it. She'd snapped, and stuck her foot in it. He was going to hate her. He'd never—

He laughed, a deep, raucous, side-splitting laugh, bending double to put his cup on the table before the ripples spilled over the edge.

"A certain...!" he repeated, then howled again, up at the ceiling, clutching his middle.

With the tension unceremoniously cut, Lucy sipped her drink with as much dignity as she could muster. The chamomile passed her lips just shy of scalding. Perfect as always for a Cross-Key kettle. And yes, she admitted, she did like it hot.

Wiping tears from his eyes, he said, "If I'd made it, it would have been cooler. The psychic field only picks up on the person's preferences who actually makes the drink. I'm glad vampire tech has some flaw."

She nodded, then asked, "Do you know if Dave's feeling better?"

His grin turned to a scowl, face set. "He's good, but the situation stinks like a pile of wolf dung after a bad batch of moon cakes."

He drew his feet up beneath him, not noticing Lucy's confused look, and continued, "He's facing charges of fraud. You know I check stock going to the Fleet? Well, supplies have been going missing, and we've got no idea how. I haven't seen anything pointing to Dave, but the Council wants someone to blame for getting short-changed, and humans are an easy target, politically." He ran a hand through his hair.

Cogs turned in Lucy's head as she ran over his words. Deciding she was underqualified to comment, she tried to play it safe. "I'm glad he's recovering."

Will gave a weak smile, blew over his cup, and took a sip.

"Physically, yeah. But last night was messed up. Remember my brother Duke? Well, he worked here before me. They placed him on the arrest squad. The only werewolf in a group of vampires. It was sick."

*And not the cool kind,* Lucy thought. The cruelty made her shiver, and Will curled up smaller. A snap decision later, she sank into the sofa next to him, reached out and pulled him into a one-armed hug. He froze, then slackened, accepting her comfort. His hair tickled her nose, adding the smell of earth to the chamomile.

"Duke's part of the Guards?" she asked, picking up threads of previous conversations.

"Duke's incredible. Once he sinks his claws into something, he's the best. Top in exams, winner of the Fleet's Programming Innovation Award, and star of our ship's Reality Boots team."

"What's reality boot?" she asked.

He gave a small chuckle. "Reality Boots. It's like Ultimate Frisbee, but it's played in a large microgravity bubble. Everyone wears special boots, and every time they touch the surface, the targets change place."

Her mouth fell open, but she gathered herself again when he pushed himself up, breaking the embrace. He took another sip and peered into his cup.

"I'll never be half the wolf he is. Never made the team. Average grades. He came here and needed a cane, but I need this thing." He motioned to his wheelchair, and her gut lurched. "I doubt they'd even let me join Guards training."

Cogs turned in Lucy's brain while waves of doubt seeped off the withdrawn teen.

"Is that what you want to do? Be a Guard?" she asked softly.

"It's what Duke did," he said, as if it explained everything.

An icy chasm opened in the pit of Lucy's stomach.

"If he's got all that attention, doesn't that mean you're free to be who you want? Do what you want?" she asked, but wasn't sure if she wanted to know the answer.

"Our papa was a lunar explorer. It brought our family a lot of prestige. But he died during a mission."

"I'm sorry," she consoled.

"Duke stepped up to help our mum earn money with his programming, on top of everything else. Then he got chosen as ambassador. Now he has this incredible job in the Guards. Everyone thinks he'll become a Councillor one day." He smiled sadly into his cup. "I'm proud of him. Really, I am. But I can't go anywhere without him being mentioned, or being compared to him. This job was my greatest achievement, and even here they're saying Duke did it first."

The words stabbed at Lucy's heart. Had she been going about things the wrong way with Ben all this time? Instead of distracting the focus from him, would she end up magnifying attention onto him?

Ben wasn't here, but Will was, and she could help him.

"You're not your brother. Everyone has their own likes and talents. To be honest, I thought he was far too serious when I met him." His head whipped up, eyes as close to puppy dog on a human she'd ever seen.

"What do you want to do?" she asked, and even more doglike, he tilted his head. Her insides squirmed.

He got a distant look in his eyes. "I've always just gone with the pack. I like people, and meeting new ones. Then last year Mum pushed me towards the off-vessel track, and suddenly I'm here. I'm not special or brilliant. People train for years to get this job, but they picked me, and I think it's only because of who my brother is."

Lucy sipped her chamomile, contemplating. "You said you like people. That's an important quality for an ambassador. You must have other skills and interests that separated you from the rest."

Will lifted his head and grinned sheepishly. *"Protekante ĝis la fino de la tempo."*

Lucy sucked in a breath, almost launching to her feet in excitement. *"Protektante ĉion kion estas via kaj mia,"* she finished.

He rubbed the back of his head. "Do you know much Esperanto?" he asked.

"Nope," Lucy admitted, her inner fangirl glowing on a pedestal. "But how could I forget the motto of Sgt. Sir's prized battalion?" she answered proudly, her lips finally putting shape to the words she'd heard since childhood. "Do you?"

"Actually, I'm a polyglot. There's not much use for other languages in the Fleet other than translating the odd old song a vampire sings. I normally learn for fun, but started Esperanto when I got my placement here. Thought it would come in handy, a universal language, but I seem to have picked up the wrong end of the stick."

Lucy's eyebrows rose in incredulity as he spoke.

"But then when you left my birthday party, I heard it coming from your bedroom and tracked the phrase back to a show called *Sgt. Sir!* I wasn't eavesdropping. Promise!" he said, raising a hand in defence. "Wolves have much better hearing than humans."

A part of her shattered. He wasn't a superfan after all, but he had done his research. Maybe she could get him to watch it properly? And the languages blew her away.

"How many languages can you speak?" she asked.

"I wouldn't know what to count. A few fluently, like old Romanian, Latin, and Greek. The vampires and wolves like their myths, and I wanted to read them in their own languages. But I could get by with modern versions." He then began listing all the languages he could hold an introductory conversation in, running out of fingers.

Lucy was shocked. So many languages meant the possibility of insulting so many more people without meaning to. Then again, in Will's case, he said it himself. There weren't many people to talk to. The positive was he could read about other cultures in their own words.

"Well now, we know why they picked you, Mr Modest. Earth uses so many languages. You're definitely in the right place," she reassured him, wondering if after her actions that morning day she did.

"You're very kind," he said, staring down into his cup again. "But I'm not sure. Since I arrived, it's all gone wrong. Nothing got lost or went missing when Duke did this job."

Images of his tall, muscular brother flashed through her brain. She remembered their first meeting, the drawing she'd made, and Hina's fawning.

She hummed, then smirked. "Duke sounds like an overachiever. That's not a bad thing. He looked like an upstanding citizen. But he's not my cup of tea. He's Hina's."

Will uncurled, relaxing into the sofa. "Really? Shame. Look, I wouldn't normally comment on something like this, but she's barking up the wrong tree."

Lucy froze. What?

Seeing her expectant look, he continued, "Duke doesn't like girls. Or anyone. He's aro. Openly so. Proudly."

She blinked.

"It's short for aromantic. He doesn't feel romantic attraction to anyone. Says he's married to the Fleet when anyone asks."

Dread dripped down her spine. "Do Guards ever need to send emails to Cross-Key & Co. receptionists?"

Will arched an eyebrow. "No. They'd only contact Earth at all if there was a criminal investigation going on, and it would be in person."

Groaning, Lucy rubbed her temples. "Then something's rotten, because Hina told me she's been emailing him at work. Said Duke picked his job especially so they could stay in contact."

With a clink, he placed his cup down on the coffee table, then locked gazes with her. "Very fishy. Unless there's a back door I don't know about in Mind Mail's programming—that's our vision of message sending—but, no." He shook his head and muttered, "I don't even think the two systems are compatible. If I wanted to contact Duke, I'd have to go through the portal first and Mind Mail him from there."

"You said yourself that it's impossible to contact Duke from here, so we'll have to..." She sucked in a shuddering breath. "...ask Hina about it."

Will uncurled, shifting his legs back to the footstool. "Sounds good. As well as accepting the morning mail drop, she also points lost delivery drivers to the relevant warehouses. I'm not sure if the missing stock and Duke are related, but it's going to kill me not knowing."

Having already been down one rabbit hole that day, she had no intention of sticking her foot down another so soon.

"There's a lot going on right now, and I need to get my head on straight before making Hina's world potentially implode. Can we keep this between us for a couple of days?"

Will bit his lip but nodded. "Alright. Dave's a good guy. Welcomed me with open arms. We'll prove his innocence. And Duke's."

Thankful, Lucy downed the last of her now lukewarm chamomile, tapping absent-mindedly on the handle. "Ready for tonight?" she asked, wanting to return to positive distractions.

His eyes lit up, and she knew she was on to a winner. "Can't wait. Dave's picking me up at 3:30 p.m. Even though it's his day off, he's coming in especially for this. I get to ride in a helicopter up the coast."

Lucy imagined Dave throwing a big stick and a fluffy auburn ball barrelling across the sand.

"Is it just tonight?" she asked.

He raised four fingers. "Whenever the Earth's moon is at 95 percent visibility or more, so four nights of frolicking."

"I hope you enjoy it," Lucy said earnestly.

The words were simple, but made Will beam, and butterflies took off again, this time reaching Lucy's chest.

# CHAPTER SIXTEEN

# CROSSING LINES

Dave's cheery tones filtered through her bedroom door at 3:30 p.m., and he left not long after with Will for the big night. Lucy stayed hidden in her room and waited, eventually turning to sketching.

Pops and bangs interrupted her shading a lily, her phone flashing up and vibrating. She bit her lip when she saw the caller. This was it.

Shakily, she swiped to answer.

"There's been a development," Alex said before she'd even said hello.

"We'll track you down. Mark my words, we will!" Kamal shouted angrily in the background.

Alex shushed his fellow manager, and his ranting faded into the distance, as if he'd walked away to continue his tirade.

"Fane's gone walkabout, and so is the prototype cam-suit that Cecelia wore to bring him in. What did he say to you this morning? Did he give you any hint about his plans? Anything at all?" "You fell?" Lucy asked, incredulously.

"Earth's gravity is tough to get used to again," he snapped. Then his gaze grew distant, and he looked down at his palms. "What a curious creature," he commented to himself. The words were soft, curious, and it dawned on Lucy in that moment that Fane was as enraptured with the tree spirit as much as she was. Her gut stirred at the thought, and she snapped back to attention.

Lucy screwed her eyes closed and shakily drew a breath. She could do this.

"No," she lied. "Just what I told you."

Alex sighed his trademark sleepy sigh, and Lucy could picture him slouching, tucking a hand into his pocket.

"That's unfortunate. On the plus side, the suit never had the chance to recharge, so the battery won't last long. Three hours at most, Dave reckons. Sundown isn't far away, but depending on when he left, it could have given him quite the head start. Not that we can do anything without Cecelia, mind. And she's swanned off to the Fleet to get her tooth fixed. Won't be back 'till tomorrow, then we can regain ground on him during the day."

Lucy arched an eyebrow as she thought of a vampire in a dentist's chair, then shook the thought away. Day?

"If he's taken the cam-suit, how can Cecelia travel during the day?" she asked tentatively, torn between rooting for his recapture and escape.

"Very good," he said, then Lucy heard what sounded like a sweet popping into his mouth, muffling his next words. "Lucky for us, Dave just revealed a secret project he'd been working on—a second line of suits with an upgrade. Twice the battery life. Considering even we didn't know about it, Fane shouldn't see it coming."

"Oh," she said stupidly.

"Lucy, don't worry. We have extra security posted across the estate. He won't get to you. He's probably long gone by now." His reassurances were lost on deaf ears.

Long gone. She'd done her part. Now it was his turn to leave Oda behind.

"Keep your ID with you at all times from now on, even off the clock. Can't be too careful."

Lost in thought, Lucy thanked the man and ended the call before jumping when her communicator beeped.

She reached for the green flashing light and swiped, opening the new message.

Hi Lucy,
There's a package for you at reception. Not sure who from. It was left when I nipped to the ladies'. It's in the drawer behind reception. Ask whoever's on after me and they'll fish it out for you. It's the end of my shift. I'd have invited you out for coffee, but Dad's on the warpath for some reason and ordered me straight home.
Hina x

Dropping the communicator, she grabbed her jacket and flew out of the building. She didn't stop jogging until she reached Headquarters. Bursting into the atrium, she bent double at reception, hands on her knees.

"A package was left here for Lucy Blakely," she said between gasps.

A young security guard picked out a brown envelope, with *Lucy* scrawled across in curly italic.

She smiled. It was big—big enough to hold a notebook. Then she frowned when she grabbed it. Too light. Her heart sank like a stone.

Retreating to the toilets off the atrium, she locked herself inside a stall and tore open the package.

Her ID fell into her palm and she pulled out a sheet of paper with the same curly script on it.

No one will know. I hacked the system and changed the code for your card, so it won't appear as yours in the system. Don't worry, I put it back again. Say you'd lost this, and someone handed it in to reception.

Lucy's heart sank. What had she done? Of course, he wouldn't hand over his only form of leverage. Thanks to her, they had no Oda and a criminal vampire was at large again. She slumped onto the toilet seat and groaned.

People were at risk.

Noticing her hands trembling, she forced her breathing to slow, turning the problem over in her brain.

Fane was a criminal, but he hadn't killed anyone yet since coming to Earth—just drank blood. She grimaced at the thought, but conceded that no one had died. Or at least she thought so. And even though he'd scarpered, he'd covered her involvement. Did she owe him the benefit of the doubt?

Rubbing circles into her temples, she resolved to fact-check that later.

Fist clenched around the paper, she strode up the flight of stairs to the Security Department. Fane was her problem now, and she was going to help solve it. Find Fane, find Oda.

Before she could knock, the door swung open to admit her, meeting the steely gazes of Alex and Kamal.

"I want to be part of the mission to bring down Fane tomorrow," she said sternly, adding, "please," as an afterthought.

Alex sighed, and Kamal raised a greying eyebrow above his black glasses. "My daughter was right when she recommended we hire you. You've grown a spine since you were little."

❧❧❧❧❧ ❧❧❧❧❧

Lucy woke to a blank inbox and balled her fists. The lying blood sucker really had done a runner! She'd expected an Oda-shaped parcel to appear in the night. Why had she believed anything he'd said?

She stormed out of her bedroom like a typhoon, furious at her own stupidity, then stopped in her tracks.

On the sofa sat Will, looking as if the sun had just been hung and he could order rainbows on demand. He looked up, spoon half raised to his mouth over a giant cereal bowl.

"Morning," he greeted her with a wave, and her freezer-burn brain melted into a warm puddle.

He looked good. Better than good, in fact, for someone whose bones had cracked and force-grew fur the night before. She's expected tired, pained, and lethargic, but he looked animated, lifting a spoonful to his upturned lips. A massive, inhuman spoonful.

Even though her rumbling stomach would never match Will's bottomless pit, she dug out her own bowl from the drying rack. It hid behind two wet ones, meaning the other guests in the building had already gone. Good. They'd be able to chat freely.

Having shifted from tempest to churning waves, Lucy took the seat next to the other teen.

"How was last night? I thought you'd be gone for a few days," she confessed, forcing out her words around a lump in her throat.

Will put his bowl on the coffee table. "It was probably the best night of my life. Indescribable, really. Sand under my paws, wind in my fur, salt on my tongue..."

He trailed off, and she glanced up and locked with his sky-blue eyes.

"If I had to describe it," he said, eyes going distant, "I'd call it freedom."

Freedom. That was a good thing, wasn't it? But it was what Fane wanted, too. Lucy blinked and forced her gaze down to her cereal.

"Dave was fantastic," Will continued. "He brought this giant pile of meat for me and a bunch of stuff to chase to keep me entertained."

Lucy fought off a snort of laughter, fearing milk would come out of her nose. She remembered her idea of a wolf playing fetch with a large tree branch. Maybe it had come true.

"I'm glad," she said, and she was. For him, and for the distraction from the escaped convict.

"The best part was I didn't need this." He reached out and put a hand on the wheelchair at his side. "On all fours, my head and my heart are aligned, so my body pumps blood easier to the head. Gravity wasn't as much of an issue."

Lucy nodded. It made sense, and she was genuinely happy for her flatmate? Colleague? Friend? Yes. Friend sounded right, she concluded, surprised. When had that happened?

"Are you going back tonight?" she asked, and shifted her gaze down to her spoon. The question was loaded, and she knew it. Will knew, too, and his face fell for the first time that day, making her heart skip.

"Yes. I heard about what happened with that night-snapper. But a wolf running through city's would stand out too much. And it would be a risk. In full wolf form, my instincts are in overdrive. I'd probably lose interest and chase cars or something," he said, crestfallen. "Or worse."

Lucy hummed, but her head shot up when she felt hot skin on her arm. Vivid amber eyes gazed into hers. "You volunteered to capture him again, even after his advances on you?" His voice was low, and his concern was touching.

She bit her bottom lip.

"Dave told me. Be careful. Please."

The hair on her arms prickled under his touch, and her breath caught at his sincerity. His closeness. He was getting closer. Her stomach coiled.

*"Protekante ĝis la fino de la tempo,"* she blurted out.

Will stopped, blinked, and drew back, his face softening back into a smile. "Protecting everything that's yours and mine," he finished. "Come back safe. I want another Lucy-cooked meal someday."

He withdrew his hand, and Lucy glanced at the warm skin on her arm, thankful she hadn't put on a jacket yet.

Oblivious to the tennis match going on in Lucy's head, Will continued to make small talk while Lucy pecked at each spoonful.

Beeping interrupted them, and Lucy pulled out the vibrating messaging device.

"Update?" asked Will.

"Cecelia's back from her...trip," she relayed, unable to bring herself to say *dentists*. "10:00 a.m. at Security. We're leaving from there."

"You'll get him, Ruĝa. Cecelia's small, but then again, aren't most people from the Middle Ages? Anyway, she'll be enough to take down Fane. He's not so big, either."

Lucy briefly wondered what language the nickname was, but she was more fascinated by his comment about size. It explained why all the vampires she'd seen at the Bureau were so small, and why the old church in Lombar had such small underground doors.

"Small but deadly," she agreed, then asked a question that had been cycling through her head all night. "Will," she asked, enjoying the ease that his name rolled off her tongue. "Why is Fane in prison?"

He sat silently for a moment, scratching the back of his neck in thought. "I'm uncertain about all the details, but Mum told us he tried to turn a werewolf. Vampires live forever, so they consume resources for eternity. If their numbers kept growing, they'd eventually use all the resources in the Fleet, on Earth, then the universe. They're unsustainable, so they voluntarily restricted their numbers."

Lucy tilted her head, trying to wrap her head around that.

"I don't know any wolf crazy enough to want to be a vampire. It's unnatural." He shuddered.

Images of wolves with red eyes and bat wings filled her head. Will didn't seem to like it, but it sounded cool, and she promised to sketch it later privately.

Will stretched his arms above his head. "I'm off to take a shower. Good luck."

Her vocal cords jammed, and she couldn't respond. Feeling herself heat up, she gave him a quick wave, then made a beeline for the kitchen and a large glass of water to cool off.

❧❧❧❧❧ ❧❧❧❧❧

"Welcome," the CEO greeted her, as Lucy strode into the Security Department, ignoring the lead feeling in her limbs. Alex nodded in her direction. He looked more awake, his back straight, making him tower over Cecelia, who as usual took a corner. She raised a manicured eyebrow above her sunglasses, absent-mindedly running her tongue over her protruding diamond-white fang.

Lucy took an offered seat next to Mrs Crossley. She folded her hands on her lap, feeling like she was back at school and had to sit right next to the teacher.

The monitors switched to a large map with one flick of a controller from Alex. In the centre was a pulsing vermilion-coloured dot. He picked up a paper and began their briefing.

"CCTV indicates Fane has travelled three hours north, taking the 20:32 express train from Garrowhead East. The vermilion light indicates he had a snack or two on the train. Our signal is getting weaker, so his collar must be starting to fail. Clearly he thinks so, too, because it's pinged back five attempts to break it in seven hours. We have to catch him and charge the collar before it dies."

Lucy examined the map and sucked in a deep breath. Between each pulse of vermilion shone a light blue airplane. "He's trying to catch a flight?" she thought aloud, starting at the sound of her own voice.

Cecelia hmphed. "Getting on a plane in broad daylight would be a death sentence. He's likely holed up in the airport's hotel until night."

A jolt ran down Lucy's spine. It was winter, so nights came early. They'd have to hurry.

"Dave and young Will are indisposed due to that time of the month," Mrs Crossley said. Alex snorted. Lucy bit the inside of her cheek. "I have to stay to oversee the fraud investigation, while Kamal takes a long-earned rest. If all goes well, his first task tonight will be reinforcing our cells."

Cecelia flashed a toothy grin. "Let the hunt begin. Do we get to take the helicopter?" For being decades old, she sounded like a child in a toy shop.

"The helicopter wouldn't be big enough to secure yourselves and a vampire fugitive, and it's reserved for Will and Dave. I appreciate speed is of the essence, though. Take the company car." Out of a pocket she pulled a set of three silver keys on a ring and tossed them to Alex, who caught them and inclined his head.

Lucy's eyes widened. How could they be safe trapped in a car with the cheat? Not wanting to sound stupid in case she was missing something, instead she raised her hand.

"You aren't in school, Miss Blakely. Speak," she prompted kindly.

"Last time, there were others. Family members..." she trailed off.

"Very good," she said, praising her unasked question. "I believe we have two branches of the family nearby, and another only an hour's drive away. The Parsons from my Great Aunt Patricia's side," she said fondly to Alex. "I'll reach out to them to meet you there."

Once again, she got the feeling that she was intruding. Alex was family, and the driver. Cecelia was a vampire with the strength and speed to take Fane down. Where did she fit?

The answer came back to bite her.

"This hunt will be quick," Cecelia commented. "After all, we have a mouse for our trap who we know is his type."

Lucy gulped.

# CHAPTER SEVENTEEN

# A ROYAL FLUSH

The 'company car' pulled around the corner: a lorry full of high-tech equipment complete with miniature research lab and vampire-proof cage, or at least Dave claimed.

Sitting in the back, Lucy jolted every time they ran over a bump in the road until they turned onto the smoother highway.

"Faster!" Cecelia snapped into a receiver that linked to the front cab. "I know this contraption is capable of more."

Being alone so near the angry vampire made Lucy shiver, but she squashed down the rising nausea. They had to get Fane back. Somehow.

"Sorry for trying to obey the laws of the road," Alex drawled. "Would you prefer to drive?"

Cecelia crossed her cam-suit-covered arms and huffed. She couldn't risk sitting in the cab and running her suit low in the sun before they got there.

"Thought not," Alex answered the silence.

The vampire grumbled. Then, Lucy glimpsed the long paper in her hands, streaming out from a printer attached to a laptop, and paled. ID card logs. Of course, they'd check!

The question is had Fane lied about changing the code, too?

Cecelia growled and crumpled the printout, clearly not finding what she was searching for, and Lucy gulped down a few calming breaths.

"Why did the mutt get priority for the helicopter? I could have swooped down and got him much quicker, then waited for this thing to arrive later."

At her words, Lucy's teeth clenched.

"Bad timing," she spat back in a tone that shocked even her.

Cecelia looked in her direction.

Lucy froze, hoping her outburst would be misconstrued as anger towards Fane instead. She didn't fancy becoming a meal.

"Feisty. Hey, Al. Our church mouse is evolving. Escaped the cat and is growing a tongue. Wonder where she'll end up?"

Alex's grunt came through the speakers. The only indication he'd even heard what she'd said.

"Hopefully not skewered," Lucy muttered.

"While there's no guarantee, I'm under contract to try to prevent that," Cecelia answered.

"Last time you had the element of surprise," Alex commented through the speaker. "You were just one in a crowd. Now he knows what you look like."

"Oh, it's much worse than that," Cecelia said in her singsong voice. "Now he'll be able to smell you coming, too. It's not just werewolves who have that ability. Vampires have to be able to smell good blood from infected, along with cortisol. It all aids in the hunt."

Great. She really was bait. But if that's what they needed, then that's what she'd do—even if his interest in her wasn't what they all thought.

For two hours, Lucy repeated motivational lines from *Sgt. Sir!* in her head, while watching Cecelia curse as she scanned hundreds of lines of door entry logs. After one particularly crude string of profanities, Alex said, "I'm not sure you're in the right headspace for this at the moment. Why don't you relax or something? Watch some animal videos?"

So, Cecelia pulled up an internet browser and clicked on a playlist of baby bat videos. Followed by rabbits, foxes, foxes catching rabbits, cats, cats chasing mice, and cats chasing laser pointers. Spotting Lucy watching, she shrugged. "Pets aren't allowed in the Fleet."

At last, they pulled into a car park a five-minute walk away from the Skyward Apple Hotel. Alex's voice crackled through the speakers. "Cecelia, hack into the hotel's wireless network and on Lucy's signal trigger the fire alarm. They're a 'modern smart' hotel, so clearly they know their security," he commented sarcastically. "Blakely, use the radar to track him to his room and distract him, then Cecelia will swoop in and secure him. I'll follow after with family members to guard and handle the police."

She screwed her eyes shut.

For Oda.

"Got a spare stunner?"

✣✣✣✣ ✣✣✣✣

"You're early," Fane drawled, as Lucy cracked the door of the hotel room open. He sprawled across the double bed, his arms leisurely folded behind his head. Even with the curtains closed, his gaze pierced through the darkened room, landing on her.

He didn't move. Well, if he didn't want to see her as a threat, that was his mistake.

She flicked on the suit's white light, eliciting a hiss from him as he covered his eyes to block it.

"To be honest, I didn't expect you until after sunset, but by then I'd already be on a flight," he admitted. "Are you even old enough to drive?"

Her eyes narrowed.

Then, in a very human gesture, he sighed. Another lie. He didn't need to breathe.

"Look, I was going to return the notebook, but only when I was far enough away across the sea. Can you blame me?"

More false words. Why should she believe a word that came out of his mouth after what he pulled? This time she wouldn't let him talk her into anything, even by quoting Oda.

Lucy clenched her left fist and raised it, giving the signal. Cecelia sprinted past her through the door and pounced.

Fane's eyes widened, then he leapt towards Lucy. He pulled her with one arm, gripping her to his front; his other hand rose to her neck, the sharp nails grazing her skin.

"How did you escape?" Cecelia growled.

"I don't believe you're in any state to be questioning me," Fane said, pushing his nails slightly more into Lucy's neck, causing a sting. "A second cam-suit? Sorry, but knock-offs are never as satisfying as the original."

"Is that so?" Cecelia said, head cocking like a cat.

"FIRE IN THE BUILDING. PLEASE EVACUATE. FIRE IN THE BUILDING. PLEASE..."

"*Argh!*" The grip on Lucy's neck released as both vampires hunched, hands covering their ears.

Then Fane smirked, straightened, and launched towards Cecelia. Lucy didn't have time to register her shock. She twisted, aimed at the man's back, and pulled the trigger.

A bright blue light flashed from the stun gun, hitting her target square in the back. Fane crumpled to the floor in a heap.

Cecelia also straightened, then barked, "Shut it off," into the radio attached to her hip.

"A thank you would be nice," came Alex's modulated voice, then the alarm shut off, and Cecelia popped out two earplugs.

Rolling Fane onto his back with her silver-toed boot, she bent to his neck and clamped a small device to the escaped convict's collar, which began glowing a sickly green—almost nuclear. Out cold, Fane was oblivious to the recharging.

Lucy scowled at the fallen man, and Cecelia held out her own taser as they waited for backup to arrive.

"Good hunt," Cecelia complimented, baring a fang in a victorious imitation of a smile.

Lucy nodded, her hands shaking with adrenalin. "Th-thanks," she stuttered, still keeping her own stunner trained on him, as well.

Less than three minutes later Alex arrived, stationing guards who Lucy supposed were the Parsons branch of the family outside the room.

"Good shot," he said. "Not exactly to plan, but it worked. Aha," he exclaimed, bending down and pulling out two blue plastic earplugs from the convict's ears. "Easy access to these at a hotel airport."

Good. At least she'd made some impression on him.

"Lia, he got the jump on you. What was that about?"

The blonde growled. "Don't call me Lia! He just had the element of surprise," she ended with a huff. "Not that it matters now," she said, prodding him again with her boot.

"Only fair since you dubbed me Al," he said, bringing out a couple of cable ties and pulling his arms behind his back.

The vampire groaned at the contact, starting to come around.

With Fane's cam-suit having ran out of charge, the group decided to stay inside the suite until evening. Although the Parsons had diverted the police and fire brigade away from the so-called disturbance, attempting to carry a vampire out in a body bag would raise too many eyebrows.

Soon Lucy's arms began trembling under the prolonged effort of holding the stun gun aloft.

"At ease, Miss Blakely," Alex intervened. "I'll take things from here." He pointed a third stunner at the convict. Lucy breathed a sigh of relief. She could only wonder at how her arms would have been burning if it weren't for the enhanced painkillers. Now her part of playing bait was over, she was determined not to be a spare part.

"I'll start looking for Oda," she stated, adrenalin making her voice sound steady even while her insides vibrated. The offer was self-serving, and it twisted her gut. Yes, she was keen to see the naive tree spirit safe and sound, but who knew what Fane would tell them? If he ratted out her part in his escape, perhaps they'd go easy on her if she was the one to recover the notebook? She disgusted herself.

With permission, she set to work, opening every door, lifting surfaces, and turning out every piece of folded material she could find. As her search went on, she became increasingly frantic.

Fane had regained some of his awareness and had propped himself up against a wall. "Your heartbeat is giving me a headache. Calm down," he grouched.

Lucy paused for a moment, then chose to ignore him in favour of turning out a navy-blue cloth bag with a hairdryer in it. If she tried hard enough, maybe she could blank out the creeping dread of Fane's potential exposé of her behaviour.

"If you're awake enough to complain, you're awake enough to answer some questions," Alex said, pulling out a notebook. Then, in a gesture that reminded Lucy of his familial connection to Dave, he pulled a pen out from behind his ear and removed the cover with his teeth.

"Seriously? I think Al Two's been rubbing off on you," Cecelia said, exasperated.

Alex raised an eyebrow above his sunglasses, Fane all-out cackled, and Lucy hid her heating cheeks behind an ironing board.

"You need to brush up your knowledge of male humans, Cissy," he chastised, like a disapproving teacher.

The blonde scowled but cocked her head at the critique.

"My apologies," Fane commented to Alex. "We picked this one up from a monastery."

"Good to know I'm Al Number One at least. As for the analogue method, we know you're an accomplished hacker. Any electronic recording could be doctored. And yes, I suppose Kamal's stiff demeanour has had an effect on me."

This time Lucy pulled down the trouser press, still unable to look at the group.

"How did you escape?" Alex demanded.

"Why would I tell you something that could benefit me again?" Fane rebuked.

Hidden behind the diamond-indented mattress, Lucy froze. He'd covered for her. Again. The evidence that suggested blackmail was stacking up.

"Yes, I expected as much. It was worth a shot. We'll have to keep a guard with you round the clock. Now where's the notebook?" he continued.

Lucy paused her search to watch as Fane cocked his head to the side, grinning mischievously. "That's a secret."

The stunner in Cecelia's hand whirred to life and Fane backed up as far as he could against the wall behind him.

"Okay, okay," he said, lifting his hands in a peace sign. "If you must know, I buried it under a tree."

The mattress in Lucy's hands dropped to the bed frame with a ringing clang, making the vampires wince. Cecelia shot Lucy a dirty look, but

Lucy's mind was too busy to register it. It didn't make sense. If he buried it, how was he going to post it back after crossing the sea? There was a lie in there somewhere but revealing that would mean revealing he'd told her as part of their promise, and she couldn't risk that happening. Biting the inside of her cheek, she mentally returned to her mantra. Silence is golden.

She looked at Alex. "Keep going," he urged. "Try using your phone's light under the wardrobe."

"Where?" Cecelia snapped, jerking the weapon again, threatening.

Draining his face of all emotions, Fane put on the perfect, blank poker face. "I'll tell you in exchange for a request."

"We don't negotiate with prisoners," Alex said icily.

While hunched on her knees, crawling, Lucy's chest squeezed in a freezing grip of guilt.

"How about this, then? As a symbol of goodwill, I'll let you in on a little secret?" His voice was all business, but it rang with an eerie, soothing cadence, one of trust and kindness.

Lucy's eyes widened. This was it. He was going to rat her out. She was done for.

"What about?" Alex asked, his voice deadpan.

The vampire's lips twitched upwards, and he spoke as if recalling a fond memory. "When I'd had enough Crossley generosity last time, I took myself on a tour of your computer system on my way out. Did you know you're housing an artificial intelligence interface?"

Oh. He hadn't he grassed her up. Why?

"It's settled in nicely between your contact book and BIOS. Looks similar to the program created by Duke Harven a few years ago when he took the IT prize for innovation."

He crossed his legs, knit his fingers together, and placed his chin on them. Alex and Cecelia moved in closer.

"You guys have an issue with a fraud investigation going on, don't you? How about I help you investigate this software in exchange for political asylum? I officially ask this in my status as second-in-line to the vampire throne."

Lucy's jaw dropped, Alex's eyes widened, and Cecelia's arm dipped as she faltered.

"Y-you can't," Cecelia stuttered. "We abandoned that system when the Charter was assigned!"

"It brings me no pleasure," Fane muttered, brow wrinkling.

"We bound you. You signed in blood—"

"Apparently, you also need to revise the exact wording of the Charter's jurisdictions, too," Fane snapped. "My quarrel is with the Bureau, not the people here. I suggest, Ambassador, that until I am finished with my diplomatic negotiations, you hold your tongue and remember your place."

Cecelia recoiled, and Alex stepped forward. "This is above my authority," he said, running a hand through his hair. "I'll need to run it by the family head."

"Put me on the phone," Fane ordered.

Alex pulled out a nondescript silver mobile, tapped to dial, and Fane snatched it out of his hands faster than Lucy's eyes could follow.

"I am Fane, second prince of the Coven, and I formally request political asylum with your family."

There was a pause, while Lucy assumed the CEO was speaking.

"I'm aware you've been monitoring the situation, Mrs Crossley. Can I call you Margaret?"

Lucy's upper lip curled at his sickening attempt at civility.

Pause.

"I'll do anything to bring down the Bureau. They're oath-breakers. The software investigation would benefit me, too."

Mrs Crossley wouldn't do a deal with this liar, would she? Lucy's hands twitched, so she set them to use, attempting to place the sheet back on the mattress, shifting her weight from foot to foot in a bid to release her coursing adrenalin.

"I'll allow my collar to be replaced, but not a bio-bomb." Pause. "Yes, as a sign of good faith, I'll blood-seal a radio tracker."

Lucy's stomach dropped. Making a deal with her was one thing, but who was he to strike a deal like this with the CEO?

"I'll only work primarily with Lucy."

Lucy's head shot up.

"She's a person who can be trusted. Oda told me all about her."

Oda again. Her heart panged, but she promised herself she wouldn't fall for it. She couldn't.

"I accept your terms. Tell those Fleet Guards that I'm still on the run. I promise not to leave the grounds."

Then, as casually as old friends, the convict passed the phone back to Alex, who held it up to his ear, and paled at least three shades.

"Put your weapons away," he said, voice wavering. "Fane's now our...guest. Cecelia, I have to remind you under the terms of your employment at Cross-Key & Co. to keep this confidential. I'm not sure the Bureau would even have a protocol or mandate covering these circumstances."

Cecelia dropped her already half-lowered gun, then took off her sunglasses to stare at the vampire directly. Her eyes flashed between cherry and rosewood. "Why?"

"You didn't think the royal line wouldn't leave themselves an out, did you?" His words were soft, and for a brief second, Lucy was almost convinced she heard remorse.

She shook her head, clearing it.

"When can we have Oda back?" Lucy asked, voice strong.

If she was going to have to work with him, she figured she shouldn't be seen as weak.

"I told your boss that I would tell you Oda's location after the fraud case has ended. With any luck, I can bring down those Council liars at the Bureau. Then I won't need my insurance anymore."

There it was again; the insinuation that the members of the Council were liars. Oath breakers. Lucy shuddered. If even a cheater like him was calling them out for their lies, how bad must it be?

## Chapter Eighteen

# Arresting the Truth

"Have you noticed the clouds look like they go on forever? But we know better. The sky's behind it, and that really seems like it's going to go on forever. Like the sea," Will rambled, wondering aloud.

It was cute, Lucy mused. Like a young, excited puppy exploring a brand new world, but instead of having his head and nose to the ground, he looked up to the grey February sky. She thought it was dull, but to Will, it was magical. She decided to humour him.

"When did that occur to you?" she asked. She was glad for the distraction. The idea of what they were about to do made her shudder. Confrontation was never easy.

The industrial estate was quiet for a Saturday morning, but it was still open for business—a few cars passed by every now and again. Lucy spotted the tell-tale metallic green of the Usmani family car and tried not to grimace.

"Just now," he answered cheerfully. "The sea and sky...they're beauties. We haven't found any other worlds so far like this one. I'm lucky to be here."

"And I'm happy you're here, too," she confessed. "Very happy."

She felt her cheeks heat. Oh boy. She had not just said that! But she had. She'd heard the words come right out of her mouth.

There was a beat of silence before Will responded.

"Ruǧa," he said softly, and her brain all but melted. "You're kind, caring, and braver than anyone I've ever met. I mean, you went after Fane. Twice."

*Yes, but,* her brain continued. If she hadn't let him escape in the first place, then she wouldn't have needed to. Not that he knew that, though, so she waited for his inevitable *but.* Waited to be the butt of the joke.

"I'm very glad to have met you," he said, and Lucy's heart pumped in her ears. "And I'd love to get to know you more—really—but if I don't get kicked out of my job, then I'll still only be allowed to stay in my post for three years. Then... Well... Wolves partner for life."

The already dwindling balloon of hope popped. It wasn't an "I love you." Why would it be? And then there was Trisha—Red—who made him blush when she was around. And to top it all off, he'd diverted the conversation with hard fact. In three years' time, he'd have to leave. Not just Cross-Key or even the country, but the planet. Then, someone else would be sent to take his place.

Biting her wavering lip, she reached out and placed a hand on his shoulder in an 'It's OK. No hard feelings' gesture, but stared off to the side at the bushes lining the path instead of meeting his gaze.

She thought over his words. *Brave?* More like stupid. *Caring?* What good was that if she always hurt at least one person to please another? And as for *kind?* Thinking about what she was about to do almost had her bringing up her morning toast.

Will began propelling himself again and Lucy pulled her arm away, forcing herself towards their unpleasant task.

They entered through the revolving door and spotted Hina at reception, exactly like the timetable Will brought had detailed. She wore a stylish crimson blazer, accentuating the fading henna on her hands, now tinged orange as she spoke into a phone.

She looked up and waved with her other hand as she finished the call. "You, too. See you next week," she finished, and put down the receiver. "This is a pleasant surprise. Congrats on yesterday's haul," she said, before delivering the trademark Crossley wink. "What can I do for you?"

Lucy's voice died in her throat. Spotting her distress, Will jumped in to cover. "It's about my brother," he said.

"One of my favourite topics. Do go on," she said, unfurling her wrist.

"Has he been in contact with you recently?" Will asked.

Hina glanced around the atrium before standing to lean over the desk and tapped a finger to her nose. "I'm not really supposed to talk about it, but yes. The special deliveries have to be kept away from our regular merchandise. Company secrets, you know," she said in a voice a shade louder than a whisper.

Special deliveries? Lucy kept her face as blank as possible as Will continued.

"I don't know a lot about what Duke does day-to-day, but when you say deliveries, you mean...?"

"The orders. That you work on sending. He sends them to me to direct," she said, her eyes casting over in a dreamy daze.

Steeling herself, Lucy gulped and blurted out, "Can I see one? An order?"

"I don't see why not. You're as good as family at this point," she said, then turned to her computer and began clicking through screens.

Lucy's brain screeched to a halt. Family. Hina considered her family. The hum of the printer dialled her heart rate up, as her fears were potentially being printed into existence.

"If you're after something specific, let me know. I heard you're having issues with stock, and I know Dave isn't doing anything wrong." She pushed a couple of sheets over the counter.

"Here's the last thing I got from him. It's a bit personal in parts," she said, cheeks turning rosy.

"You've been a big help. We'll make sure everyone gets what they ordered," Will said as Lucy picked up the sheet. She blanched as she read it.

```
Little Star,
Not a day passes when I don't think of you.
You continue to be a beacon of light among
the darkest recesses of space.
Don't worry. It will be soon.
I'm happy to hear that Lucy seems to have
settled in well. I look forward to meeting her
when I get the chance. Any friend of yours is
a friend of mine!
I've attached another list of special deliv-
eries for you.
Continue to shine!
Yours,
Duke
```

Lucy bit her lower lip and handed the top sheet over to Will, before pouring over the list of items on the second. She didn't know what half of them were, so quickly handed over that list to Will as well, who'd turned green.

"This may have just solved all of our problems," she said.

Will looked up from the sheets and grimaced. "I'm sorry, but this isn't my brother."

Hina's right eye twitched. "What? Of course, it is. I've been in touch with him for months. He got a job at the Imports Section so he could contact me directly." She pivoted her computer monitor around so they could see. Months of emails from sender Duke Harven. Then in January, orders attachments began.

"He doesn't work in Imports. He's a Fleet Guard, like your police," Will explained.

"Well, that's just a job title," Hina snapped. "How do you know he can't be both?"

Lucy inhaled slowly, then breathed out the truth. "That can't be Duke. He said he looks forward to meeting me one day, but we already met at the Bureau. You know I did. You saw him in the picture I drew for Will's birthday."

Hina stepped back, hand clutched to her chest, tears welling.

Lucy launched herself at the crumbling teen, pulling her into a hug. Her nose wrinkled at the mix of apple shampoo and lavender perfume, but she didn't pull away.

"Then..." Hina paused, fighting back sobs. "Who have I been speaking to?" she choked out.

"I don't know, but we'll find out. Don't worry, nothing bad is going to happen," Will reassured her.

Lucy looked up over Hina's shoulders and spotted Will making a series of hand gestures to the camera above the reception desk.

"He's real. He has to be," Hina argued, and Lucy held her tighter, her insides shattering as she knew what she had to do—had to say.

"You saw the picture I drew. I could do that because I met him," she repeated.

"How do you know it wasn't someone else? That you didn't get confused?" she pleaded.

"Dave introduced us. I'm sorry. And Duke doesn't seem like the type to forget someone like that. Or Will his brother."

Hina slumped in her arms, the fight leaving her. Lucy shifted her weight and supported the girl into her chair behind the desk.

Lucy pivoted the screen back around and Hina glanced up at it, the sight sending her into a fresh round of sobbing.

"What have I done?" she wailed.

"You did your job. How were you supposed to know it wasn't him?" Lucy answered.

Hina took out a white silk pocket tissue with the Cross-Key logo embroidered into the corner. "You're right," she said, dabbing away the mix of tears and running mascara. "I knew what he said in the email didn't make sense. About meeting you. But I ignored it and..." She waved a hand, unable to speak, and Lucy, too, choked, as once again something she'd said caused the girl to crumble.

As a SWAT team of security entered the reception room, Lucy had never felt so useless. "What happened?" Alex asked, leading the group.

Will held out the email to him. "Cyber security breach. Hina's been receiving instructions for redirecting delivery shipments for weeks. They impersonated my brother—looks like for months. Dry food packs, vaso-constrictors, hydration tablets, water, blankets... They match the missing orders."

Alex stared down at the list then at the crying girl. "Well found. Miss Usmani, please come with me." He turned to the Guards and ordered, "Take it in turns to cover the reception desk. Two-hour rotations. You two, find the key to Warehouse 23B and report back what you find."

The Guards nodded and divided themselves.

Alex pulled his radio from a belt at his hip. "Fane. Please run a check on Hina Usmani's emails. Find out all you can about the sender called Duke Harven."

"My pleasure," drawled a voice through the speaker, followed by a crack of knuckles.

A hand on her wrist made Lucy jump, and she followed it to Will, who had joined her side. Without thinking, she twisted, pushing their palms together and interlacing their fingers.

Hina, however, remained slumped and frozen, unable to respond as the world shifted around them. It was excruciating to watch.

Realising the teen wasn't moving, Alex froze and crouched down to her level. "We can't do the interview here. Come upstairs and have some tea. I have a new pack of bonbons that I need someone to share with."

"Are they O negative flavoured?" crackled a voice through the speaker.

"Even if they were, you're not the one crying here," the security manager snapped back.

"True. Pretty sure this is the first case of intergalactic catfishing ever recorded. The account's fake," Fane confirmed.

Hina whimpered. "I thought he loved me," she choked out, before doubling over into sobs again, and Lucy's heart ripped in two.

Alex placed a consoling hand on her shoulder.

"I'm sorry you're going through this. I promise we'll catch whoever this is and they'll be punished, but I need you to come upstairs and answer some questions. Then the CEO and I can get to work."

"Oh no—Great Aunt Marge!" Hina wailed, and Lucy turned her head away from the excruciating sight.

"Auntie's fair and lenient, and you're a good worker. With a bit of luck we can get this finished long before your father arrives for work. Come on."

Hina said nothing but shakily stood—the threat of facing her father finally pushing her into action.

"You two," Alex ordered Lucy and Will, "Good work. You can go, but stay close. It'll be nice for you and Hina to grab lunch all together, won't it?"

Lucy nodded automatically, but what comfort could she dare give? She'd just ripped her friend's feet out from under her, again, with her words.

Her breath quickened, and she felt it pulsing in her ears. The sound of the world faded in and out, and she only caught snippets.

"...AI created a profile..."

"...engineered back through the portal..."

"...someone at the Fleet, no doubt about it..."

Something gripped her hand. She blinked, the sensation pulling her out of her head. Will's warm fingers clenched around hers, and she looked into large, concerned eyes.

She blinked at him, thankful for the grounding, but couldn't muster a sound as her freeze took hold—her thoughts overrun by a single chanting mantra: *Off with her head.*

⚜ ⚜

Lucy and Will sat on a bench a block away, staring away from the industrial estate to the rolling countryside. Cars roared by, breaking the heavy silence once in a while, when Will wasn't trying to mutter unfounded reassurances. His heart was in the right place, Lucy mused, but the picture of an angry Queen of Hearts kept popping up, causing her confidence to cower in a corner.

Her shoulders ached from her hunch, but she couldn't bring herself to care about posture, all things considered.

Consumed in thought, she barely noticed the time pass until Will answered a call.

"Mr Matisse has finished his questioning," he explained. "Let's go get Hina, then try out that little canteen around the corner."

Standing, Lucy followed the self-propelling teen for a time. She wanted to reach out for the handles—to ask if he wanted help—but she stopped, right arm half outstretched, and lowered it again. He wouldn't want help. She'd just make things worse.

Hina greeted them with a shaky smile, rubbing mascara onto her sleeves as she dried away her tears. "Lunch?" she asked, voice wavering, and Lucy stared in amazement at her friend's attempt at composure.

The trio shared a subdued lunch together in the nearest canteen to headquarters.

Hina stared down at her plate, played with her food, and looked like she was about to burst into tears at any moment.

"You'll be alright. Don't worry about it," Will said, jabbing at a potato with his fork. "We found the missing stock, and that's what matters, right?"

Hina said nothing.

Lucy didn't know what to do. They hadn't spoken since they were children, and she realised that other than for the past couple of weeks, they were pretty much strangers. She didn't know who this girl was or how to help her, but she desperately wanted to.

Lucy's communicator buzzed in her pocket and she pulled it out. Will and Hina moved at the same time.

Miss Blakely,
We invite you to attend a meeting currently being held at Chief Executive Officer Margaret Crossley's Office. If you are attending, please arrive as soon as possible. If you must decline, please respond immediately.
Signed, Mrs M Crossley, CEO's Office

"Did you get the invite?" Lucy asked, voice barely more than a whisper. Her gut wrenched.

On arrival the trio were ushered straight into Margaret's office.

Alex stood next to Cecelia—their expressions blank and unreadable behind sunglasses. Mrs Crossley sat in her chair behind her desk and to her right—

"How lovely to see you again, dear. Although I wish it was under better circumstances."

Trisha stood to Margaret's other side, and behind her were a group of three pale men, all wearing grey suits and sunglasses, the Fleet Guards insignia on their chests. Then the lady turned and walked around the desk, placing her hands on both of Hina's slumped shoulders in support.

"You'll be alright, Cuz. I'll make sure of it," she said.

The teen sniffed in response, relaxing into the redhead's touch.

The door closed behind them, and Lucy started. She forced her face to stay as neutral as possible, as if she hadn't just jumped through the ceiling and her cheeks burned. But her embarrassment was immediately quashed when she saw Hina by her side, eyes glistening with a fresh batch of tears.

Thankfully, Trisha had gotten there to comfort the teen first. She was the girl's family. Lucy felt cold. Separate. Like the infringing outsider.

Mrs Crossley sighed, knitting her hands together on her desk, her brow furrowed into lines. "Alex has briefed me thoroughly on today's events, including Miss Usmani's testimony from this morning. Thank you, Hina, I know it was difficult for you."

The girl raised her head.

"I'm pleased to report that we've found all the missing stock. The warehouse in question has not been in use for months and we've had it earmarked for demolition in spring. It's safe to say that whoever the culprit is knew that."

Lucy shifted her weight, taken aback by the implication. It was someone on the inside? The air in the room was thick as they all hung on to Margaret's every word.

"After discovering the security breach in our systems, I immediately reported the incident to the Bureau, who could confirm that the creator of the rogue software was Duke Harven. Upon hearing this, he voluntarily submitted himself into custody for questioning as a suspect."

*Thunk!*

A glass rolled onto the floor, spilling water at the pool of Will's chair. His hands shook.

Lucy stepped forward but stopped as the aged woman raised her hand. She gulped—a black hole opening in the pit of her stomach as the CEO locked eyes with Will.

"Mr Harven. These Guards are here to escort you to the Bureau."

The three stepped forward. One was holding handcuffs. From their small stature and the fact that they could stand upright against the force of gravity, they must have been vampires.

"As it stands, you are the one here with the connection to Duke, the software's apparent creator, and you have had extensive access to the orders going through the HAT machine and shipment process. I'm sorry," Mrs Crossley said as the trio of vampires stepped forwards, one holding a collar that she recognized.

Lucy gasped.

"You're under arrest for attempted fraud, illegal use of Fleet technology on Earth, and unauthorised communication via the portal network," said the Guard on the left.

Trisha stepped forward, her face pale around her blusher. "Is this really necessary? He's in the middle of his moon cycle. Can't we just—"

"You know the rules," Mrs Crossley cut across her. "In accordance with our treaty, we must hand him over."

"It's alright," Will said. A steely glint of amber flashed across his eyes as they surrounded him. "Like my brother, I want to get myself cleared quickly so they can find the real culprit."

A Guard secured the collar around his neck, while another took the handles behind his chair and the third opened the office door.

Lucy stood, jaw gaping as she watched Will get wheeled away, her dinner making itself known.

"I'll do what I can to get him back," hurried Trisha. "I'll pull in every favour I have if I have to," she said, then bolted out the door behind them.

Lucy couldn't move. Her throat constricted. She needed to move. Why couldn't she move? Why couldn't she do what Trisha had?!

"Miss Usmani," the CEO barked, startling both girls out of their reveries. "You failed to double-check the authority of the orders you were being sent. That naive and grievous misjudgement put the integrity of our entire operation at risk."

Hina looked as if she'd been slapped. She covered her face with her hands and crumpled into a mess of tears in the chair opposite the CEO's desk.

"The Guards will return to speak to you later. You can see how serious this was not just for ourselves, but for the Fleet, too, to send vampires to Earth in broad daylight, when they didn't send them to recapture an escaped convict. This is now an interspecies matter. As for Cross-Key, you are hereby suspended, and an official investigation into your conduct is being launched."

Then, the older woman's expression softened with her voice.

"I've informed your father. Kamal will be coming in the next half hour to take you home."

Clenching her hands, Lucy's nails dug into her fisted palms. Hina's father was a security manager, and this was a major security issue. It was no wonder Hina had gone from flushed, to red, to grey.

"Miss Blakely." Lucy glanced up at her name. "Thank you for your continued support in this case. We recovered the missing stock because of your due diligence. I'll be arranging a suitable bonus for you." He smiled, like the fleeting smile her parents gave her when she abandoned her best friend last time.

Hina suspended. Will arrested. Was losing friends always going to happen when she opened her stupid mouth? She'd been right all along. The freezes really did protect her from herself. Silence was golden.

The self-berating lasted all the way back to the residential building—alone—where she collapsed into a heap on her duvet.

Images of Hina, as empty as a broken rag doll, flickered behind her closed eyelids. Her father furiously tugging her out of the CEO's office and bundling her into his car.

Guitar ripped through her thoughts, followed by bombastic brass. But this time, the *Sgt. Sir!* theme failed to raise her spirits.

Words had wrecked her life again. She didn't need more. Couldn't take more.

Weakly, she pulled the phone out of her pocket.

Dad flashed across the screen.

Her hands shook as she swiped up to answer, and her throat closed, choking off any attempt at a greeting.

"Lucy!" His voice rumbled like rolling thunder. "How dare you not turn up to babysit? Your mum invited you to that conference for free, and this is how you repay us?"

Lucy bit her bottom lip to stop it from trembling.

"Passing us off to strangers. Do we mean that little to you? Don't let that big job of yours go to your head. Your mother works tirelessly for our sake. I was a deputy editor. The least you can do is pitch in."

Big job? But he'd been so proud of her before...hadn't he? What was she meant to do—split herself in two, to be in two places at once?

"We didn't raise you to be ungrateful. You never call. You don't offer support. And you didn't have the decency to say goodbye to your own mum at the conference. Yes, I heard all about that."

It was true. She didn't get to say goodbye. But surely saving her mum's life from a vampire on the loose counted for something? But even if it did...no. She didn't call. Why would she? Nothing she'd ever done was enough. Cancelling, changing, rearranging her own plans was never enough. She was never enough.

"I was so worried about finding a stranger to babysit that I couldn't properly prepare for my job interview. Next time before passing the buck, try to think about the knock-on effect of your words on people other than you."

A long dial tone beeped, and the call was dead.

Rising waves of tension racked her body, then exploded in a torrent of tears.

Her parents angry—and that was in writing never mind speech. Hina was suspended. Will arrested. Oda missing. And there was no guarantee Fane would ever give the notebook back. She'd messed that up, too. Why would anyone want her around? She was a liability.

Squinting through floods, she scrolled through the options on her phone before escaping into the brass bravado of the *Sgt. Sir!* soundtrack on repeat, loud enough to drown out her sobs.

# CHAPTER NINETEEN

# THE NATURE OF THINGS

The night came and went with one less vampire on the loose, and one less werewolf on Earth. That would have made her feel better before she'd got Will as a flatmate.

She went about her morning routine on autopilot. But there were only so many lessons she could pre-plan for the tree spirit. Her feet aimlessly took her back to Oda's empty underground dome. The commute had the eerie calm that only Sunday could bring, bar the odd car on the main road outside of the estate. The wind bent bare branches—empty of leaves and life—like her missing tree spirit, arrested flatmate, and suspended best friend.

Before her job at Cross-Key & Co. she'd been fine on her own. She'd often turned down after-school invites with her classmates, to run to get back to cook dinner, or look after Ben instead. To keep her parents happy.

The industrial park was as ghostly and bereft as she felt. Misplaced. Wrong. It needed life. People. Movement.

A sudden, powerful gust pressed against her back, sweeping her forwards down the path towards a line of trees that she couldn't identify. They bowed and danced in the breeze, like responding to a conductor. She wanted to know what type they were but would have to wait until they sprouted leaves to know.

They'd come back budding, fighting harsh weather to burst into life again, and Lucy admired their fight.

What would Oda do right now? Go wherever the breeze led them? Or stand rooted, firm but flexible against the wind?

Her imagination showed her the answer.

A single apple dropped from a branch, thrown so enthusiastically people would have to duck to avoid being hit.

What would Hina do?

The feisty girl came to mind. She'd wipe her tears on her cuff, then punch one fist into her other hand.

Then what would Lucy do in this situation? What should she do? What could she do? Should, would, could. That line of thinking led nowhere. She rubbed her eyes in frustration, let out a deep breath, and tried again.

What did *Lucy* do? Lucy drew. That was her dream job, and she'd been doing it, albeit briefly. It was the first time she'd ever stuck her neck out for something that she wanted, instead of giving in to parental expectation.

She stopped, as if struck by lightning. She'd gotten her job when her dad hadn't. It wasn't lack of preparation for the interview that lost him his interview but his failed business. That meant he wasn't upset with her. He was jealous of her.

So adults, even parents, made mistakes too. How many words or lies of theirs had been down to mistakes?

Just like Hina not checking her emails; and Dave and Will's arrests? And mistakes could be rectified.

It was time for Sgt. Sir!'s steps for success.

Goal: Keep her job.

How: Rescue Oda. Get her friends back.

Resources: One fraud case. One Security Department. One vampire hacker in the basement.

Clutching her satchel tightly, she turned, changing trajectory from the underground dome to Headquarters, taking the stairs two at a time to Security.

❦

Raised voices came from the Security room.

"I want to stay. My daughter's failure led to this security breach. It's my duty as her father to put things right," he stressed.

"Kamal," Alex intoned with a sigh. "I understand that's how you feel, but it's not your place. Hina needs you at home to support her, and you need rest. Let us take care of things here. This is my jurisdiction during the day."

Lucy coughed to announce her presence, and the pair turned to look at her. She took a deep breath then asked, "Is there any news?"

Kamal unfolded his arms. "Nothing yet. Thank you, Miss Blakely, for helping my daughter to see the lapse in her judgment." He looked as haggard as Alex after a double shift.

"Alex is right. I think you should get some rest. If we've found the supplies, who knows what the person behind this will do next? What they needed them for? We'll need you at your best for whatever their next move is." Lucy wasn't sure when she thought she could start talking to the man as an equal, but when Mr Usmani's face softened, she knew it had been the right line to take.

"You make a good point. I'll be back for my usual shift tonight. Call me if anything comes up. Anything. I want to be ready."

Alex nodded, then the balding man strode out of the room, the door sliding closed behind him with a heavy *thunk*.

"Thanks. I made the same point. But he'll listen to you, since you helped his daughter."

Lucy's fingers ached as she clutched her satchel tighter. "I don't know about help. More like caused a world of hurt and trouble."

Alex ran a hand through already unkempt curls and slouched against a desk. "Look, broken hearts can mend. Who knows what else this mysterious Harven interface messed up? For all we know, Hina's emails were the tip of the iceberg."

"Any news on Will?"

The blond leaned back onto his counter and pulled out a bag of chews. "Trisha's on the case, and that's the best we could possibly hope for."

Lucy squirmed. "She mentioned using favours..." she trailed.

"Ah, yes. About that. Dave and I were born six months apart. Given our ages and the age of the CEO, we were prime candidates to start training to take her place when we grew up. Not that we knew we were being trained for it at the time."

After pulling a computer chair over, Lucy sat, her eyes fixed on the manager.

"Then, ten years later, Trisha arrived. Growing up, she saw what we didn't. What our parents had in mind for us. She wanted in, but a ten-year-experience gap is hard to fill. So, she climbed her way up the only way she could. Collecting favours. Then two years later Hina came along, and Trisha has a soft spot for her, probably sympathising with another Crossley child who missed out on the succession race by age."

So, she was empathetic, smart, and ambitious. Lucy was outclassed on all fronts. After all, she couldn't lift a finger to help Will, but Trisha could and would. And Trisha was a Crossley, so she could remain close to the Fleet. Wasn't that the sort of person Will deserved to be with?

It was too painful to think about, so she brought the conversation back on track.

"Has our *friend* found anything yet?" she asked, conscious of any listening ears. Thankfully, there were only a couple at the far end of the room and they were on the phone. She figured the rest must be on patrol.

"According to Kamal, our *friend* has been asking for you. He refuses to talk to anyone else. Given his current political asylum, I'm obligated to pass on his request. I appreciate after what he pulled last time if you want to say no, but we really could use his help." The day manager looked weary, with a wrinkled, pained expression as he said the last part. His unspoken plea was all too clear.

"I'll go find out what he wants," Lucy replied, straightening her back to fight off the jitters creeping up. Being in the same room as the convict freaked her out. She strode over to the door in stiff, jerky movements.

He nodded. "You'll have access to your panic button at all times. If he tries anything funny, his asylum ends." His eyes narrowed and Lucy thought she was lucky to have such protective...friends? Were they friends?

She smiled at the possibility, and woodenly walked down to Fane's personal dome. When this was all over, she mused, she was going to buy the manager a large bag of powdery purple fruit bonbons. The bag beneath the monitor looked almost empty.

***

"Finally, someone I can actually talk to," Fane exclaimed as Lucy entered his sub-level dome.

The sight of the escaped vampire convict flooded her system with fight, flight or freeze.

Lucy forced herself to move through the sludge, raising an eyebrow and pushing herself to approach and perch on a chair inside the horseshoe of monitors.

It was silent other than the back wall, where towering grey processors whirred and hummed, filling the space with the smell of burning plastic and dust. Thankfully, Lucy spotted a well-placed air vent, which reminded her to breathe.

Fane lifted his hands off a keyboard and gave a mock bow.

"Knocking your friend down a peg was a marvellous performance the other day. I applaud your logical thinking."

Her spine tingled the way it always did when he spoke to her, as if layered with ASMR. It was mesmeric.

She forced herself to look at the screens, not rising to the comment in case it was bait. "You said that the emails were generated by the system?" she probed. After all, all that computer stuff was beyond her.

Fane wrinkled his nose. "Duke took modules in computer science as part of his scholarship pathway. For his final project, he created an artificially intelligent program to aid engineers in reporting bugs and mechanical failures across the Fleet. Impressive stuff. His award was well deserved."

Lucy narrowed her eyes as he talked, saying silently, *get to the point*.

"Anyway," he continued, message received, "I found it installed in Cross-Key's systems. It's created a false email address, assigned Duke's profile to it, and created a back door into the mainframe where all the Fleet's orders are processed."

Lucy's mind reeled, trying to catch up.

"So, they think Will installed the software?" she asked.

"Yes."

"Can you find out when the software was installed?"

"I like you more and more each time I see you," the vampire said, flashing a toothy grin at her.

Lucy shuddered.

"I thought the same thing, so I've already checked."

He tapped a couple of buttons and the monitor to her left blinked to life, showing lines of code.

"The software became active on the day Will Harven began his internship with Cross-Key."

She sucked in sharply.

"However," Fane all but purred, "it was installed six months before he arrived, lying dormant."

Lucy sat up straighter. "So, Will couldn't have installed the software because he wasn't here," she said.

"Yes," he replied, holding up a finger to pause her. "But that doesn't mean he wasn't complicit in this scheme. The timing indicates he may have known about its existence and activated it as soon as he arrived. It was installed during Duke Harven's tenure as ambassador."

Her shoulders shrank.

"Maybe the software could have had a delay on it, to activate when Will arrived to frame."

A devilish smirk appeared on the convict's face. "Very good," he said, waving his forefinger.

"That is also a possibility we cannot disprove. What we can prove, however..." he trailed off and pressed a few more buttons. The screen shifted again to a blurry CCTV image of a beach. 1:26 a.m. was timestamped in blocky white letters, and a massive outline of something huge and furry filled the bottom left corner. "...is that Duke Harven was very much indisposed during the time of installation. That lessens the link to Duke, and therefore your wolf's involvement."

Heat rose to her cheeks. She opened her mouth to object, but the words died in her throat. Her wolf. She liked the term but knew it didn't belong to her, and shook the image of Trisha out of her mind. They had work to do, and she would not let her love life, or lack thereof, become a source of entertainment for this vampire.

"This is important," she said, rising out of her seat. "We should tell Alex."

"Not so fast, little one," Fane said, waggling his forefinger again.

Lucy grit her teeth.

"That leaves us with a very big problem of who did plant the software if it wasn't the Harven brothers? It means that the true culprit is still at large."

Cogs turned in Lucy's brain. "A set-up of both Harven brothers—who knew they'd be coming? Who oversees the selection of ambassadors?"

Two pointed fangs bared as Fane grinned nastily, his face transforming in disgust. "The Councillors and the Grand Bureau Member," he spat.

"So, it could be the Grand Bureau Member?" she asked tentatively. Fane's pupils narrowed to black pinpricks in a swirling pool of blood and vermilion.

"That's what I'm trying to understand, but there is no solid evidence yet of her involvement. But there will be. I'll find it."

Lucy shuddered again, less from thrall, and was suddenly very aware of how close she was to a furious predator.

Playing it safe, she tiptoed around the topic instead.

"Is Oda alright?"

The vampire's face softened, along with his icy tone.

"I checked in with our little friend earlier. Oda's doing fine." Lucy's scalp tingled. She was calm again, dropping back and melting into her seat. She shouldn't be this calm, should she?

"I'm being honest when I say I don't want to keep you separate for much longer. I think you're good for one another."

A lump rose in Lucy's throat. It sounded good. Having Oda back. It was what she wanted.

"When?" she asked, just as softly. No. This was code red. A *Sgt. Sir!* code red mission. She needed to snap out of whatever relaxing trance Fane was putting her in. Code red demanded action.

*One, two, three!* She bit her lower lip harshly, and pain ran through her, sharp enough to bypass the painkillers she'd taken. Her brain cleared of fog, and she sat upright.

Fane shot across the room, hands against her shoulders, wheeling the office chair and her up to the wall.

His eyes were wide. Wild. He licked his lips, running a tongue across his fangs.

"Clever but stupid. You're playing with fire," he said, gripping her coat jacket.

Lucy stared back, frozen, but then felt the distinct tang of metal, copper, in her mouth. Her lip was bleeding.

Her right hand whipped to her mouth, the other to the communicator in her pocket, ready to hit panic.

Fane sniffed. And again. But he didn't move.

She pulled her hand away from her lip. Just a split. That was all. She could do this.

"That coconut lip balm is disgusting," he said, withdrawing. "I don't need those chemicals polluting my system."

Lucy slumped in relief and promised to buy her mother an entire bag of replacement coconut balms.

They were off track. Again. She balled her fists.

"What do I have to do to get Oda back? What are you waiting for?" she demanded, too shakily for her liking, but it was something.

The vampire turned away, crossing his arms as he walked back to the monitors. "I already said. Oda's my insurance policy. The Crossleys are harbouring me on the condition that I help them solve this fraud case. I want to make the Grand Bureau Member and her loyal dog followers squirm. Until I can track this fraud case back to them, keeping Oda out of their hands is one of the best ways to make them squirm."

It was hard to see how Oda could make anyone squirm. They were too caring, and it wasn't as if Oda could actually speak.

"I don't think Oda poses any threat to exposing your existence to humans. The tree spirits, maybe. But who would make the leap to vampires? Or werewolves?"

The prince, in an uncomfortably human gesture, ran a hand through his hair.

"Werewolves, and especially vampires, like to think they've already discovered everything worth knowing. Oda is new. And new means they don't know something. It challenges their position as top dog in the universe. To them, anything new is unnatural, so our friend's nature, I'm afraid, will be misunderstood completely."

"That's not fair," Lucy stated, crossing one knee over the other and folding her arms. "Surely if they exist, then there's a species even more intelligent out there? Like an alien or something?"

Fane's eyes darkened, changing from vermilion to hardened coal. His voice dropped to a pitch just above a growl. "They've spent so much time thinking of themselves as the next stage of evolution that anything other than themselves is automatically deemed a threat to their progress. Both species are as bad as each other."

Anger radiated off him in waves as he turned and punched. *Crack!* Lucy shielded her eyes from a storm cloud of dust, lowering her arms to see a fist-size chunk of rock carved out the wall.

"I loved a woman," he said, voice cracking. "A werewolf. She came to the end of her natural lifespan, and I couldn't bear to watch her leave. I tried to give her eternal life. The Council executed her as an abomination of existence—something unnatural. A vampire-werewolf hybrid. I've been stuck in prison ever since."

Lucy couldn't hold back tears as Fane spoke. The utter sorrow in his voice sprang tears in Lucy's eyes.

"That's disgraceful," she said. "She didn't do anything wrong."

Fane's frame trembled—taut—beneath his skin. They locked eyes. His black irises swirled with strips of red again.

"And that's precisely the reason I like you so much. You care. I think it's something most of my kind forgot how to do long ago with no humans around to teach us."

# CHAPTER TWENTY

# ALPHA

M elodic chimes rang over the din of computer processors. Fane reached into his lab coat pocket and pulled out an old-fashioned radio: a chunky black brick with a thick antenna poking out the top.

"Can I help you?" he drawled, back to his usual pompous self, but at this point Lucy suspected it was a mask. At least she'd like to think so.

"Hello there! It's Dave from Head Office," Dave's voice crackled, enthusiasm radiating from him in waves.

"And what do you want, Dave from Head Office?" Fane deadpanned.

"Now, now," Dave admonished, and Lucy could imagine the finger waggling. "I decided to come in early since my shift tonight is uncertain, and I came across a delightful bit of footage that I'd like to share."

The man's ability to sound positive while things were so turbulent genuinely impressed Lucy.

"Well, get a move on and send it," Fane huffed.

"Great. Lucy, I know you're down there. I think you'll enjoy this, especially." She cocked an eyebrow in curiosity as Fane accepted the file, beginning the transfer. A few more clicks and the wall of monitors switched from displaying multiple video feeds to one large image.

The bright white timestamp flashed across a dark scene: 01:04. In the centre hunched Dave, who waved jovially at the camera, then pointed at something over his shoulder. He shuffled out of the way, revealing a large stretch of beach. The waves shimmered against the shore, lit under an enormous round moon.

Then came a sharp whistle and a large stick went flying across the screen, followed swiftly by a hulking furry blob.

Lucy burst into giggles. They actually played fetch.

Clearly unhappy with the stick, the auburn-and-mahogany wolf came trotting back into focus, dragging a large tree branch in his mouth, tail wagging.

Behind him was Dave, who laid down a large sheet of tarpaulin on the sand, before tipping bucket after bucket of items onto it in an enormous pile.

The wolf sniffed the air, dropped the tree branch, then loped towards the pile with an excited growl. Dave made a hasty retreat, arm raised in a peace gesture as the wolf raised his hackles at him before sticking his head into the pile. From the middle of the meat pile, he prised out some sort of leg with a hoof on the end, then lay down with his prize between his paws before ripping it apart.

Dave picked up the camera, and tried to approach the wolf but stopped as the wolf froze, staring him straight with glowing amber in the darkness, lips curled in a snarl.

Fane pressed his hand to the screen. "A rare treat; a pure wolf-child out to play. But I don't remember ever seeing one that large or with anything other than yellow eyes. Very unusual."

Dave's voice crackled again from the brick like receiver. "We saw this phenomenon happen once before with Will's brother. We believe the separation from the other wolves is forcing an alpha change—a sort of survival technique to establish a colony in a new area when—" Distorted ringing cut across his speech and they heard Dave answer, "Cross-Key

International Operations, Dave Crossley speaking." Then the radio shut off. Apparently, the future CEO in training was as in demand as ever.

"I liked it when things were simple," Fane reminisced, rubbing his goatee. "When vampires could hunt humans, and werewolves could roam the mountains, picking off hermits and lost travellers…" He trailed off as a loud crunch rang through the room as Will's canine-filled jaws splintered the leg in two, cracking through the bone.

Clearly done, the wolf then pawed at the tarpaulin, shoving it aside, then continued to dig a hole and promptly started burying the goods. At the other side of the pile, Dave dangled a chicken in the air, waving it. Will stopped in his tracks, transfixed, before Dave launched the chicken forwards. The wolf sped after it, kicking up sand as he raced to reach it before it hit the ground. He was a territorial playful puppy.

Even when Will wasn't physically there or human, he still found a way to cheer Lucy up. A warm glow lit in her chest.

But Dave's words echoed round and round in her head.

"Fane?" she asked tentatively.

After receiving a grunt in response, she asked, "I thought having werewolf ambassadors here was tradition, so why would only Duke and Will become alphas?"

Fane scratched his chin. "Never given it much thought, myself. Genetics, maybe? You're better off asking someone who cares."

Lucy's brain buzzed as she mentally raked over what she knew of Will's history. A pack thing. What constituted a pack? A group of friends? A family unit? Was it genetic? And if so, why did it pop up in this generation?

Something niggled away at the back of her brain, and she scrunched her nose in annoyance as it danced just outside her grasp.

The two sat again in companionable silence with the sound of Fane's clicking keys accompanying the image of a happy werewolf on his haunches, digging a hole and burying bits of leftover meat.

When it was clear that Fane had returned to his work and she wasn't going to get anything more from him, she took a seat and pulled out her future lesson plans for Oda. But as much as she tried to concentrate on the insects she was sketching, her eyes kept drawing up to the looping footage of Will, like a moth to light.

It took her a while before she realised what was off about the playful canine. Dogs expressed themselves in their faces, using their eyebrows in a very human-like way. But Will's face was fixed, his gaze straight and penetrating. His stare was stern, with all his emotions on display in his flaming, amber irises. Will was all wolf.

After a few hours, Lucy pulled herself away from the footage in search of some food, Oda's lesson plans all but abandoned. The mystery of the alpha circled in her brain as she distractedly meandered to the canteen. She'd sat down and barely touched her jacket potato before Dave came rushing in with an enormous grin plastered all over his face.

"Hey! Good news. Are you finished eating? Never mind. Bring it with you. Come on," and with that, he grabbed a carton, pushed the contents of her plate into it, and had her herded out the door before she could protest.

The route was a well-travelled one, to Margaret Crossley's office. "Wait here. There's someone in there dying to meet you," Dave said, leading her into the waiting room and pointing to the office door.

As usual, arms folded in the corner, stood Cecelia.

Glimpsing an empty reception desk, Lucy took her chance to approach Dave.

"Thank you for the video. I loved it," she said.

The grinning scientist clapped his hands together. "I knew you would. He's so playful, even if larger than we're used to. We thought it might be the case after his brother, so we took extra food provisions, and I'm glad we did."

The butterflies in her chest took flight as the conversation went in the direction she wanted it to.

"You mentioned Will's brother was also an alpha when he was here. Fane said it could be genetic, but he also said it could be a pack thing."

"Yes. It's quite the mystery! Nothing so complete as this though. So far as we can tell, genetics have little to do with it. I'd say it's more about upbringing and personality, at least as the foundational building blocks."

"A pack thing indeed," Cecelia said in disgust, folding her arms. "Vampires tend not to get involved in such convoluted dynamics. Too much drama."

Dave beamed. "Indeed! Wolves are a very social species but with a strict hierarchy. In the strictest of sense, the pack in this case would be their immediate family. A pack within a larger community. In any case, I believe Mr Harven will have told you about his upbringing by now."

Lucy's fist clenched, and she raised it to her chest. Although her mother disappeared for weeks for archaeological digs, and even though her parents were distant, they were both alive, and cared for her in their own ways. But for Will to lose his papa... A lump formed in her throat.

"I read in the case files that Mr Harven, the father, went missing during the *Lunar Voyager X2* crash fourteen years ago. That would certainly change the dynamics of a family unit. Wolves typically navigate family matters from a top down alpha pair." Cecelia commented as if it bored her, and Lucy narrowed her eyes at the woman.

"Very much so," Dave picked up sympathetically. "Take Duke. He's always been serious about his studies, and his drive to protect people is second to none. With his immediate male alpha gone, he'd be the prime candidate to take over in his pack. However..." he paused, and removed a pen from behind his ear, tapping it against his temple. "Transformed, Will is the larger wolf."

Cecelia cackled, and Lucy shivered. It reminded her of how similar Cecelia and Fane really were. "Now there's some gossip for you, Little Miss. It seems like our little alpha feels like he has a new pack to protect now. Even bigger than his brother, who became a Guard."

Protect? She had Ben and Oda to protect but dreaded to think about who that would be for Will.

She turned away from the vampire's gaze, which she felt even from behind her sunglasses. Dave, meanwhile, whipped out a pad of paper from the inside of his lab coat and scribbled furiously.

Cecelia's cackle turned into a giggle and Lucy began examining the diagonal wood pattern on the floor.

Mrs Crossley's door swung open, cutting the tension.

"What's so funny?" asked a deep, masculine voice, and Lucy's head shot up in recognition.

Will propelled himself through the doorway, spotted Lucy, and waved. She met his gaze with a genuine smile. "Hi, Will."

He beamed. "They let me off. I told them what I know, and they let me go due to lack of concrete evidence. Everything was circumstantial, apparently."

Lucy wanted to say, *that's great news* but the words died in her throat as Trisha strolled out behind him, head high like a swan.

She ought to be thankful for the woman's help, but inside she smouldered, and bit her cheek instead.

The redhead turned to Dave. "That's another one you owe me. I pulled in my last favour to get him released so he won't have to miss his last full moon of the month. They were going to keep him overnight. Absolute disgrace."

Dave scratched the back of his head. "I appreciate it, Cuz. Thank you."

Trisha gave a hmph before turning to Cecelia.

"Thanks for holding down the fort here. It's chaos here without a strong woman taking the lead."

Cecelia stayed silent but bowed her head.

Then she turned to Lucy, who wanted to curl up under the gaze.

"I have to get back now. Send Hina my best wishes. I'll see myself out."

Lucy bristled at the abrupt dismissal and watched as she approached Will.

Placing a hand on his shoulder, the redhead leaned forward and planted a kiss on his cheek. Lucy resisted the urge to huff as she watched the redhead walk out of the room, and was pleased to see Will flustered, wiping the cherry smudge off.

Even if she was relegated to temporary flatmate status, it didn't mean she had to enjoy others approaching Will, especially so blatantly. If Will were interested in her, didn't she have enough decency or respect to keep it behind closed doors? Couldn't she see how embarrassed he looked?

Dave coughed, drawing their attention. "I'm sorry you had to go through that. We're getting to the bottom of it, though. Still on for tonight?" he asked, a twinkle in his eye.

Will's eyes flashed from blue to amber and back. "Oh yes," he said, cracking a smile. "Nothing on Earth could stop me."

From her corner, Cecelia smirked.

Pre-flight checks took place at Cross-Key's heliport.

Lucy turned up to watch Will climb on board, only to be turned away by Dave. "Stand too close to a helicopter taking off, and your ears will rattle for days," he'd said, so she'd made her way to Security to watch via CCTV.

On-screen a wide-eyed flight engineer climbed out of the cockpit and lifted his radio. The radio at Alex's hip crackled to life.

"This flight is a no-go. Contact the police. The black box is missing. They've doused the engine with petrol and the seat belts have been slashed."

Lucy's jaw dropped.

The day manager's brows furrowed, and he raised his own radio. "Write up a thorough report from your pre-flight checks. Thank you for your time."

"Roger that," came the curt response.

"Security Department to Dave Crossley. Come in Dave," Alex continued.

Dave's jovial voice rang through the speaker. "You called?"

"The helicopter has been compromised. Your flight is cancelled. I've got to go speak with the boss."

There was a pause before Dave's professionally calm voice responded, "I'm enacting plan B. I'll inform Will and get the site ready."

Plan B? What was plan B? It was already 3:35 p.m., and the moon was due to rise in just over thirty minutes in the early February nights.

She knew how much the trips to the beach meant to Will, and was relieved there was a plan B at all. But her mind raced.

"I don't think this was just vandalism," Lucy voiced to Alex, who zoomed in on the CCTV.

"Oh?"

Her heart pumped in her ears through the silence before she forced out her words. "I think it's someone who knows Will needs it tonight. It's too coincidental otherwise."

"Your reasoning?"

Lucy turned it over in her head, like she did when teasing out Oda's thinking from their drawings.

"I'm not a pilot, but even I know the black box records what happens during a flight's journey. They're picked out of wreckages. If that's missing, then someone doesn't want people to find out what happened."

Alex hummed.

"But I'm not sure a crash is what they're after," she continued. "It's illegal to fly without a black box. If they didn't want to alert people to there being damage, they wouldn't have made it so obvious by slashing the seat belts or dousing the seats."

Alex grunted. "You've been hanging around with the vampire in the basement too much."

# Chapter Twenty-One

# INSURGENCE

Kamal turned up dutifully early for his shift, which was fortunate considering all the developments Alex had to hand over. But her stomach still squirmed at his presence. She hadn't heard from Hina at all, and knew if she hung around long enough, she could ask about her...friend? Former friend? Shortly rekindled bestie?

Lucy kept her ears open to the room as she half-heartedly attempted her lesson plans as cover.

Alex finished, handing over his shift to Kamal. "In light of plan B, I've brought in the family on guard duty for tonight. We can't take any chances."

Kamal drew himself to his full height and raised a hand in salute. "We'll get him. Mark my words."

Any other day, Lucy would have laughed at the unintentional *Sgt. Sir!* reference. She wiped her drawing tablet blank and started afresh while Alex at the other side of the room groaned.

"Mrs Crossley gave us level 3 clearance to investigate, which should keep the authorities from breathing down our neck. Which would help, if only we had any leads. Even the CCTV didn't show anyone going near the helicopter all day."

Her chest clenched at the words, then she stilled, stylus hovering over her spread.

"CCTV has deceived us once before. Even Miss Blakely can tell you that," the night manager said.

Lucy tilted her head but tried not to make it obvious she was listening.

"Good luck. If you need me, I'll come straight back." With that, Alex clapped Kamal on the back.

"It's not easy, but go and rest. And take this pack of diabetes with you," Kamal said, shoving a pack of fruit chews into his arms. "I've got this."

Then, finally slumping in exhaustion, Alex slunk from the room. After issuing his own orders to the Cross-Key security staff, Mr Usmani sent them all on their way, leaving only himself and Lucy remaining.

"Now, this should be interesting," the manager commented, unusually chatty. "Have you ever seen a wolf stuck in an empty warehouse?" He chuckled and began searching through the displays for the right camera.

An empty warehouse was plan B? With no beach or branches to entertain Will, she knew Dave was going to have a massive job on his hands containing the giant ball of furry energy.

"Can I stay and watch?" she asked.

"It's probably safer for you here than it would be wandering around with a gigantic wolf so close by."

So Lucy sat with Hina's father, waiting for the big moment, and took her chance.

"How's Hina?"

She saw the man's eyebrows droop below the top rim of his sunglasses. His expression was poker-straight. "She's upset," he intoned. "A bit of time sparring, some quality time with her mum... And she's asked to see the imam. She's a tough girl, and I'm sure she'll find her own path soon."

That was, if nothing else, unexpected. Hina had never been the religious type. Not that her parents had pushed her or anything, not when they held differing beliefs themselves. Relieved that her friend had support, she smiled at the girl's father and vowed to drop her a text message. She'd already burnt their bridge once. If there was anything left at all of the floating debris, this time she'd work hard to collect it all and rebuild it herself. It was the least she could do.

Then a flash of movement caught Lucy's eye, and she sat up straight. On-screen, Will wheeled himself into a large warehouse lined around the edges with sandbags, and in one corner, Dave rummaged through what looked like a large fridge freezer.

Dave turned, waved, then jogged over to slide shut the heavy metal door to the warehouse before padlocking it.

Will said something too quietly for the cameras to pick up, and Dave directed him to a large round clock on the wall.

Biting her lip, Lucy watched as Will stood, shakily, stepping out of his wheelchair and bending forwards, arms out for balance, before...

Heat raced up her cheeks, and she hastily covered her eyes as Will began to strip.

Kamal barked out a laugh. "I'll let you know when he's finished. You didn't think he'd transform with his clothes on, did you?"

In truth, Lucy admitted to herself that she had thought about it but would never say so to another soul.

Then came a scream that morphed into a solid, yearning howl, accompanied by bones cracking and popping. She imagined them shifting, popping in and out of sockets as his new body formed, and cringed.

"It's beautiful, don't you think?" Kamal said in awe. "It's an honour, it is, to be trusted to guard this secret—out of all the people in the world. You can look now."

She looked up and an enormous wolf stood in Will's place. He shook his entire body as if it were wet, then gave an enormous victory howl.

"Plan B works because there's so many people and noise, they'll think he's just a dog off in the distance."

Hiding in plain sight. Lucy applauded the ingenuity.

She stared, transfixed, as Will began sniffing around the warehouse before finally noticing Dave again, setting him with a stare.

As he had last time, Dave grinned and calmly raised his hands, showing he was unarmed, then he crab-walked over to the fridge.

Will growled.

Tugging the door open one-handed, his eyes never leaving the wolf's, he pulled out a chicken and dangled it like a toy for a pet. Will followed the movements, mesmerised, before Dave hurled it high in the air.

The wolf launched himself into the air and snatched the carcass with his teeth, before trotting happily to the other side of the warehouse to a heap of blankets; curling up with the peace offering.

Lucy clapped as she watched Will rip into his prize, collapsing it between his jaws with a loud snap.

"He won't have the space to run in the warehouse, so making him jump will be excellent exercise. We briefly thought about bringing in a treadmill, but there wasn't time to source one for his size," Kamal said, sounding relaxed for the first time since Lucy had known him. He had his arms on his hips and a smile on his face, and Lucy could tell that this was why the man worked so hard; for the privilege of being privy to this spectacle.

An hour ticked by, in which Dave gained Will's trust enough to approach him and pat his furred head.

A myriad of ideas ran through Lucy's brain. "You should hang joints of meat from the ceiling for him to jump up and reach. Or maybe get a big pool and fill it with fish."

The man smiled. "I'd love to see that. You have good ideas, you know. You should tell that to Dave. Knowing him, he'd build some incredible contraption combining the two."

Lucy stilled. Had she spoken her own mind again? This wasn't anything to do with the case. But when it was about Will, it felt easier somehow.

Pushing the mystery thoughts away, she changed topic while on-screen Dave cut into a few of the sandbags, creating a huge mound that Will took great pleasure in burying bones.

"Does he still recognize Dave?"

"You see how he growls, but then cuts off after a couple of seconds? That shows Will's trying to override his instincts. The trick is to calm them down after they've first transformed. That allows the human mind to slip in again."

"So that's what Dave was doing with the chicken at the beginning?" Lucy pondered out loud.

"Mr Dave Crossley is one of the best in the business. He's been witnessing these transformations since he was a child—a Crossley born and raised. He knows them in and out." Kamal said, then breathed a sigh tinged with envy. Having married into the family, the man would never be in line for a position that close to the action. He was an outsider brought in, just like she was.

The pair watched for hours in their unspoken shared outsider kinship. The last delivery left the estate at 6:45 p.m., leaving empty roads and a silent night to sweep in.

At 8:42 p.m., Lucy stretched, her throat parched. She remembered a time when she would have brought her own drink to avoid asking others their orders in case she froze.

"Do you want a hot drink? I'm making coffee," she asked, standing up.

"Just milk, thanks. The first cup in a long night," he grunted.

She turned the doorknob to the kitchenette when red lights flashed across the room and a siren blared.

Kamal swore and launched to his feet. Cecelia's voice rushed out of his radio.

"We have a situation. Unauthorised activation of the HAT machine. I'm trying to shut it down, but it won't let me. The rogue AI's in control."

A jolt ran the length of Lucy's spine, freezing her in place.

The night manager switched the monitors to show the floor-length mirror of the portal. At its side stood Cecelia, typing furiously at the controls.

Kamal barked down his radio. "HAT machine breach! All guards in areas 3 and 4 report immediately for backup. Guards from 5 and 6, the main atrium. Area 7: guard the CEO's office. Miss Cecelia—"

Trisha walked out of the now rippling mirror, a crimson pistol in hand. Lucy counted at least ten behind her, all armed.

The redhead lifted the gun, yanking the slide with a click. Gold streams glowed down the length of the barrel. It emitted a high-pitched beep. Then, with two practised hands, she aimed.

*Bang!*

A laser ripped through the air.

Lucy covered her mouth, but the scream had already died in her throat.

A chunk of the pillar next to Cecelia exploded, leaving a charred hole.

That was not the stunner she'd used before. She stared at the monitor, slack-jawed as the group staggered—hunched—towards the lone vampire.

Lucy recognised that gait. They couldn't cope with the gravity, like Will.

*"Na uzo billah,"* Kamal said, as they watched in sickening horror.

The groups' fingers elongated around their triggers. *Beeep! Beeep! Beeep!* The laser devices came online one by one, then bangs flashed and tore through the air, accompanying the sound of snapping and resetting bones.

Covering her ears from the noise, Cecelia dodged the onslaught like a ballet dancer on fast-forward, fangs bared in a snarl.

Unlike Cecelia, the werewolves didn't flinch at the noise. But why? Lucy knew from Will they were just as sensitive.

Glancing closer to the screen, she squinted, then paled as the blood drained her face. "Earplugs," she choked out.

"What?"

"They're wearing earplugs!" Lucy repeated, voice warbling, and pointed at the monitor. Her mind ran a thousand miles a second. Trisha hadn't been there for Fane's recapture. She hadn't even known.

The night manager found the answer first, turning as grey as Lucy felt.

"That stupid, stupid girl!" he roared, voice cracking as he finished, and it clicked. Hina and her emails to the impostor.

Cecelia's words rang around her head. *Loose lips sink ships.*

"Trisha! You back-stabbing, self-serving—" A fresh round of firing cut Cecelia's tirade short. Having reached their perfect mid-transformed state, the group's aim had drastically improved, only needing one hand to fire.

One, two, three holes punctured the vampire's left shoulder, each causing her to jerk backwards.

Lucy placed her palm over the screen's static, as if willing a protective barrier there. But thoughts weren't enough.

Lasers sailed, shot after shot.

The blonde crouched, grit her teeth, removed her hands from her ears and pounced towards the remaining human in the group. She launched through the onslaught, nails sharp as claws, fangs bared. Her crimson eyes glared daggers through her shattered black lenses.

Three metres. Two metres. One metre.

A tall female with ocean-blue eyes and mahogany fur jumped in front of the human, racked the slide of her device and fired. Again. And again.

Chest. Chest. Hip. Leg. Leg. Ankle. The vampire crumpled as her legs gave way. Blood ran out of her in streams.

*Clatter.*

The wolf held out her gun, shrinking, and Trisha took the weapon with a toothy grin and holstered it at her hip.

She took a step forward to the downed blonde, as behind her the pack clawed their suits to shreds, limbs shrinking, tails growing.

The redhead flashed the hunching, shrinking wolf her own toothy grin. The wolf at her side clawed open her suit, in time for her arms to shorten and tail to grow.

Trisha dropped to her knees, coming down to the same level as her pure wolf guard, the level of the vampire ambassador's temple. The crimson weapon beeped.

*Bang!*

Lucy retched.

Trisha yelled her victory, joined by an unearthly cacophony of howls at her back.

❧❧❧❧❧ ❧❧❧❧❧

"Would someone tell me why Cecelia's aura just disappeared? What on Earth is going on up there?" Fane's angry voice broke across the radio.

Kamal, ashen-faced, rushed out, "HAT machine breach from the rogue AI. Cecelia was on duty but couldn't shut it down before intruders came through. Fourteen Fleet and one Earthling. Trisha Crossley and a pack of wolves. They killed her. Miss Crossley killed her."

On the monitor Lucy watched as the Crossley family guards finally arrived. They froze, bumping into one another as they spotted Trisha standing in the middle of the pack of wolves. A few lowered their weapons in confusion, which Lucy recognised as the stunner Cecelia used to bring down Fane.

Trisha grinned, swung herself up onto the back of her female companion, and pointed. "Charge!"

The pack lunged as one, raining down on the Crossleys, who screamed and fell, writhing under teeth, claws, and fur. Clothes shredded, limbs tore, and blood pooled.

Words didn't just harm. They killed.

"They're taking out family members," Kamal said into his radio. The man's hands trembled around his handset. "Dave, do you hear me?"

Fane growled in a way impossible for a human. "Those wolves have declared war against the vampires and the humans. This attack against my people is unacceptable. Lucy, get down here. I have a job for you."

Lucy looked up at the aged man, who nodded. "Take the fire escape to get out of this building and keep this with you. If you're not back in twenty minutes, run as far away as you can!" He pulled open a drawer and tossed her a spare radio. "Stay safe, child. *Fee aman Allah.*"

Lucy grabbed it and bolted for the door. A thousand thoughts swam around her brain.

Trisha. Trisha, who knew the Cross-Key systems. Who worked with the Grand Bureau Member. Who knew Hina well enough to know she liked Duke!

She sprinted down the corridor.

Hina. Hina was a Crossley. It could have easily been her there with the wolves too.

Her airways stung and her legs burned as she leapt down the stairwell two steps at a time.

She made it to the Research and Development building in record time, and sprinted all the way to Fane's hidden dome.

When Lucy flung the door open, she found Fane typing furiously at the keyboard, jaw set. Her eyes zoned in on a monitor in the top left corner, showing a live feed of more Crossley family members. They knelt behind a reception desk, stun guns at the ready, pointing at the door that Lucy recognized as leading down to the HAT machine's cavern.

The rest showed lines of code and a percentage bar at 5 percent, beneath the title: Operation Silver Star.

Fane wiped a hand through his hair. "Those bloody meat bags!" he exclaimed, then turned around to face Lucy.

"Operation Silver Star cannot happen. It takes twenty minutes to launch, so we have little time."

"What's Operation—" Explosions lit up the monitor and Lucy's breath caught. The group had left the HAT Machine and were shooting their way closer to the exit.

"Self-defence," Fane answered. "You don't think Cross-Key would keep vampires and werewolves around without some sort of protection? The Silver Star is humanity's own genetically coded bomb, designed to take down every vampire or werewolf in a fifteen-mile radius. If the Fleet finds out it exists, they'd launch a full-scale interspecies war."

Lucy's head spun. So that's why they were so confident about having Fane there. Who launched it? The CEO? Security? But Will was still in the area. He was innocent!

She clenched her fists. "We have to stop it. How do we stop it?"

"We don't. Either I'm out stopping the pack or here working on the bomb, but there's no guarantee I can crack it's coding within the time. We need backup. Vampire backup. Cecelia was never going to be enough to take down a pack that size and neither am I," he admitted. "This problem is bigger than us. We need help, but I can't set foot in the Fleet without immediate arrest. It's imperative that I am *not* there. There's something on Earth I need to do. Vitally important."

Although Lucy's curiosity peaked, it was slammed down as a horrifying realisation dawned.

"Don't worry. I won't run away. I'll stay here and fight." He raised his hands and counted on his fingers. "Mr Usmani is coordinating the Crossleys. Alex is off-site. Dave's locked in with a transformed werewolf. Margaret Crossley is off-site. Any one of those had Operation Silver Star clearance. Lia is dead. That leaves—"

"But they'll never listen to me," Lucy protested. "They wouldn't even let me in last time with Dave. And even if they did, the Councillors wouldn't be quick enough to do anything."

The plan was insane. Surely, he knew that? Nobody would listen to her.

"As soon as those egotistical mutts breached the contract, the chain of command reverted to the old ways. The vampires will come if the command comes from the royal bloodline," he explained, then reached out and poked her in the ribs.

"If you carry my blood, you'll hold command. You just have to say the orders."

Lucy's mind scrambled for more protests, but a fresh round of screaming cut it short.

Trisha continued her assault on her own family, gun in hand, as they trekked through the building to the main atrium, a trail of bodies in their wake.

"Won't that make me like you?" she said. Images of her parents and Ben flashed through her mind.

"To transform someone, I need to drink them almost dry and then give them my blood. This is only going to be a one-way thing. You'll get some vampire abilities for a short amount of time, but it'll wear off in a few days."

"But long enough for—"

"Yes, twenty minutes is a lot shorter than a few days. But without help, we're doomed anyway. You could run away, or you could act. Preserve peace. Maintain order. Save more innocent lives."

Innocents like the Crossleys. Like Hina. And Will. Will couldn't even speak for himself in his current state. Just like Oda. She was their mouthpiece. If she didn't act, wouldn't she have the blood of those people on her hands from Trisha's rampage?

Steely resolve settled, she clenched her fist.

"What do I do when I get there?"

An ear-splitting howl wrenched through the speakers, drawing Lucy's eyes back to the screen.

The Crossleys lay dismembered across the floor. Trisha held out her arm in offering and her werewolf companion bit into the flesh. The pack howled around the pair, and Trisha flashed them a toothy smile. Her eyes turned pink, and she began to grow.

Fane shouted over the din. "Don't bother with that jumped-up check-in bot. Contact the vampires on board the Bureau using ERT. You remember the mind link that you and Oda have? That's a sort of bond all vampires have. Emotional resonance transmission. That's what my blood will give you, and it'll give you weight behind your words. No vampire in a mile can ignore that voice of a royal."

Her voice. They were relying on her voice. But what if she froze? What if—

The howling stopped, leaving deafening silence in its wake. Lucy turned to the screen, and staring straight back into the camera stood a wolf that towered over the others. It was at least a foot larger, with fiery red fur and amber-pink eyes. It blinked, sniffed, then ran towards the exit, the pack following at its heels.

Fane reached for his radio. "They'll be heading for their stockpile of missing items at Warehouse 23B. Mr Usmani, I'm on my way up. I'm sending Lucy for backup."

Kamal's gruff voice spat back, "So, now you want to talk? Fine. I hope you're not planning any funny business."

Lucy lifted her own radio. "Nothing funny. It's alright," Lucy reassured him, trying not to stumble over her words. At least she hoped so. "How's Will?"

"He's gone crazy. He keeps howling when he hears the pack howl, and now he keeps running into the warehouse door trying to break out. Dave's having a horrible time in there."

Her heart clenched. Red. Will was trying to join Red's pack. Tears prickled, but she rubbed them away with her sleeves.

No. Even if Will wanted to join the pack, he'd never killed anyone. He was still innocent, and as a wolf, he couldn't even speak to defend himself. Like Oda and Ben. She had to speak for him. Get help. Save him.

"I'll do it," she said to Fane, steeling her shoulders. "What do we do?"

Vermilion eyes glinted. "An eye for an eye, a tooth for a tooth." He raised up a hand, lowered his chin, and jerked. Blood pooled in his palm, spilling out of the tear. "Drink this. It carries no human viruses, and I washed my hands before you arrived. I'll tell you when to stop. And beware stomach cramps for the next couple of hours."

She tentatively stepped forward, icy with horror, and closed the distance. The blood hit the back of her throat, and her veins pumped liquid fire.

# Chapter Twenty-Two

# Operation Red Promotion

Hot. Everywhere. Burning. Then something cool touched her. Yes, she was a *her*. More than a writhing mass of pain. The cold grabbed her arms. She had arms, and they were being pinned to her sides.

*"Shhhhhh,"* she heard a voice in her head. *"You're OK. It's almost over."*

The voice was male and comforting. It washed over her, settling her limbs and dowsing her panic. She tried to grab it, but it slipped from her mind before she could catch it. She clenched her fist in frustration, then hissed at the ache it caused.

Where was she? How long had she been there?

Like the voice promised, the pain gradually dulled. Experimentally, she flexed her hands and toes, working out the residual pins and needles.

She opened her eyes, and bright white pain had her jamming them closed tight again.

"Here," a voice breathed into her ear. The male voice. But it was distant. Apart from her. "Put these on." Something smooth fell across the bridge of her nose and settled behind her ears.

244

Lucy chanced opening her eyes again, this time seeing Fane's underground cavern tinted in a soothing grey. No pain. The frames tickled behind her ears and she recognised them as sunglasses.

Fane stood in front of her and she realised with a squirm that he must have been the one holding her so tightly. Blood marked the cuff of his sleeve, but there was no sign of the wound on his palm at all.

"Use these indoors. The night is more forgiving, but watch out for those damned estate floodlights. Whoever invented them needs to be made an enemy of all vampire-kind. I'm amazed none of the ambassadors complained before now." Fane stepped away from her, letting her find her balance. Lucy was thankful for the chat, defusing the awkward tension in the air.

"Vampire eyes?" Lucy asked.

Fane nodded. "Now try to use ERT. We don't have time to stand around and chat. Fifteen minutes left now."

Lucy blinked at the double standard before the reality of her situation crashed back down onto her shoulders. What felt like eternity had only been minutes. Precious, valuable minutes.

ERT. Right. Like she did with Oda.

Her mind scrambled. She didn't have an illustration to project and enhance this time, so she tried to concentrate on words.

*"I've got to get to the HAT machine. We need help. I've got to get backup."*

"Good," Fane said. "I can hear you, but you're muffled. Probably the human blood distorting it. I could make out what you said, though. Remember, use your emotions to amplify the transmission and let your mind sing."

*Crash!*

On-screen, a million shards of glass scattered all over the floor of the central atrium at Headquarters as the wolves burst out into the night. The pack was loose.

"Let's go," Fane commanded.

Lucy nodded once, then the pair dashed out of the door, taking the steps with powerful gazelle-like leaps. She'd felt nothing like it as she kept up with the vampire prince.

The night air no longer felt cold, and her lungs no longer burned from the exertion she'd felt on the way. But as they ran down the estate streets, she knew Fane was still more powerful. Every three or four steps, he'd gain a metre in front and have to rein himself back in. Aside from the rapid thump of her heart in her ears, her brain pieced together that he was trying to stay by her side.

The estate roads were empty, punctuated only by barking and howls in the distance. Three blocks later, Fane stopped ahead of her at a junction, and she attempted to stop—slowing down to only overshoot a few yards away.

"I'll head straight to the stockpile," he said, motioning in the direction of the barks and howls. "The Crossleys and I will try to barricade them inside. They'll expect someone calling for backup. Ordinarily that would take a bureaucratically long time to arrive, which we don't have. But you with my blood? You're our ultimate trump card."

Lucy shivered as vermilion eyes connected with hers through her lenses.

Even as the superhuman strength flooded her muscles, the weight of the task settled on her shoulders and constricted her throat. She froze. But just because her vocal cords couldn't move didn't mean she couldn't speak.

She flashed a thumbs up sign, then ran left towards the tunnels leading to the HAT machine's cavern.

Copper filled her nostrils as a trail of limbs and Crossleys lay unmoving, marking her way.

Stifling waves of nausea, she told herself not to look down as she ran.

The smell in the cavern itself was even worse. She gagged, then noticed a dribble on her chin. Saliva. That damn vampire blood! It was gross. Wrong. Inhuman.

Until she smelt a wave of iron. Strong iron mixed with copper. Too much iron, mixed with hints of other metallic compounds she couldn't identify. It wasn't appetising at all. She looked down.

Burgundy matted Cecelia's blonde hair as she lay broken like a doll. There were no eyes to close.

This was wrong. This was the work of a real Queen of Hearts.

Tears ran down her cheeks.

No more.

With a guttural snarl she continued her journey, launching herself at the humming mirror wall and red eyes staring back.

⁂

Lucy braced herself as the chrome-panelled wall hurtled towards her. With no gravity dial, she hurtled forwards in the microgravity.

Instinctively, she drew her feet into a ball, covering her head from the oncoming impact.

*Smack!*

At the last second she pushed out with her foot, accidentally catching the custom program's drawbridge, making it clatter open.

"Hey—gentle with the hardware! Now, how many in your party?" Be intoned but Lucy ignored it, too busy concentrating on not flying head first back through the mirror she'd just come out of.

Mentally cursing the recoil, her brain flashed back to Will and how he bounced around the ship. She needed a surface to grip.

Then she spotted it. Closer. Closer! She flung her arms and legs out like a starfish and her plimsoll caught on to the edge of the portal's frame. With her new vampire strength, she kicked off the surface, rebounding back towards the drawbridge.

"I repeat. How many in your party?" Be chirped.

Waves of nausea rolled over her as she flipped back, and she clung to the drawbridge.

"Party detected but no verbal response. Assumed vocally impaired. Bio-scan for numbers travelling commencing."

Blocking out the robotic voice, Lucy forced herself to concentrate on her message. Chanting. *Need help. Come quick. Werewolf attack on Earth. Cecelia killed.*

A hum started in the room around her as Be began doing whatever it was doing, but nothing else happened. She thought hard about her message. Still nothing.

Her hands slipped off the drawbridge, covered in sweat, making her lurch sideways. Strands of hair floated in front of her face and tickled her nose. She blew the offending lock away and scrunched her nose in frustration.

Words weren't working. Maybe she was too far away? What if Fane was wrong and his blood didn't work? What if this was a deterrent, and he really was running away? Playing her for a second time?

No. She didn't have time to think like that. Lives were on the line.

She jammed her eyes closed. If words weren't enough, then she'd do it her way. The way she did with Oda.

Multicolour strands of rainbow flickered behind her eyelids, dominated by shades of red, vermilion at their core.

She wove them, drew them with her mind, into the image she wanted to make: Trisha and the werewolves coming through the mirror, guns in hand.

Letting out a deep breath, she clung to the image, pulled it close, then launched it.

The waving swirls behind her eyelids rippled with the force of the outwards projection. Her body tingled.

"SCANNING IN PROGRESS. DO NOT MOVE."

As it faded into the inky black, three silver pinpricks of light formed behind her eyes. In seconds, they'd grown into small dots.

The dot on the left spoke, its voice that of a young woman. *"I do not understand. Your picture is blurred. Who are you? What do you want?"*

Lucy's heart leapt. It had worked. But it wasn't enough. How could she get through to them? Rising panic swept away the mini victory. They needed help. She had to ask for that help!

For once, she was glad her vocal cords wouldn't be necessary, because silence at this point wouldn't save anyone.

Filling her mind with emotion, the same way she did with Oda, Lucy used words again.

*"Cross-Key has been invaded,"* she said, laced with urgency. *"We need help. A pack of werewolves are on Earth with weapons. It's a full moon. We need backup."*

*"Fane?"* a warbling old man questioned from the orb on the right.

The left orb, the young woman, responded, *"Yes, but no. Like Fane but not. Very shaky. Also sounds female."*

Lucy interrupted. *"No time! I'm Lucy from Cross-Key & Co. Fane sent me. We need your help."*

Her chest clenched, and she reminded herself to keep breathing. A headache was setting in.

*"Our prince summons us to Earth?"* the male voice asked. *"Is that right? You're tuning in and out like a primitive Earthern radio."*

Lucy's eyes flew open in shock. Fane was right. This might actually work!

"ANALYSIS COMPLETE. ONE HALF HUMAN DETECTED. ONE HALF VAMPIRE DETECTED. NO OTHER LIFE FORMS. FLOATING CORPSE NOT POSSIBLE AS HEAT, MOVEMENT, AND RESPIRATION DETECTED. DOES NOT COMPUTE. SCANNING BODY ID."

Lucy tuned the voice out again as she suddenly felt the already tenuous connection weaken. She screwed her eyes shut again and concentrated even harder.

*"Send help. Werewolves invaded. Crossleys dead. Cecelia dead. Charter broken. Fane sent me."* She heard her pulse in her ears and her body grew hot—liquid fire engulfing her veins again. *"Please listen to me! Please help us!"* Her blood boiled, sparked, then ignited.

*Boom!* Her distress rang out like a vermilion and gold bomb, rippling her message out in a tidal wave with Lucy as the earthquake.

Last, the orb in the middle spoke. It was a young man's voice. *"I hear you. The Charter is broken. Whatever our prince commands. We're on our way."*

The young female was also all business now, issuing instructions. *"I'll contact Sector 1. Hiroto, take 2. Matthew, 3. We're on our way. Give us fifteen Earth minutes and we'll slide to the Cross-Key & Co. HQ portal. Hold on, young one."*

The elderly man from the second orb spoke, *"Cecelia will be missed and avenged. We'll make sure of that."*

The orbs reduced back to pinpricks, and the voices went quiet, random swirls of colours fleeting across the dark mindscape again.

Lucy panted, wiping sweat off her brow. She'd done it. Help was coming! She opened her eyes, tuning back into the world around her, hearing Be speak.

"ID MATCH. WANTED FUGITIVE. FREEZE. REMAIN WHERE YOU ARE. YOU ARE UNDER ARREST."

*Not likely,* thought Lucy, as she rolled in mid-air, avoiding a bio-collar shot at her from the lowered hatch. Sirens blared, and she covered her ears in pain.

She pivoted herself upright, touched a toe to the floor, then launched herself away again through the mirror.

There was a wolf to save.

The once tantalising blood in the air had staled with the stench of death and charred remains. After one gulp, Lucy refused to inhale again. Pushing her legs to the limit, she sprinted across the cavern, took the stairs three at a time, and burst into the icy February air with a gasp, bending double from the assertion. Definitely still human, then.

The estate floodlights glared and Lucy took refuge from them beneath a tree's shade. Shutting her eyes, she faded into her mindscape.

*"Fane!"*

A glowing ball of vermilion twined with gold erupted in her head. *"Lucy? We have the wolves surrounded at 23B, but they've barricaded themselves in. Is backup coming?"*

*"Fifteen minutes,"* Lucy called. *"But Be registered your DNA, and tried to arrest me."*

She mentally felt the man grimace, and wondered if it was because of the time limit, her potential arrest, or both.

A howl bellowed from her right, pulling her out of the mental conversation and back to the estate.

Scratches and bangs came with increasing frequency from a cargo warehouse on her right. The door shuddered with force every few seconds until—

*Crash!*

Lucy recoiled as the door swung open. Out barrelled a frenzied, towering mahogany-and-auburn furred wolf. Behind him ran a startled-looking Dave, who saw her and went white.

"Will!" he shouted, but the wolf didn't respond—staring Lucy dead in the eyes. Lucy froze as he sniffed. Then he flicked his tail and growled.

"Run!" the scientist shouted, and it sounded like the best idea she'd ever heard.

Lucy bolted.

*"This way!"*

Lucy hurtled towards Fane's voice, praying her vampire-fuelled legs would keep her out of reach of the jaws-with-legs.

She leaned forwards and straightened her hands into points like she'd seen sprinters do. She accelerated, but the wolf responded with a burst of his own speed.

Her heart leapt when she saw Fane with a group of five humans surrounding the warehouse. A few had weapons drawn: knives, metal bars, and a couple of the tasers the primary Crossley guards had carried. Their martial arts training showed as they moved as one to raise their weapons to Will.

The wolf stopped and glared at the group. Amber eyes locked with Lucy's and she paused. He may have chased her, but he hadn't snapped at her. Maybe he was still in there? She threw her arms up, standing between the wolf and the family. A standstill they didn't have time for.

Then Will howled an ear-splitting aria, joined by a chorus from inside the warehouse.

Lucy winced. What was he doing?

Then, the metal door to the warehouse screeched open and a regal fiery red wolf padded out.

"What have you done?" Dave asked, voice cracking. "Cuz...why?"

The she-wolf locked gazes with Will, then slowly slunk her way around to his side, and Lucy felt light-headed.

The group stiffened—a couple raised their silver knives to cover their chests.

Trisha sniffed Will's fur, then lifted her snout and gingerly rubbed it under Will's chin.

A vice gripped Lucy's chest at the pair.

Then Will leapt, pushing Trisha with his two front paws, reversing their positions. Trisha yelped as she smashed on the asphalt. She batted at him, but he leaned in and growled. She reached for his neck, rolled them over, and the pair continued to battle for dominance. They barked, gnashed, and swatted.

Blood rushed through Lucy's ears as she readied herself to jump between the two when Will bit Trisha's ear and she squealed. The sound paralysed her sensitive, inhuman ears. Then she saw them.

Fourteen wolves darted towards them. Trisha's auburn-haired beta leading the backup attack.

They were outnumbered.

Three recognized Fane and their combined weight knocked him to the ground.

Thanking her temporary vampire strength, Lucy hurled herself out of the way of a grey wolf, leaving him snapping empty air. It turned back to her, snarled, then charged. She dived out of the way, causing the wolf to run headfirst into the blue metal storage container behind her.

Lucy winced as the wolf made impact, then screamed as pain shot through her ankle. A black wolf had their jaws jammed around her ankle. She choked on her voice and froze—too scared to move in case the action tore off her foot like paper.

Arms flailing, she just dodged a large auburn mass of fur that latched on to the black wolf's throat. Lucy hissed as her ankle was released. A quick yelp later and the auburn wolf had the black one pinned to the ground. Satisfied as it dropped limp into submission, the victor's amber eyes turned to Lucy.

Lucy met Will's gaze head-on. She was there to save him, but in the end he'd saved her.

She staggered forward, but as soon as she stepped on her right leg, she crumpled in place.

Will bounded over, turned, and stood guard. Tears filled Lucy's eyes as she realised that yes, he was still in there.

The Crossleys, even with their combat skills, were easily outmatched. Other than a couple of stunned wolves, and a pair that was busy wrestling Fane, the rest fell in behind alpha-Trisha, who advanced towards the pair.

They didn't have time for this. They were all in danger!

*"We're here, young one. Where are we going?"*

It took a moment for Lucy to realise she heard the voice in her head. She recognised the young female voice from the Fleet.

*"Cecelia, I hope you find some rest,"* came the elderly male voice.

They must have just appeared through the portal.

Fane stayed silent—too busy grappling his opponents to concentrate.

Lip trembling, Lucy closed her eyes. She had to believe Will would keep her safe while she sent her message.

Drowning out the sound as best she could, she followed the strands of colour behind her eyes to her mindscape. Fane's orb glowed gold not far from her. She pushed, reaching out as far as she could until ten or so faint pinpricks of silver faded into existence, huddled together. They were so far away, and she knew her signal was weak, but they would die otherwise.

She hummed the bombastic *Sgt. Sir!* theme tune, hyping herself up to the task. The electric guitars and brass reached a crescendo and the blood in her sang. *"Follow the trail of bodies. They'll lead you outside. Then follow the noises. Blue shipping containers. Hurry! Please!"*

A harsh yip broke her concentration, her eyes shot open, and she froze.

Two wolves dug into Will's back. He shook, struggling to shake them off. They whined and barked as he rolled, clawed, batted, and snapped.

"Well done!" Fane shouted over the din before executing a perfect German suplex on one of his wolf assailants. The wolf screeched on impact and didn't move. The second, smaller of the pair ran, loping back to the safety of the pack behind Trisha.

Finally free, Fane disappeared—moving faster than Lucy could see—and the next thing she knew she was being set down on top of the blue metal container out of harm's reach.

Lucy's blood hummed as she heard Fane call to the incoming vampires. His voice and blood resonating as strong as a trained opera singer.

*"May we seek our revenge against this pack who has blighted our allies and robbed us of our own."*

The call cloaked Lucy in calm, then stoked a fire in her.

"*Yes, Prince,*" came a mental chorus.

Yes. She had to get vengeance. It was a brilliant idea!

Lucy pushed herself up.

"Not you," Fane said to Lucy, and gripped her arm. His real voice broke through the thrall and her thoughts cleared. The urge to jump off the shipping container and join the fighting vampires all but disappeared.

Her eyes widened as she took in the rogue. Vampires alone were dangerous, but his abilities of suggestion were on a completely other level.

Without a second glance, Fane jumped back down from the shipping container, and three wolves attacked him at once.

In the centre of the fray, Lucy recognised Will and Trisha going tooth and claw again. Her heart wrenched, but she knew with her injured ankle she'd only get in the way if she tried to intervene.

Then, multicoloured blurs came into vision, closer and closer, until people appeared in their place. The vampires. Like the Crossleys, they ranged from old to young, with varying genders and ethnicities. From her vantage point she counted thirteen, and they each targeted one wolf to fight on an even keel.

But the difference was staggering. The vampires, almost methodically, tackled, restrained and tased their chosen wolf before placing bio-engineered collars around their necks.

As they apprehended their wolves, they then turned in confusion to the two alphas at each other's throats. Both wolves' fur was knotted with matted blood, and they staggered, yelping and snarling. It was a deadlock, both evenly matched, and they showed no sign of stopping until one or both killed the other.

Lucy searched for Fane. He needed to tell the vampires to stop Trisha! But she couldn't see him. In all the commotion, the renegade prince had disappeared.

She didn't think twice before closing her eyes. With her palms clenched, she pictured Trisha in her human and wolf forms, and pushed the image out. *"She killed Cecelia! Stop her!"*

The vampires turned to look at Lucy once before a pair leapt forward, grasped Trisha around the neck, and tased her. She fell to the floor with a thump.

Will howled into the silence—a haunting mix of loss, betrayal, and victory.

Wincing, she dragged herself towards him. Thankfully, he noticed her and padded to her side, bending his neck down to her face. She grabbed him with both arms, buried her face in the crook of his furry neck, and shook.

Time was up. Any second, there'd be an explosion. Or a pulse. She didn't look up—not wanting to find out if the blast that killed them was silver. Her shiver racked the length of her body and Will whined.

A gentle touch to her arm made her flinch, then Dave's gentle voice said, "It's all over now. No more fighting. No more death."

She blinked into the fur before pulling away to look up at the scientist. His face shone with sweat and he clutched his left arm.

"The vampires say we have you to thank for their being here. We owe you a great deal. Nice eyes, by the way."

Reaching up she found her glasses had been knocked off somewhere in the fray. But more importantly, he sounded earnest, and Lucy believed him.

Operation Silver Star had been stopped. She sagged as the night's events took their toll. She'd made it.

The next thing she knew, the solid neck she'd been clinging to wriggled away and a cold wet nose prodded her ankle. She reached out and stroked his snout. His fur tickled her palm as he nuzzled into it.

"It looks like this male already found his alpha, eh?" a young looking vampire commented. Will's ears flicked, and Lucy gave a small smile.

Another vampire whistled as she looked inside the warehouse. "They're got everything they'd need for a morning getaway here. POTS meds, ration packs, fluids, minibus. Even ammunition."

"We suspected as much," Dave replied cordially, as if he spoke to vampires every day of the week. "Our supplies have been going missing for weeks."

Lucy shifted her weight and hissed as pain laced up her ankle.

Will nudged the wound again, opened his mouth to lick it, then was promptly hit on a hind leg by Kamal.

"Oh no, you don't! Who knows where that mouth has been? She could get infected."

The alpha looked thoroughly chastised, lowering his ears at the lecture. Lucy's heart lifted, though. Hina still had a father returning home. And surprisingly, Alex was at the man's side, holding him up.

Seeing her questioning look he said, "Good thing I decided to come in early, even without the fifteen distress messages. You lot climb into the bus in the warehouse and go get cleaned up at the medical centre. I'll oversee this mess. What a night..." he trailed off, and ran a hand through his hair. "I'll catch up with you all for statements later. Shoo."

No one needed telling twice.

# CHAPTER TWENTY-THREE

# WHERE THERE'S A WILL

E ven in their state of grief, the Crossleys pulled together to patch up the wounded, including cleaning and dressing Lucy's ankle.

Kamal had converted a few of the ground floor research bays into makeshift hospital wards, and tended the injured like he would on the front line in a war. This wasn't a victory. It was a family tragedy, and Lucy counted herself lucky she still had parents to go home to—even if she couldn't tell them a single word about what happened.

The night manager turned to Lucy, who had her leg propped up on a table and an ice pack to ease the swelling. He grunted. "Honestly. What were those wolves playing at? They ought to know better than to go spreading their infection to others." The semi-balding man handed her a glass of water that she used to down a pain med. It was the same one Cecelia had prescribed for her cat scratch and arm ache, and she felt cold inside.

Dave sat in the testing cubicle opposite, with a large sleeping wolf curled at his feet. He'd made the wolf a makeshift nest of blankets and had insisted on locking the pair in together 'just in case.'

Will initially protested, tugging at Lucy's sleeve, whining, before she coaxed him to follow. They picked a cubicle where he could still see her through the glass door, before watching her with the intensity of a hawk. Eventually, even he succumbed to the exhaustion of the day's activities.

The scientist spoke softly enough not to disturb other patients but loud enough so Lucy and Kamal could hear him across the three or so metres. "Those we saw tonight are about seven generations removed from the original Earthen wolves, who spread with bites. These guys have only ever known breeding as their method of reproduction. With their fully formed instincts driving them for the first time, they frenzied, killing everyone they bit outright other than Trisha. Saying that, remarkable control from the beta there. And of course, there's our own Miss Blakely."

Lucy dropped her cup as if it were a bomb, though the real explosion happened in her mind. *I was bitten and survived.* "Does that mean I'm going to..." she trailed off in shock.

"Not quite," Dave piped up again from his confinement. He kept stroking Will's head and fur to keep him relaxed enough to sleep and said, "Fane told me he gave you his blood so you could fetch backup. That vampire blood is potent. Certainly strong enough to wipe human grade pain meds out of your system from the look of things."

"Should have said sooner. What a mess. I'll fetch stronger ones," Kamal said, then left.

Lucy smiled at the man's back sheepishly. No wonder she'd been in so much pain.

"Anyway," Dave continued, "by the same logic, I believe the vampire blood is currently at war with the werewolf infection."

Lucy stared at her propped-up ankle. "So, what happens when the war ends?" she asked, shakily.

Dave scratched his chin. "By nature, it's easier to make something living dead than it is dead living. I imagine the vampire blood in your veins would cancel out the infection before it could convert you. It's a fascinating idea. In the same way, I'd imagine a vampire could turn a werewolf to some degree—perhaps even make some form of hybrid..."

A cog turned in Lucy's head as Dave excitedly rambled. Would Fane's lover have actually become a vampire-werewolf hybrid? Or something else? It didn't sound like she'd lived long enough after the attempt to find out.

"... and without a top-up to fully convert you, I'd say your part-vampire status will probably fade in a couple of days. Perhaps longer since the blood was royal."

Her stomach unclenched with relief then gurgled loudly, announcing to the entire department she was hungry. She felt her cheeks grow hot.

Kamal popped his head out from the medicine cupboard and said, "Someone fetch this girl a sandwich. And maybe something for all of us, too. It's been a long night. I need caffeine."

It had, Lucy mused. The clock on a wall ticked over to 3:00 a.m.

The awkward position of her foot propped up on the table from her chair made it too uncomfortable to sleep, so she let her mind wander.

What would have happened if she had become a werewolf? She glanced at Will across the room and her heart panged with a thousand possibilities.

While the humans recovered, the vampires and Alex rounded up and transported the tased werewolves to Cross-Key's underground holding domes. According to Kamal, they'd stay there until sunrise, so it would be easier for the Fleet Guards to apprehend them in their weakened human forms. All but Trisha, that was, who Alex had argued that Cross-Key should get first right to interrogation as a Crossley family member. His argument made in the middle of the medical bay had the support of most of the awake Crossley members there.

Alex had also bartered for help to clear up the estate of blood and bodies, and for unrestricted access for the vampires to take Cecelia's remains.

261

*Knock. Knock.* "Lucy?"

Lucy blinked blearily, hobbled over to her bedroom door, and opened it. Alex's face swam into view. The man looked like a panda with deep rings around his eyes, and he held out a pair of crutches. "Sorry to wake you up, but Will could use some support. Would you mind coming with me?" Turning, she saw the clock flash 8:46 a.m. Had Alex worked a third consecutive shift?!

Taking the crutches, she hobbled behind him out into a bustling common room. The remaining Crossley family must have stayed overnight. She briefly wondered if any of them had carried her back to her room, when a flash of memory hit her—of warm soft fur beneath her hands and cheeks.

The smell of toast and eggs broke through the embarrassing but hopeful thought. Alex, however, was in a hurry. "Breakfast?" he asked, before picking up a box of croissants and walking out of the room with them.

"A car's waiting outside. I'll hold the doors for you," he said, clipped.

As she hopped by with her crutches, a few Crossleys gave her solemn nods and small waves.

Once in the car, she took a pastry. "How's Will?"

Alex's tone was low and dull as he replied, "Not good. When he transformed back to his human form, he demanded to see the prisoners on CCTV. He didn't take it too well and asked to see you."

"Why me?" she questioned honestly. "Why not Dave?"

"We saw last night that you're the closest thing he recognises as family here," he said, and Lucy squirmed, deciding to take another bite. The security manager handed her a cup from nowhere and she washed away the dry flakes from the roof of her mouth.

She felt a pinprick of pity for the man, but when she saw Will's ghostlike expression as they arrived, it turned into a well.

He sat beside Kamal in the Security Department, and she shuffled over as fast as she could on her swollen ankle and buried her head into his neck.

"Thank you for coming," he croaked into her ear and she pulled back. His eyes were back to their regular sky blue as he looked her up and down, then paused on her bandaged ankle.

Breaking the tension, Lucy raised her crutches. "Fancy giving me a ride? These are good, but I think you'd be better company."

He barked out a laugh and patted his thighs. "Oh, I don't doubt that. But my human form is quite fragile, and your red eyes are kind of...freaky."

Lucy gave him a mock pout while wondering how long the vampire blood would be around for.

"Come on, you two. Stop flirting. We're going down into the domes," Alex said. "You're lucky that Mrs Crossley, Fane, and the Grand Bureau Member have allowed this visit."

"The Grand Bureau Member? But wasn't she the cause of all this?" Lucy asked. "She ordered Fane to steal Oda and then ordered Trisha to attack."

Alex sighed. "The Grand Bureau Member was as shocked and disappointed as any of us. Yes, she told Fane to steal Oda, but it was for the sake of protecting her own kind. Trisha planted the idea that the Crossleys wanted to expose Oda to the human world, which would highlight the existence of paranormal-kind. She would never have risked a large-scale invasion like that."

Lucy's eyes grew wide at the revelation. "So, all this time, it was Trisha?"

Alex looked like he had visibly aged a couple of decades. His tone was lifeless and Lucy thought it was as much a response to the betrayal as it was the tiredness.

"Trisha played on Astra's chronic fear of human discovery as a distraction from the supplies going missing. It was a ruse."

As they made their way into the lift, Lucy's head spun. Trisha hadn't just pulled the wool over the Crossleys' eyes, but she'd fleeced the Fleet, too. A true wolf in sheep's clothing. Her eyes narrowed as they walked, and looking at Will, she re-evaluated how offensive that saying was. Trisha had played on peoples' hearts, and painted the streets in red.

When they reached ground level, the group entered another lift, taking them deep underground.

Throughout all of this, Will had again lapsed into subdued silence.

"So," Lucy broke his reverie, "are we visiting anyone in particular?"

Will let out an uncharacteristic sigh and sagged. "Yes. My mum."

# Chapter Twenty-Four

# RED

Lucy's back went poker straight. She shouldn't have asked. She'd stuck her foot in her mouth again. He'd be upset. He—

Will's warm fingers wrapped around her wrist, and she snapped back to reality.

"That's why I wanted you here. I don't think I could face her alone, but you...you ground me. I'm not sure I could do this without you. Please, Ruĝa," he admitted simply.

Oh. She lowered her hand and placed it on top of his. Maybe she hadn't messed up yet.

His blue eyes had turned to ice, and she hoped that if he believed her presence would help, then she'd be there. She was sick of abandoning people who asked for her help.

Alex led them underground through a series of domes. She heard short bursts of chatter from behind doors leading to other domes on their left and right, passing regular workers going about their experiments, completely unaware of the paranormal guests or the massacre of the night before.

They finally stopped at one unremarkable dome that was just as indistinguishable from all the others, but Alex, undeterred, led the way as if he did it all the time. Since none of the domes had any signs or identifying marks, Lucy assumed he must have them memorised.

The security manager knocked once, popped his head around into the room, and announced, "Enid, you have a visitor. It'll have to be quick. The Guards are due any minute to take you back."

Then, Alex opened the door and Will propelled himself in. Lucy recognised the dome as the same sort of cell that they had kept Fane in. A slim woman with Will's auburn hair and ocean-blue eyes lay propped up on the bed.

Lucy's eyes narrowed when they landed on Trisha's right-hand wolf. She was the one who'd brought Cecelia down, but right now, it didn't look like she even had the energy to sit up against gravity. A pile of food lay neglected on a white Cross-Key & Co. branded tray at her side.

Will positioned himself by the bars running the centre of the dome and Lucy stood behind him, hands clasped firmly on his shoulders.

"You stupid boy," she admonished in a raspy, exhausted voice. Her eyes narrowed. "This was the perfect opportunity, and you ruined it."

Beneath her palms, Will's shoulders tensed, so she massaged them with her thumbs. She bit her bottom lip.

"Why?" Will asked simply.

Enid's eyes narrowed, and she coughed. "You know the poverty we were plunged into. I took all those extra jobs to keep food on our table. It wasn't enough. We lost everything when your father died. Our reputation. We were nothing but borderline strays without him. I knew to dig us out of our hole, I had to raise leaders. Produce an alpha."

"You can't manufacture an alpha. It's nature," Will argued.

"I researched the old scriptures and took a chance. Hardship, segregation, and a strong mate were the key. I pushed Duke as hard as I could to get him his Earth internship. Then what does he do? What does he do?!"

she screeched. "He refused to take a mate. That stupid son of mine had so much potential, but he squandered it."

Will raised his voice. "Just because Duke isn't attracted to anyone doesn't make him any less of a leader! He's a brilliant Guard and one day I think he could be the Grand Bureau Member."

"You cannot rule alone!" Enid shot back. "He may become a Councillor, but he'll never be elected Grand Bureau Member."

Will shook his head, his face stony. "That's not true."

"I saw those reports. Yes, Duke was had alpha potential. He managed a partial transformation. But he couldn't complete it because he couldn't find his other half. Since Duke was a hopeless disappointment, I turned my sights on you. Our last hope."

Lucy sucked in a breath but forced herself to keep the tension out of her fingers to help keep Will calm. She concentrated on drawing small circles with her thumbs on the back of his shoulders.

"You should have taken Ichigo. She knows Earth. She has ambition and was willing to take risks to rise to the top. With you."

"Ichigo? Who is that?" Alex asked.

Shaking, Enid lifted her arms in a grand, open gesture. "Our newest pack member. Her hair is as red as a blood moon. She was going to lead us into our reintroduction to Earth."

"Trisha," Lucy blurted.

"Formally known," Enid snapped. "How was I to know you'd already shacked up with someone else?" Her voice shook. Lucy clenched her jaw, tight. The urge to shout at the woman was difficult to restrain, but Will needed her calm, to keep him calm. She exhaled.

"So, that's why you pushed me to come to Cross-Key as an intern?" Will's voice shook, and Lucy's heart went out to him. "You always favoured Duke for his grades and academics. I thought when he moved out you'd just gotten lonely or something, so you started paying attention to me. Was I just a last-minute replacement to you?"

"Ichigo introduced herself to us lowly cleaning staff as human ambassador and immediately recognised our ambition. Even though you never excelled physically or academically, that beautiful creature still persuaded the Councillors to consider you as Duke's replacement. You're too arrogant to see when people are sticking their necks out for you."

Alex coughed softly in the doorway. They looked at him and he looked up at the ceiling, obviously not wanting to intrude on the mother and son moment.

Will prompted him, "Go on."

Alex took the opportunity. "I want to know what role Duke's software played in all of this. You seem disappointed in him but that doesn't wipe out any involvement from him completely."

For the first time, Lucy heard the woman speak warmly and with pride. "Duke's genius was recognised everywhere across the Fleet, and the potential for his AI interface is limitless. Ichigo mentioned wanting a way to stock supplies without being noticed, and I asked if an IT solution would help. The clever girl made it work when I gave it to her."

Will's voice was deadpan when he spoke next. "I think we're done. I have nothing more to say to you."

Enid's voice cracked from the bed. "I only did the best I could for my pack. One day you'll understand."

"Just because you struggled when Dad died doesn't mean other people can't thrive alone. Duke is a success, in IT and as a Guard, even being aromantic. Thank you for what you did for us growing up, but that's come to an end."

Internally, Lucy yelled her victory. Will glanced back at her, and she realised she'd squeezed his shoulders in excitement. She grinned a shy smile back, and his face softened.

"Duke's drive to protect has always been strong," Will warbled, and Lucy stepped to his side, taking his hand. "There may not have been a single alpha before, but he started the transformation. With his love the Fleet, I bet he'll finish it." Will's grip tightened around Lucy's fingers. "You know what? I'm glad Dad's not here to see this. You're delusional. Go back with the Guards and don't let your pride hit you on the way out. Let's go, Red."

Lucy's world tilted on its axis. She stopped, and Will's hand broke from hers as he wheeled forwards before stopping.

"Are you OK?" he asked.

"What did you call me?"

"Red. You never had a problem with it before. You know—like Red Riding Hood? You fed me," he said with a sheepish grin. "Ruĝa is red in Esperanto."

Red. *She* was Red, like wolf-tale *Little Red Riding Hood* Red! Her heart swooped. He held out his hand again, and she took it. She was an idiot.

"At least you're interested in having a mate. There's hope for you yet, cub."

Will barked out a laugh. "Well, if there's no hope for Duke I'll be sure to tell him you don't need his paycheck anymore."

They left, and Alex closed the heavy door behind them with a thud. Then Will crumbled, and Lucy wrapped her arms around his sobbing frame.

An hour later, Lucy escorted Will to the CEO's office, having received a summons from Dave.

Astra herself had turned up with the Guards, and part of Will's role was to meet her.

When they arrived at the CEO's waiting area, two shorter than average men in sunglasses and lab coats, stood frozen at either end of the room. Lucy guessed that to the uneducated, the pair resembled two eccentric Cross-Key scientists gone rogue. They saluted Will, who gave a small wave back, and one opened the door to Mrs Crossley's office to let him in.

Lucy sank into one of the plush waiting room chairs.

Twenty minutes later, Mrs Crossley's door opened. What looked like a sun goddess, with frizzy black hair and broad athletic shoulders, sat tall in a wheelchair, pushed by Alex. Astra's black hair fell in tight curls down around her broad shoulders, and her muscular wolfish frame transferred to her human form.

As she passed, the Grand Bureau Member's eyes fixed on Lucy; her eyes flashing from yellow to amber. She raised a hand. "Well met, Miss Blakely. I am sorry you found yourself in the middle of this tragedy. We appreciate your confidentiality in this matter."

Lucy licked the inside of her mouth that had replicated the Sahara. "No problem. Um... Thank you for coming—for your help." Silently, she followed it up with *not that you offered any.*

The Grand Bureau Member flicked her wrist. "It's my job to maintain order and protection. You may want to wear a pair of sunglasses, dear, unless there's a new trend on Earth I haven't heard about."

Lucy brought a hand up to her face in horror. She hadn't noticed that she didn't need to wear sunglasses anymore in the bright light. Had she really been waltzing all over the estate with red eyes? Was that why Enid had called her interesting?

The leader clicked her fingers and barked, "Sunglasses!" One of the Guards pulled out a pair from the pocket of his lab coat and held them out. Lucy took them and fumbled in her attempt to put them on fast enough.

"Much better," Astra complimented. "Much more natural. The way things are *meant* to be."

Will pushed himself out of the room after her, and she turned her steely gaze on him. "You proved yourself loyal beyond measure last night, Mr Harven. If you ever wish to join the Guards like your brother, I'll make sure to drop a good word in for you."

He bowed his head. "Thank you. You honour me."

"I'll take our guest down to the cells. You should rest. Well done on the recommendation," Alex said.

Will shut his hanging jaw and grinned. "Thanks."

Astra lifted her left palm upward, raising it to the right side of her face. At her signal, Alex and the incognito Guards left.

Lucy smiled. She knew how much Will adored his brother. The recognition that he was just as suited for the position would do wonders for his self-esteem. Still, she felt a pang at the thought of an eventual Will-free future.

"Of course," he said, turning pink, "I couldn't join the Guards right now. I still have two to three years left here, depending on how long they take to find and train my replacement."

Lucy's inner butterflies waltzed. They had time. Limited, yes, but it was better than nothing. Being his friend was better than nothing, she reminded herself. She had to be happy with that, even if Will liked her back, too.

"You're incredible. You know that? Not just anyone would get involved with races they've never interacted with before, and travel to an entirely different world alone," he said, making Lucy's cheeks heat, too.

"You've just described yourself," she replied, and wondered what it would feel like to kiss him on the cheek. She clenched her fists. It wasn't fair.

"Why, if it isn't our favourite pair?" Dave said from the office doorway. His smile didn't reach his eyes. "Here's the state of play. We have first rights at questioning Tri—sorry —Ichigo; then the Guards will take her back to the Fleet to stand trial. Now's your chance if you want to talk to her."

Lucy grimaced and Will scrunched his nose. "Not after the morning I've had. No offense, but I can't believe Mum tried to set me up with her."

Lucy's butterfly squadron performed a victory flyover.

"None taken," he replied, then sighed and scratched his head. "I'm sorry you got dragged into Crossley politics."

"And I'm sorry you got dragged into Harven politics," Will answered.

Dave clenched his fists. "Yes, I heard about that. Your mother is certainly a person to be reckoned with. My cuz is also ambitious and had a good head on her shoulders. The CEO was working on a brand new role for her, but..."

Lucy stared as he trailed off, then shook himself out of his reverie.

"Something's not right with her at the moment. We'll get to the bottom of it, though. Why don't you two head home and rest? Thanks for your help. We'll let you know if we need you."

"Back home?" Will asked, tilting his head.

"Back home," agreed Lucy, grabbing on to the handles and pushing him out the door into the lift.

Hina's voice echoed loudly around the reception area. "Vandals really did this?" she asked a security guard loudly, motioning to the taped-off broken windows and doors. "Wow. What a mess! I hope they catch them soon." She laid the act on thick before spotting them.

"Lucy!" The human firework waved enthusiastically, crossed the room in a shot, and drew Lucy into a tight hug. Lucy squirmed, but was eventually released into vice grips on her shoulders as Hina looked her up and down.

"Cool glasses," Hina said, then promptly exploded. "I'm so glad you're safe. I couldn't believe it when Mum told me. We were lucky. My mum was visiting a friend up north when the call came in for family members, so she couldn't respond. I wanted to play my part, too, but I'm still suspended—and that extends to 'family matters,' you know? I can't believe I missed my chance to use my jujitsu and karate."

She turned to Will. "I heard you played your part well last night in keeping my BFF safe. You'd better continue to do that or else."

Will's nose scrunched up in confusion. "BFF?"

Not believing her luck, after everything she'd put the poor teen through, she said, "Thanks! You're my best friend forever, too. I'm glad you're alright."

Ignoring Will, she continued, "You have got to show me what's behind those glasses. Alex said it was spooky. Oh—your satchel's damaged! I'm sorry. I know you loved that like a baby."

Glancing at the scuffed bag at her side, Lucy marvelled at how observant the girl was. The bag had been abandoned when she had responded to Fane's call. She'd attempted to cover the tears with tape and markers.

"Are you free this weekend? We could go shopping for a replacement," Hina asked.

Lucy's heart leapt while her brain tried to shoot it back down. Then the familiar tennis match of her childhood started up again.

She couldn't. Her family needed her.

She had to. This was her last-ditch attempt to get her friend back.

Her family needed her.

Her friends needed her.

Forcing her shoulders to relax, she took a steadying breath and looked into Hina's hopeful eyes—the ones she'd couldn't look into without guilt for more than a decade.

"How's 8:30 a.m. outside the cafeteria?" Lucy asked. The words sounded strange as she said them, but as they registered in her ears, they lifted a weight from her.

"Perfect. Now, though, I'm off to find Trisha. I have a bone to pick with her." Her eyes narrowed, and she punched one fist into her other palm. Yes. Hina was definitely the daughter of the night security manager.

"Good luck," Lucy said, though she didn't think the teen would need it.

Hina beamed, hugged Lucy again, then strode away like a boss.

# CHAPTER TWENTY-FIVE

# RECOVERY

A buzz swam around her head, like a fly that wouldn't go away. She wanted to swat it away, but couldn't reach it. She followed it, tracing it back to a familiar glowing ball of vermilion and gold that pulsed out into the darkness.

*"Lucy Blakely!"* the light screamed, and she jumped awake, heart pounding. *"Come on, sleepyhead, wake up or I'll leave without you."*

She flung her eyes open and looked around at nothing but darkness. The clock read 2:13 a.m.

With a hand on her chest and her breathing settled, she reached out with her mind. *"Fane? Where were you yesterday?"*

The voice huffed. *"If you must know, I was watching Astra's every move from my underground dome. She has no authority to take me back because of the political asylum. Not for lack of trying, though. She may look cool on the surface but that insurgence was a blemish big enough to destroy her career."* A pulse of glee rang behind his words. *"I think a little more pandemonium and questioning of her judgment might just force her out of the job. My disappearance and the tree spirit's reappearance might just tip the scales."* He gave a haughty laugh.

*"What?!"* Lucy sat bolt upright. *"Where are you going? What about Oda?"*

*"Calm down, Miss Blakely. I have some business to attend to over on the continent. As for Oda, I think this is the perfect time to reintroduce our optimistically naive friend back into the mix."*

Lucy sucked in a breath. *"Where is Oda?"*

*"Here,"* he said and projected an image as detailed as any photograph into her mind. It showed the large iron gate to the park on the other side of Garrowhead. Then came an image of the lake that shared its banks with the Step-Ahead Hotel. A small yellow ribbon was tied around one branch.

*"Dig here, and the kodama is yours. By the way, you know my species has a capped number. Now that Cecelia is gone, there's an opening. Would you be interested in filling the position? We could do with someone more...human."*

Lucy fervently shook her head, then remembered he couldn't see the action.

*"Why would I want anything to do with you? You lied to me. You used me. You marched your own people to their deaths by sending them towards the bio-bomb! Don't you have any remorse?"*

*"Says the one who willingly summoned them to save their precious wolf!"* he shot back. *"We played our pieces. You knew as well as I did it was a calculated risk, and you still did it, too."*

The words were a sucker punch to the gut. He was right. She'd still played the willing part of the messenger, but it hadn't sat well with her. Risking her own life was her choice but lying by omission? Weighing up one life over a small group or all-out war?

*"As for remorse, of course I do,"* he said sternly. *"As a royal, I have abilities other vampires don't, including emotional manipulation. Evolution deigned to give us said emotions more potently so we could understand them better to lead our people."*

Lucy shrank from the rebuttal. It made sense, all those times when she'd been unnaturally calm around him. More manipulation. But then he'd loved once. And he'd tried to prevent a full-scale war. Scratching her ankle absent-mindedly where the bite had been, she brought her mind back to the images he'd sent.

*"I thought you said you were taking Oda with you to the continent and planning the return journey by post?"*

*"I lied."*

Her point had been made. She couldn't trust him.

Lucy felt her lip ache and unclenched her teeth before she broke through the skin. She cocooned her duvet covers over her head, as if it would keep prying ears out of their silent conversation, then asked what she'd kept secret from everyone else.

*"What happened to Operation Silver Star? Did the backup we gathered convince them to stop the program?"*

There was a pause before Fane replied, *"The Crossleys did not cancel Operation Silver Star. Only the top brass know it exists and they're currently scrambling to work out why it crashed. They're lucky it did."*

A lump gathered in Lucy's throat.

*"No. They wouldn't have let it continue. They had time. Maybe Trisha knew about it all along and crashed it before they—"*

*"No. She lacks the clearance to access the program. Assuming she knew about it, then she'd have been banking on human compassion for it to never be used. The fact that it was indicates apples don't fall far from their tree. Let that be a warning to you, Miss Blakely, about the company you keep."*

The warning sent a chill down Lucy's spine. So, who did launch it? But there was a more pressing question. *"So, how was it stopped?"*

*"Well, aren't you awake now and full of questions? In short, Duke's rogue AI identified it as a threat as soon as it was engaged, and began working out how to disable it. By my checks, it was a close thing. It was neutralized at 95 percent start-up. At least I've got some great blackmail material now."*

*"Please don't tell anyone about it!"* she begged.

*"I'm not stupid enough to spark an intergalactic interspecies war. I think even you'd know that by now. But if you don't and you'd like more time, the offer's still open for a one-way ticket to Fang City."*

Silence.

*"Shame. Farewell, Lucy Blakely,"* he finished, and then the golden light faded away.

A weight settled on Lucy's body and she slumped at the sudden energy drain. She dropped her duvet hood, arms weak. The bedroom lost its focus. Pine no longer wafted from her bedside table. Her room was silent without the hum of the common room's fridge. And she was alone with her thoughts again. She looked down and could barely make out her own hands in the din.

That was the end of Lucy Blakeley's vampire adventures. She hoped.

Raising her two-tonne arms with her returned human strength, she fought her way over to the table lamp and flicked it on. Layer by layer, she peeled back her bandages, revealing a shiny, fully healed ankle.

Grinning, she picked up her sketchpad and pen from the nightstand and sketched as fast as she could.

Satisfied she'd gotten all the important details, she set her alarm, rolled over, and went to sleep.

❦❦❦❦❦ ❦❦❦❦❦

At 6:30 a.m. Lucy bounded into the common room, satchel in hand and a smile on her face. It fell slightly when she saw a couple of Crossley family members with circles around their eyes.

They looked up, smiled, and offered her a croissant from an open packet. The breakfast had Alex's name all over it.

Lucy took one in thanks, then said her goodbyes, heading for the door.

The bus pulled outside the Cross-Key industrial site at 6:55 a.m., and Lucy made her way across Garrowhead. Twenty minutes later she hopped off, jogging past dog-walkers and the occasional runner who nodded at her.

When she arrived at the entrance to the park, she closed her eyes and called. *Oda!*

The call rang hollow in her own brain. Of course, she didn't have vampire blood anymore. Oda was the one who had ERT abilities to pick up her thoughts.

Setting off through the park, Lucy kept calling. Again and again. Nothing.

Shivering, she walked to the highest point of the park she could find, and pulled out the sketch she'd made of the location Fane had shown her. Five minutes later, she set off towards a cluster of trees and bushes that looked recognizable.

*"Oda?"* she called. This time, the thought reverberated. She was in range, but there was no reply. Then she smacked herself on the forehead.

What sort of translator was she? Oda didn't use words! Changing tactics, she pictured herself with her hand pressed against a tree trunk, and loaded it. Longing. Protection. Yearning. Love. She clenched her hands, eyes screwed shut, and propelled the thought like a slingshot.

A tidal wave of warmth and joy washed over her, knocking her a step back, making her practically melt under the winter sun. Oda was close.

Through the prickling tears, she searched the trees and branches until...found it. A yellow ribbon waved in the wind, perfectly matching Fane's memory. She parted the bushes, stepped through, and crouched down by the roots, concealed from passers-by. The soil was wet and cold, but she ignored the slime on her fingers as she dug. It was loose.

Her insides vibrated as she kept scooping until she heard a rustle. A spot of white poked out from the earth, and she pulled, dislodging a plastic bag with a familiar size and weight.

Upon opening the bag Lucy saw a brown envelope protecting the book. After cleaning her hands with a wipe, she carefully slid the notebook into her lap.

Back against the trunk, she flipped open the book, pulled out a marker pen, and drew a sun in the middle of the page.

The image faded, and Lucy wept. Openly. It was over. At last.

An image of apples raining from the sky made her laugh, and she slumped back against the tree.

With one hand, she reached into her pocket, pulled out her phone, scrolled down to Dave, and hit call.

"It's Lucy. I've got Oda."

Clutching her charge, she stared up at the sky, towards the universe beyond the clouds.

❧❧❧❧❧ ❧❧❧❧❧

A Celebration of Life event took place one week later in a private mansion out in the countryside. The event was invite only, and Lucy held herself as tall as she could as she pushed Will through the crowds. To be recognised and called here to take part was a humbling honour she could not refuse.

Margaret Crossley, CEO and head family member, led the ceremony. A lily wreath lay for every Crossley family member who lost their life, as well as a bunch of purple tulips for Cecelia. Lucy swallowed as she passed by the memorial. It could have easily been Will lying there.

Stepping up to her side was Alex, dressed all in black, but without his sunglasses. Lidded bags under his eyes.

"We need to talk," he said, voice low.

Curious, Lucy followed the guard to a small side room away from the assembly hall. She motioned to the door handle, but he shook his head. "Leave it open. The chatter of the other guests is better cover than silence."

He took a long gulp of water and eyed her, steely gazed. "Did you think we wouldn't find out?"

Lucy gulped but stayed silent. He couldn't mean...

"You talked to Fane, then he escaped, and your ID badge just happened to go missing."

He stared, eyes searching hers, and she refused to look at him. "Of course, we ran a search on the badge codes. Yours didn't appear, but two did that didn't exist before, then vanished the same day. Unauthorised. Advanced hacker that Fane is, of course he could have changed the codes. And that fact that you don't seem to hate the convict means he likely didn't just steal yours."

This was it. She was done for. They'd never keep her now.

Lucy exhaled raggedly, and the stretching silence was all the confirmation Alex needed. He ran a hand through his hair in trademark Crossley fashion.

He shook his head. "You know, it was Cecelia who discovered it and reported it to me. Never told another soul."

The unspoken words lingered between them. She'd kept Lucy's secret to the grave.

"I didn't tell Kamal, just like I promised. But I have told my aunt and gave her my recommendations for you. You lied, and you're impulsive to a fault. After everything with Trish... Well. You're a danger to our family, and I'd rather you not stick around."

The words hit like bullets to the chest. Tears welled. It was the end of the line for her. She knew it. There was no going back from this now. She'd lost.

"Alex?" a soft voice called from the corridor outside.

"In here," Alex shouted, and a small brunette appeared, bouncing a newborn in a baby sling at her chest.

"Hello," the lady said. "I hope this lug hasn't given you much trouble?"

"Actually, it's the other way around on this occasion," Alex said, and took a sweet from a packet the lady offered. "Lucy, meet Eleanor, my fiancée, and my ten-week-old daughter, Eve."

"P-p-pleasure," Lucy said, holding out a hand to shake. No wonder he was so tired all the time, with a newborn. And his comments about family hit home all the harder. She didn't belong after all. Not with this family unit. A mother, father, and baby. Just like home, and the people she'd disappointed there, too.

"I got the new baby formula. Dave said it was nutritionally balanced, but we don't have a clue what it'll taste like. Just a guarantee Eve will like it," she informed.

"And if all goes to plan we'll never know," Alex said bluntly. "They'll be too young to discuss the flavour, and should have forgotten by the time they grow up. Another perfect product by the sound of the trials. Same vein as the pet food. If she doesn't take to this one, she's not a baby. We should try plant food next."

The corners of Eleanor's lips turned up a fraction, but Lucy wasn't allowed to laugh at the joke. "Come on. We've got a quick five minutes to feed her before the speeches," she said, and tugged Alex out of the room.

Lucy wished she was invisible, like an imposter, and crept into the back of the hall. But her solidity was confirmed when Hina swiftly found and herded her to a pair of seats next to Will's. Will, who she was also about to lose.

Different branches of the family read speeches and eulogies, holding the audience in a rapt silence of loss.

Lucy sat between the pair. All three broke into tears at some parts, though Lucy's was for a unique set of grief.

"Our family has been trusted and tasked with a great boon, and we recognise the heroes that laid down their lives to protect us from the hatred that sprang up from inside one of our own. But out of the darkness dawns a chance to begin anew," the CEO intoned. "This week I have met with the Council of the Bureau and a new Charter is being forged between ourselves, one bigger and stronger than ever."

She paused as a wave of applause scattered through the audience, heads lifted and tissues on laps. The leader paused, letting her words sink in before continuing.

"As you know, we recently welcomed the very first non-family member into our secrets. Lucy Blakely." Lucy wanted to shrink in her chair at her name. "Why did we break our protocol of silence? Because we needed help, after discovering a brand new sentient species, hence Project Oda was launched."

Whispers spread around the room liked wildfire.

"This new entity will be shown to you all shortly. It was discovered by a Crossley, and as such it's up to us to bring them into the Charter. Due to the nature of the species we recruited outside of our family for the very first time. Also for the first time, the Charter was disregarded completely by one of the parties."

Solemn rapturous silence rang around the room.

"The new Grand Bureau Member wishes to increase this level of coop-eration between our races. To that end, we are replacing Project Oda with an independent embassy for our newly discovered species, allowing them a voice and a place in the Charter with ourselves and our friends in the stars."

Lucy's eyebrows arched.

"Cross-Key will play an integral part in supporting the foundation of this new organisation. We will dedicate our resources to finding and befriending as many of these people as we can. As is tradition, their embassy will also play host to an ambassador of each race. I hope you will all support me in suggesting our very own Lucy Blakely for this role, who will aid us as translator, and herald the news of our new ally to friends."

The audience launched into applause at the CEO's words and Lucy's face burned as they recognised her as one of their own.

So, Alex was right. They were getting rid of her but in an entirely different way. Maybe the CEO saw something in her after all. She glimpsed Alex in a back row frowning. She couldn't tell if it was in response to the news or the occasion itself. Maybe this was a role they'd been inventing for Trisha.

Will prodded her with his elbow, snapping her out of her rumination. "Lucy—you might get to take Oda on a tour of the Fleet. They're going to need an embassy there, too, so maybe you can visit?" He always managed to lift her spirits. Maybe she'd have more time with Will than she'd thought. Inside, she beamed.

As the CEO began talking again, Will leaned in and whispered, "Dave said he'd take me to visit an Earth café on one of his next free weekends. Maybe you could join us? Then when you visit us, I could take you to our best eatery—The Point."

Lucy's butterflies took off in an aerobatics routine, drawing loops and hearts.

⧽⧽⧽⧽⧽ ⧼⧼⧼⧼⧼

The day after the Celebration of Life event Lucy sketched, pouring her heart out on paper to process it.

So much death and injury, and why?

She glanced down at the portrait in progress—a curly redhead pointing the barrel of a gun downwards as she climbed up a ladder. It seemed like everyone had family problems.

She turned the page and sketched herself holding Oda, with Will and Hina at her side, and wondered what Ben would look like at her side, too.

Shading her jacket red, she promised to talk to people about expectations to avoid crossed wires. She needed a work-life balance, especially being given a second chance by Hina. They'd wasted too many years already.

Glancing down at her sketch, she bit the pad of her thumb. Deciding she was happy with it, she flipped the page and started something new.

Sketching her own form, she drew her mother, her father and...she paused. What was Ben up to right now?

She pulled her phone out of the side pocket of her new navy blue satchel and lifted it to her ear.

"Hi Dad, it's me. What's Ben up to?"

...

"Did Mum tell you? I'm getting a promotion."

...

"Yes."

...

"To celebrate, I wanted to treat you all to a meal."

...

"Friday night. I'll come around early to play with Ben."

...

A stone dropped in Lucy's stomach.

"What do you mean, rearrange her appointment?"

...

"Who's Dr Wentworth? Is something wrong?"

...

Her heart crawled its way up to her throat as everything clicked into place. Her mother wasn't staying late every day after work. She'd been sneaking out for counselling sessions, attempting to hide the toll of the miscarriages from her. Trying to shield her.

"Thank you, for telling me. You don't have to rearrange. We can wait for her to get home. So, what about you?"

...

"A new magazine? Sounds good. I think you'd be great self-employed."

...

"Sure, I'll ask if anyone's good with websites. Mine worked, but it was pretty basic."

...

"Thanks. Apology accepted."

...

"Love you, too. Good luck with your writing. Bye."

*Click.*

Grinning, she glanced down at her notebook, feeling lighter than she had in months. The family portrait she'd been drawing had disappeared, replaced instead by her, her mother, and her father all sitting in the branches of a tree. And at its foot lay a cluster of apples and a small tree sapling.

She giggled at Oda's attempt to fill in the blank, and slowly began sketching Ben, lying curled up at the foot of the tree.

So what if her words froze every now and again? She could say what she wanted to in different ways.

A knock on her bedroom door made her pause. She looked up, crossed the room, and opened the door to find a pink-cheeked Will. He grinned sheepishly and held out a bouquet of red roses. Her jaw dropped.

"For you. Grown here. On Earth. In actual soil, without stem cells or solar lamps. Real red roses. Dave took me to town, and we passed a flower shop and—"

Lucy bent down and found Will's lips with hers. "They're beautiful, thank you."

"Like you, Ruĝa. Will you be my Valentine?"

It was Lucy's turn to feel her cheeks heat. She dipped her head into the bouquet, gathered up her courage, then looked up again and nodded. "So..." she said. "Do people get dressed up when they go out in space?"

# TRANSLATIONS

## *Esperanto* to English

*Protekante ĝis la fino de la tempo*
= Protecting until the end of time

*Protektante ĉion kion estas via kaj mia*
= Protecting all that is yours and mine

*Ruĝa* = Red

## *Arabic* to English

*Na uzo billah* = We seek refuge in Allah

*Fee aman Allah* = In the safety of Allah

# ACKNOWLEDGEMENTS

They say it takes a small village to write and publish a book. This is true.

To my wizard: Daniel KD, the digital illustrator who worked miracles with what I gave him, and elevated my front cover to something exceptional. Thank you.

To my guardian of grammar: my editor, Anne-Marie Rutella. I learned so much about Track Changes, grammar and the Chicago Manual of Style from you. Thank you for working so diligently, and your enthusiasm for my novel!

To my defender of culture: my Muslim friend who offered their services as a sensitivity reader. They know who they are. Thank you for allowing me to ask many cultural questions, sharing your experiences, and translating for me.

To my story-tellers and bards: The #WritingCommunity on X (formerly Twitter). From my very first tweet asking about how to plot a novel, you have turned up day after day to answer questions I had, and show your support as I got to grips with being chronically ill. And to my friends of AuthorTube who have kept me company for the past 5 years on YouTube; such a dedicated group of writers! You showed me being a writer was possible, and illuminated the path forward for me, every step of the way. Thank you all.

To my feline helpers: my two cats Kuriboh and Thelonius, who sprung onto the scene in spring 2023. Even if your attempts at writing weren't exactly helpful, you forced me away from my keyboard to rest, often by lying between me and my laptop. Thanks for all the memes!

To my cheerleaders: my family, my alpha and beta readers, who I also bounced cover designs off. Your enthusiasm to read and reread my work, as well as your financial support, made me believe I could do it. Thank you.

And to my provider, Mr Spence, who was there every step of the way: as a supporter, a believer in my abilities, to make me food, and help me manage my fatigue. Your support has been unwavering and this book wouldn't exist without you.

# ABOUT THE AUTHOR

**Adara Spence** is an autistic and disabled writer. She lives happily with her husband and two cats, Thelonius and Kuriboh, in the UK. Adara wanted to be an author since she was 6, or so she'd been told. Other options included: plumber, scientist, Pokémon trainer and pilot. She wrote *Drawing Red* as an escape from her increasingly housebound life, and to low key raise awareness of one her more annoying conditions: POTS. Primarily afflicting women, it kicks in during the teenage years and post-illnesses (or after forays in space, which sadly Adara has not visited).

## Connect Online:

email: adaraspence@gmail.com
www.adaraspence.com
X (Formerly Twitter): @AdaraWrites